Praise for the novels of Sheila Roberts

"A delightful celebration of the joys of small-town life and a richly rewarding romance sweetened with just the right dash of bright humor."
—*Booklist* on *Home on Apple Blossom Road*

"Engaging, sweet and dusted with humor, this emotional romance tugs at the heartstrings as a headstrong pair who were always meant to be together find their way back to each other."
—*Library Journal* on *Home on Apple Blossom Road*

"*The Lodge on Holly Road* is the ultimate in feel-good family drama and heart-melting romance. Plus there's the added bonus of getting to celebrate the season with a community that couldn't be more devoted to Christmas."
—*USA TODAY*

"This amusing holiday tale about love lost and found again is heartwarming. Quirky characters, snappy dialogue and sexy chemistry all combine to keep you laughing, as well as shedding a few tears, as you turn the pages."
—*RT Book Reviews* on *Merry Ex-Mas*

"*Merry Ex-Mas* is the absolute perfect holiday book to begin the Christmas season with! It has everything great women's contemporary fiction should have—a great storyline filled with romance, humor and a bit of mystery tucked in here and there, fabulous personable characters filled with charm."
—*Sharon's Garden of Book Reviews*

"Witty characterization, slapstick mishaps and plenty of holiday cheer."
—*Publishers Weekly* on *The Nine Lives of Christmas*

SHEILA ROBERTS

Three

Christmas

Wishes

MIRA

ISBN-13: 978-0-7783-1969-6

Recycling programs
for this product may
not exist in your area.

Three Christmas Wishes

For questions and comments about the quality of this book, please contact us at
CustomerService@Harlequin.com.

www.MIRABooks.com

Printed in U.S.A.

For Katie and Addie

Dear Reader,

Merry Christmas! I assume you picked up this book because, like me, you love Christmas and enjoy reading stories about holiday high jinks and happiness. I hope I've given you plenty of that with my three friends and their various holiday challenges, not to mention my mysterious Santa. This is a busy time of year, so I appreciate you spending some of your precious time with me.

I wish you a season filled with joy and sweetness. I hope the only drama you experience is on the big screen and that Santa brings you everything you want and then some. As the song says, may your days be merry and bright.

I love hearing from my readers, at Christmas and at any time of the year! Find me on Facebook or visit my website, www.sheilasplace.com.

Sheila

Three
Christmas
Wishes

Chapter One

Riley Erickson's life was perfect. Happily, there was no other way to describe it. She was engaged to a perfect man—good-looking, easygoing, kind to little old ladies, liked her friends—and they were getting married during her favorite time of year. (Christmas weddings were the most beautiful.) She had an equally great family—generous, fun-loving and supportive (now that she and her bro and sis had outgrown the sibling-rivalry stuff)—and a job she loved, teaching fourth grade at Whispering Pines Elementary School. Kids still liked their teachers at that age, so it was fun to go to work. And you couldn't beat the vacation time since teachers got summers off as well as spring and winter breaks... which made getting married in December, well, perfect.

Riley smiled as she took the small ceramic turkey off her desk and substituted a snowman. The wedding was only three weeks away. By Christmas, she and Sean Little would be hanging their Christmas stockings side by side. Humming Christmas carols as she worked, she took down the rest of the Thanksgiving decorations in her classroom and put up her Christmas-themed ones. The children would return from their Thanksgiving weekend to find the classroom all ready for the holidays.

Once her decorating was finished, she took a moment to admire her reindeer and Santas and candy canes. Yes, it looked very festive here in Ms. Erickson's fourth-grade classroom. It was oh, so satisfying to be organized.

Speaking of being organized, she wondered how her friend Emily was doing. Riley knew Emily was getting ready to visit her family in Portland for the weekend. Maybe she could use some help putting her classroom in order. Riley wandered down the hall to Emily's room.

Emily Dieb was new to the school, new to the town of Whispering Pines, Washington, in fact. But settling in well. The other teachers liked her and so did her students. Actually, all the boys in her fifth-grade class had a crush on her. This was hardly surprising, since Emily looked like a Victoria's Secret model.

Having a pretty friend was no threat to Riley. Granted, she'd never be mistaken for a model. She certainly wasn't as glam as her sister, Jo, the fashionista, whose hair was always styled and highlighted, but with her round face, freckles and long, light brown hair, she was cute enough. Cute enough for Sean Little to fall in love with, anyway, and that was all that mattered. Sean thought she was cute, adorable even, and had told her so on plenty of occasions.

Besides, it was hard to be jealous of Emily when she was so nice. Like Riley, she loved to read and watch old movies. Unlike Riley, she enjoyed working out and had the size-four body to prove it. She was going home to Oregon for the holiday, where she'd spend the weekend playing indoor volleyball and hitting the gym. Yuck, but to each her own.

"I don't want to get too fat for my bridesmaid's dress," she'd said when Riley teased her once about being obsessed with the gym.

After Jo had gotten pregnant, she'd resigned from her position as matron of honor, so Riley had upgraded her best buddy, Noel Bijou, to maid of honor status and brought Emily on board to step into Noel's bridesmaid shoes. "I'd love to be a bridesmaid," Emily had gushed.

Emily didn't seem as gushy about being in Riley's wedding lately, but hey, Thanksgiving was coming, and Riley was sure that Emily was preoccupied with her looming family drama. Her parents were divorced and she was going to have to deal with parent rivalry and eat two Thanksgiving dinners—no easy feat for a size four.

She entered Emily's room to find her friend perched on her desk, looking gorgeous in a red knit dress and high boots, talking on her cell phone. Her cardboard Pilgrims and turkey were still hanging on the wall, and there was no sign that Christmas was right around the corner. Good thing Riley had stopped in.

Emily gave a start at the sight of her and said to her phone, "I've got to go."

"Sorry. Did I interrupt something?" Riley asked.

"Oh. No. I'm just, um, getting ready for the weekend."

"I thought you might be in a hurry to get on the road so I came by to see if you needed any help setting your room up for Christmas," Riley said.

"Oh. Well. Thanks." Emily seemed distracted.

"Is everything all right?"

"Yes. Um, everything's fine."

Poor Emily. She was obviously trying to make the best of her upcoming family visit. "Must be hard having to go home and try to keep everyone happy," Riley said.

Emily nodded.

"I wish you were going to be around. I'd sucker you into going out and getting something to eat tonight. Sean has to work at the gym." Sean owned a Fit and Fine franchise, and when you owned a business, it actually owned you. Of course, once they were married it would own both of them. Sean was giving Riley a membership as a wedding present. She could think of better ways to work up a sweat together but oh, well. She'd learn to love treadmills. Maybe someday she, too, would be a size four.

"Yeah, I'm afraid I'll be busy tonight," Emily said.

"I hope your mom doesn't try to match you up with someone again."

According to Emily, last Thanksgiving her mom had tried to set her up with her yoga instructor. Emily had just broken up with her boyfriend and had been in no frame of mind for a new man. The fact that the man had been fifteen years older could've had something to do with it. Emily's mom wasn't a very good matchmaker.

Neither was Riley. She kept trying, though. "Sean's friend Guy is going to be in town this weekend," she said casually. Maybe Emily would like to come back early. They could all go out on Saturday night.

Emily was already shaking her head. "I appreciate the thought, but…"

Riley sighed. "I know. You're not interested. But, Em, you don't want to wind up alone, do you?" Honestly, Emily wasn't even trying to fix her love life.

Emily blushed and bit her lip.

Now Riley had made her uncomfortable. "Sorry," she said. "I guess I just want to see everyone as happy as I am." Maybe Noel and Guy would hit it off. Noel needed someone new in her life.

"You're such a good friend," Emily said, her pretty blue eyes filling with tears. "I don't deserve you."

That seemed a little over-the-top but it was Thanksgiving. Everyone got sentimental at Thanksgiving. "You're right," Riley joked. "Come on. I'll help you get your Christmas stuff up. Then you can enjoy yourself this weekend without that hanging over you."

Emily stood up. "Thanks, but I need to get going."

"Okay. If you're sure."

Emily nodded. "I'm sure."

They walked to the parking lot where a few of the teachers' cars were still parked, and Emily got into her snazzy Honda Fit (even her car was fit!) and zoomed away. Riley got into her Toyota and went home by way of her sister's house.

She found Jo busy putting together a cranberry salad for the family gathering.

"That's enough to feed a multitude," Riley said after they'd hugged (not easy to do around Jo's current baby belly).

"We *are* a multitude," Jo said.

Yes, it would be a big gathering. In addition to a couple of aunts and uncles, some cousins and a grandma, Riley's brother, Harold, would be there with his wife and daughter. And, of course, so would Jo, a Wilton by marriage but forever an Erickson at heart. However, she'd be minus her husband. Mike was in the navy, stationed on a sub, which was out at sea.

Jo rubbed her back. "This kid needs to come soon."

It was her constant lament lately. Understandable, though. The baby was due any day.

"First babies take their time," Mom liked to say.

"Well, this one's taking enough time for two babies," Jo would respond. "At the rate I'm going, it'll be Valentine's Day before I have this kid."

Then Mom would say, "Maybe she's waiting until her daddy comes home."

Jo never found that remark cute. "Mike won't be here until the middle of December. Don't say stuff like that, Mom! If I don't have this baby pretty soon, I'm going to explode." Jo was a little dramatic these days.

But Riley wasn't going to point fingers. She'd spent some time on the drama-queen throne a few months ago when Jo backed out of being her matron of honor. "Thanks a lot," she'd grumbled like a true loving sister. "You couldn't have waited a few months to get pregnant?" She'd been all excited about the baby—until Annabelle Rose upset her wedding plans. Not one of her finer moments, she had to admit. It became easy to kill her inner Bridezilla, though, after Jo asked how she'd like it if her matron of honor went into labor in the middle of the wedding ceremony.

Everything had worked out just fine, anyway, and she had her two BFFs to stand up with her.

"Have you made your pies yet?" Jo asked her.

Riley shook her head. "I'm doing them tomorrow so they'll be fresh."

"Ms. Organized," Jo teased.

"I want them to be good."

"They will be. You're the queen of the kitchen, for crying out loud."

"We all have to be the queen of something," Riley said. As a personal stylist, her sister had the clothes market cornered. She claimed that since this was her business she had to look good. But really, she'd look ready for an ad in *Vogue* no matter what she did. Jo had flair.

"So, are you and Sean doing anything tonight?" Jo asked.

"No." Riley shrugged. "He has to work at the gym."

Jo frowned. "He sure seems to work a lot of overtime lately."

"He has his own business," Riley reminded her. "You know what that's like."

"I do, but I still make time for the important people in my life."

"Sean makes plenty of time for me," Riley insisted.

Jo shrugged and changed the subject. "Want to stay for dinner?"

"What are you making?"

"I was going to ask you the same thing," Jo said with a grin.

"I should've known there was a catch," Riley said, but she was grinning, too.

She dug a couple of frozen chicken breasts out of Jo's freezer and baked them with an orange sauce, then put together a tossed salad to go with them. It was what she'd planned to make for Sean. Before he informed her he had to stay at the gym. Sigh.

After dinner the sisters watched a movie. Actually, Riley watched it and Jo napped through most of it.

In spite of her evening nap, Jo was looking pooped so Riley cleaned up the kitchen then said her goodbyes and went home to her apartment. It wasn't all that late. Maybe Sean would like to come over for a while now. Surely he could leave the gym by nine.

She tried his cell but it went to voice mail. Double sigh.

"Hi. It's me. Just thought you might like to come over when you're done working. Call me," she added.

He didn't.

She tried again an hour later and got his voice mail. "Oh, well. I'll see you tomorrow. Mom wants us there at three so we'll need to leave by ten to. Love you."

She ended the call with a frown and plugged her phone in to recharge. Leaving a voice mail was so unsatisfying when you were in love. She turned on her electric fireplace and plunked down on the couch. A fire in the fireplace was romantic, even if the fireplace was electric and mainly for show. Too bad Sean wasn't here to cuddle with her and enjoy it. Well, tomorrow night he would be. The gym would be closed on Thanksgiving, and she'd have him all to herself. Tomorrow was going to be wonderful.

The day certainly started out that way. Her pumpkin pies—the first she'd ever made, thank you very much—came out beautifully. She decided to celebrate with a homemade eggnog latte. (If she kept doing that, she'd be a size ten forever, but so what? Sean loved her just as she was.)

She was taking a sip when her cell phone rang. "Let's Hear it for the Boy," Sean's ringtone.

"Hello there, Mr. Little," she answered.

And now he'd say, "Hello there, future Mrs. Little."

Except he didn't. He said, "Riley, I need to talk to you." He sounded serious.

Oh, boy. She knew what that meant. He was going to weasel out of going to her parents' for Thanksgiving. For some reason, lately he didn't like hanging out with her family. He'd actually canceled on attending her brother's birthday party the month before. When she'd asked him what that was about, he'd used work as an excuse. "Anyway, I don't think your brother likes me," he'd added.

Which was ridiculous. Harold liked him just fine. Okay, Harold thought he was a tool. But what did Harold know?

"You don't want to go to Mom and Dad's?" she guessed.

"It's not that."

"Then what?"

"I should come over."

"You're coming over in a few hours," she pointed out. Not that she'd mind seeing him now, but it was only ten in the morning and she'd been busy baking and hadn't gotten around to showering yet and she hated it when Sean didn't see her at her best.

"I know, I know," he said, but not to her.

Now she heard a voice in the background. Who was he talking to? "Sean, what's going on?"

"I'm not sure how to say this."

Riley felt the blood start rushing from her head.

Something bad was about to happen. She could feel the impending doom buzzing in the air around her. She fell onto the nearest bar stool, bracing herself.

There was that voice again, decidedly female. Riley suddenly felt as if she'd swallowed a block of ice.

"I am," Sean said, again not to Riley. "Riley…"

"Yes?" Her voice came out in a whisper.

"There's no easy way to say this. We need to break up."

"Break up?"

"I'm sorry."

"But…we're getting married in three weeks. And two days," she amended. Three weeks and two days to go and Sean wanted to break up. Now the ice was melting and pouring out of her eyes.

"I'm really sorry. But if we get married it'll be a big mistake."

It would? This was news to her. "What do you mean? I don't understand." She had to be asleep. That was it. She was asleep and this was a nightmare. She pinched her arm. *Yowch!*

"I've met someone else."

"Three weeks before the wedding?" Three weeks and two days, but who was counting?

"No, I met her before that. Things have been, uh, growing between us. Our feelings."

Three weeks before the wedding? Only a year ago he'd gotten down on one knee in front of all the other diners at Bella Bella's Italian restaurant, produced a diamond ring and declared he'd love her forever. What had happened to forever?

"How could you do this? We were in love." At least one of them was. "You thought I was adorable." Didn't adorable count for anything these days?

"You are. Shit, Riley. I hate to hurt you like this. I feel awful."

He felt awful? "Who is it?" Who had stolen her groom three weeks before the wedding?

"This is awkward."

Awkward? This was a catastrophe. "Who is it?" she demanded.

"It's, uh, Emily."

"Emily? My bridesmaid? This is a joke, right?"

But Sean wasn't laughing. He wasn't even there anymore. Now someone else was on the other end of the call. Emily herself. Emily, Riley's fellow teacher, lover of small children, friend. Bitch.

"Riley, I'm so sorry. We've been trying to figure out a way to tell you."

"How long have you been trying?"

"All month."

All month. This whole month Emily had listened to her prattle about how lovely the church was going to look decorated with red and white roses and candles, how her grandma was making her garter, how Sean had someplace special picked out for their honeymoon. It was going to be a surprise.

Well, he'd certainly succeeded in surprising *her*.

"You were supposed to be my bridesmaid," she protested. *You were supposed to be my friend.*

"I know. I really am sorry. It just…happened."

"Where did it just happen?" Oh, wait. She knew. Sure enough. "At the gym."

That explained those extra-long hours Sean had been putting in. When you owned a business…blah, blah. The only business going on had been Emily in the business of stealing Sean. "You thief! You rotten, man-stealing thief. I thought you were my friend."

"I was. I am."

Not anymore. "Have you been sleeping with him?" It was Silent Night on the other phone.

"You've been sleeping with my fiancé. Seriously?"

No wonder Emily didn't want Riley to match her up with someone. She'd already matched herself. Was that who she'd been talking to when Riley walked into her classroom the day before? *I need to get going.* Yeah, she'd gotten going—right over to see Sean.

"Riley… Oh, here's Sean."

"I hate you," Riley said as soon as he came back on the line.

"Come on, Riley. Don't be like this."

"And why isn't she in Portland?" Or Timbuktu. Or Antarctica. The North Pole. No, scratch the North Pole. Santa would ban her.

"She was going but her plans changed."

Just like Riley's. No more wedding, no more wedding reception, no honeymoon with the perfect man who'd turned out to be anything but. No more life. And breaking up with her on Thanksgiving? Who did that?

Sean Little, that was who, the man she'd loved with all her stupid heart, the man who'd just broken that stupid heart. All that was left of her perfect life was her pumpkin pies. If Sean and Riley were here, she'd hit each of them in the face with one.

"Riley, I wish this hadn't happened," he said.

That made two of them. "I can't talk anymore," she said. "I have to get ready to go to my parents' and be thankful."

Chapter Two

Riley ended the call but made no move to go anywhere. Instead she stayed on the bar stool and hyperventilated. *Get a bag. Breathe into a bag.* All she had was plastic bags. Probably not the best plan.

So she switched to crying at the top of her lungs. Good thing most of her neighbors at the Pine Ridge Apartments were out of town for the long weekend, having fun with their families.

Or their boyfriends.

Her crying increased in volume. How could this have happened to her? It was like getting hit by a tidal wave. She grabbed a box of tissues from the bathroom and, hugging it like a long-lost friend, planted herself on her couch and cried some more.

The fold-out turkey centerpiece she'd found at Daily's Drugstore sat on her dining room table, mocking her. She'd envisioned Sean and her starting their happy life together, sitting at that table every morning, having breakfast before they went off to work, then enjoying a cozy dinner for two when they returned home.

Sean would still be enjoying a cozy dinner for two. Just not with her. She grabbed another tissue.

It only took her half an hour to go through every tissue in the box. She needed something sturdier. Paper towels.

There on the kitchen counter, next to the paper towel dispenser, sat the pumpkin pies. She wished she hadn't offered to bring them. It had seemed like a good idea at the time. She loved to bake, and Mom had her hands full with the rest of dinner. She'd been excited to show off her culinary artwork to the rest of the family, imagined the oohs and aahs as everyone savored each pumpkiny bite.

No way did she want to go to the family dinner now, not when life as she knew it had come to an end. She put the pies in the fridge and called her sister.

"Hey, there," Jo answered. "Gobble, gobble."

Gobble, gobble. Happy Thanksgiving. "I can't go to Mom and Dad's," Riley wailed.

"What? What's wrong?"

"You have to come get the pies."

"What do you mean? Are you sick?"

"It's Sean. He…he…"

"He's sick."

"No."

"He's dead!"

"Nooo."

"Then what? Oh, no. He broke up with you," Jo guessed, quickly arriving at the correct conclusion. There was only one thing as bad as Sean dying, and he had done it.

"Y-yes," Riley sobbed.

"What's his problem?"

"Emily."

"Emily?"

"They're...they're..." Riley couldn't finish the sentence.

"That be-atch," Jo growled. "That sneaky little fake friend. I'll be right over."

The pie problem solved, Riley took the roll of paper towels and returned to the couch. Maybe she'd see if Jo could bring home some leftovers for her... in case she ever wanted to eat again. She hated to miss Thanksgiving dinner but the thought of facing everyone was more than she could bear. She'd be a real dinner buzzkill, sitting there like the world's biggest loser, crying into her candied yams.

Ten minutes later Jo was at the door. And not only Jo but Mom and Grammy, too, neither of whom would leave the kitchen on Thanksgiving Day unless the world was coming to an end. Oh, no. This was so humiliating.

Until they rushed her and gave her a group hug, everyone standing in the entryway like a giant amoeba.

The amoeba slowly moved to the living room, Grammy and Mom flanking Riley on the couch, and Jo and her giant tummy settling in a nearby chair.

"That boy," Grammy said in disgust. "I never liked him. He was selfish." This was because at Thanksgiving the year before, Sean had eaten the last piece of huckleberry pie, which Grammy had planned on taking home and having for breakfast the next morning. It hadn't mattered that he'd been unaware of her plans for that piece of pie. As far as she was concerned, he still shouldn't have eaten it.

More evidence of how unworthy Sean was began to come out. "Remember how cheap he was on Valentine's Day?" Jo reminded Riley. "A bag of M&Ms instead of a box of chocolates."

"But I like M&Ms," Riley said.

"It was still cheap. And he didn't even take you to a nice restaurant. Bubba's Bar-B-Q? Really?"

"You're well rid of him," Mom agreed. "Heaven knows who else he's cheated with this past year."

"Now, there's something to be thankful for," said Grammy.

"That he cheated on me?"

"That you discovered what a weaselly cheater he is before you got married."

"He had to wait till three weeks before the wedding to do it?" The humiliation, the disappointment. Oh, the wrongness of it all.

"That is a little inconvenient," Mom conceded. "But nothing we can't handle. We'll start calling the guests tonight."

"I'll text all the cousins," Jo offered.

"See? It's going to be fine," Mom assured Riley.

"And look on the bright side," Jo added. "Now you don't have to work out at the gym."

No. Emily would be doing that, right alongside Sean. Riley sniffed.

"One less Christmas present to buy," Grammy said with a nod that made her glasses bob on her nose.

Christmas. Riley had been envisioning their first Christmas as a married couple—getting up in the morning and drinking hot chocolate, opening their presents. She'd already bought Sean's, a tool set she'd found online with everything from wrenches to Phillips screwdrivers. Well, she needed a tool set. And she could still drink hot chocolate.

All by herself. She burst into fresh tears.

"We're not going to let this ruin our Thanksgiving," Mom said firmly.

Was she kidding? "I'm not coming," Riley said.

"Not coming!" Mom and Grammy chorused.

"I can't." How could they expect her to face everyone after what had just happened?

"Now, baby," Grammy said, putting an arm around Riley's shoulders, "When you take a fall you have to climb back on the horse."

"I didn't fall," Riley protested. "I was dumped."

"Doesn't matter," Mom said. "Your grandmother's right. You don't want to be alone at a time like this. You need your family. And besides, if you sit here and mope, think of the power you're giving him."

"I'm not giving him any power. I'm just... Guys, can't you let me mourn?"

"Absolutely not," Mom insisted. "Now, go shower and dress. We'll wait."

Once Mom and Grammy made up their minds,

arguing did about as much good as trying to stick to a diet in a bakery. Riley trudged off to the shower.

As she went, Grammy started singing some old song about washing that man right out of her hair. Funny.

After Riley was cleaned up, Mom and Grammy loaded her and the pies in Mom's car and hauled her back to the house while Jo went home to put the finishing touches on her cranberry salad.

"How's my girl?" her father asked, folding her into his big arms.

"Miserable."

"Don't be. Forget about that clown. Anyone stupid enough not to want to be with you doesn't deserve you. I never thought he was good enough for you, anyway."

And that was the general consensus as the family gathered for their annual Thanksgiving feast.

"Men are beasts," said Aunt Gertrude, making Uncle Earl frown.

"Good riddance," said Riley's brother, Harold. "He's a tool."

"That's bad," explained his seven-year-old daughter, Caitlyn.

Harold worked out at Sean's gym a lot. "Did you know he and..." Riley couldn't bear to mention her false friend's name. "Did you know what he was doing?"

"Would you pass the stuffing, Aunt Gert?" Harold said, trying to dodge the question.

"Harold, did you?" She knew the answer before he even spoke. Guilt was painting a red flush on his face.

But he shook his head. "Not for sure. There was a lot of flirting going on and I thought that was tacky. You're well rid of him, sis."

Maybe she was, but the loss hurt all the same and it was hard to be thankful.

Still, by the end of the day she felt somewhat better. Everyone had complimented her on her pumpkin pies. Her aunt Ellen told her how nice she looked and asked her if she'd lost weight. She'd played Go Fish with Jo, her sister-in-law and her niece and had actually managed to forget her miseries for an hour or two.

Until she got back home to her empty apartment and realized it was going to stay empty for a long time to come. Maybe forever. Oh, there was a comforting thought.

Mom had sent home the last piece of pie with her, along with some stuffing and gravy and turkey. She'd planned to have them for lunch the next day. But, like the saying went, life was uncertain. She decided to eat dessert first. Maybe tomorrow she'd bake pumpkin squares. To heck with never eating again. She was going to eat away her sorrows, turn herself into a blimp. Who cared?

She took one bite of the pie and then tossed it in the garbage. Pumpkin pie was a poor substitute for a fiancé.

She was working up to another good cry when her sister called. "I know you're feeling sorry for yourself again."

Sometimes older sisters could be real stinkers. "I'd say I have a right to."

"Yeah, you do, but I have a better idea than sitting around feeling miserable for the next six months."

She wasn't planning on feeling miserable for the next six months. More like the next six years. "What?" Riley asked suspiciously.

"Girlfriend party. Pack a bag. Noel's on her way to pick you up."

"You told Noel?"

"Yeah, since she's your oldest friend and your maid of honor. Thought she'd need to know."

Yes, of course, Noel had to be told. Still, this felt as if her sad news was spreading faster than gossip on Twitter. In fact, it would probably be on Twitter before the day was over. Maybe it already was. Maybe Sean had tweeted. *Happy Thanksgiving. Dumped my girlfriend. Gobble, gobble.*

"You wanted to give her the happy news yourself?" Jo retorted.

Good point. She supposed she should be thankful her sister was telling people so she wouldn't have to.

"Come on, we'll drink eggnog and play Farkle. Then tomorrow we can hit the Black Friday sales and get you some new clothes, give you a breakover."

A breakup makeover; that did sound tempting.

"You don't really want to be by yourself, do you?" Jo continued.

"No," Riley admitted. She had enough of that being-by-herself stuff looming in the future.

"Older sister knows best," Jo teased.

"Sometimes." In this case she probably did. Who better to help Riley recover than her sister and her best friend?

Noel, who had gone through a breakup a few months earlier, understood exactly how she felt. "It sucks," she said as Riley dropped her overnight bag in the trunk of Noel's old clunker. "I swear there aren't any decent men left out there," she said once they were in her car and on their way. "Jo got the last one. No, I take that back. My sister did. Which is great, of course. I'm happy for Aimi." Noel sighed heavily.

Great. She was almost as depressed as Riley. Before the night was over they'd probably both wind up stretched out on Pine Street in the middle of downtown, praying to get run over by a reindeer. Except it was too early for Santa and his reindeer to be out cruising.

"I think the male population in Whispering Pines is shrinking." Noel heaved another sigh. Then she cast a guilty look in Riley's direction. "But you know what? We're not going to think about that tonight," she said with a determined nod.

"Thirty-one, and there's still no one, not even a glimpse of someone on the horizon," Noel said a millisecond later.

Jilted brides and empty horizons—oh, yes, this was going to be a fun evening.

Another guilty glance shot Riley's way. "I'm sorry. Listen to me, going on like Princess Pitiful when you're the one who's suffering. I'm sorry, Riley. I'm sorry Sean was such a jerk and Emily was such a rotten friend. But like I said, we're not going to think about that. Tonight we're going to have fun."

Fun.

Noel pointed a finger at nothing in particular. "You know, I never really liked her. Remember when we were at her place and she had that box of chocolates on the counter? She never offered to share. And they were Godiva! What kind of friend doesn't share her chocolates?"

That had been last month. Had those chocolates come from Sean?

They drove through downtown (which took all of five minutes). Santa's elves had already been busy because twinkle lights now dangled over Pine Street, and the light posts were decorated with giant candy canes and red ribbons. Everything looked festive and happy. Happy holidays. *Bah, humbug.*

"But you know what?" Noel continued as they turned the corner onto Jo's block. "Tonight is all about forgetting your troubles, and we're not—"

"—going to think about it," Riley finished with her. She was glad when they reached Jo's house. Maybe now they really *could* stop thinking. And talking.

Jo was still looking picture-perfect in her maternity jeans and black sweater, an Italian charm bracelet dangling from her wrist. No matter how tired she got, she always managed to look perfect. The eggnog was ready, spiked for Riley, alcohol-free for Jo and Noel, who wasn't much of a drinker.

"Eggnog!" Noel cried happily. "That's enough to make us forget our troubles."

"Until we step on the scale tomorrow," Jo cracked and took a sip of hers. "Except I'm drinking for two. Probably for another nine months at the rate I'm going. This baby's taking her own sweet time."

"She'll be here any day," Riley said. Her sister was having a girl and had the ultrasound to prove it. She also had a dresser full of cute outfits so her little girl could be as stylin' as she was.

"I'm ready. I'm more than ready. I have cleaned this house from top to bottom."

"It looks great," said Noel.

Jo's house always looked great. It was like an ad for Crate & Barrel. Chocolate-brown leather sofa and matching chairs, an expensive, thick throw rug over hardwood floors, her cupboards stocked with artisan stoneware. Tonight an arrangement of fall flowers in a long vase sat on her antique dining table, and she had a balsam-scented candle burning.

"I even cleaned the grout in the shower," she told them. "Mom says it's that final burst of energy before the baby comes. I sure hope she knows what she's talking about. I'd like to see my feet again."

"I thought expectant mothers were supposed to, like, glow," Noel said with a frown.

"I left glowing behind two months ago," Jo informed her.

"But you're going to have a baby!"

Jo did smile at that and rubbed her bulging belly.

Wait a minute. What was wrong with her sister's smile? The lips were in the right position but something was missing.

"Are you all right?" Riley asked her.

"Me? Of course I'm all right."

"Are you sure?"

Jo's chin went up a notch, a sign that she wasn't all right at all.

Riley's stomach started churning her eggnog. She set down her mug. "What's going on?"

Jo shrugged and downed the last of her drink. "Nothing."

"Okay, something is definitely wrong," Riley said.

"Not really wrong, just…not right. I don't know if I want to stay married to Mike."

Riley could feel her eyes bugging. "*What*? You and Mike have a great marriage. What are you talking about?"

"There's nothing great about him being gone all the time," Jo snapped. "He wants to re-up."

"Reenlist? You guys already talked about that," Riley said.

"We did. And I thought we had it settled. Obviously, we don't, not according to the email I just got." Jo frowned. "All he can see is that big bonus he'll get. He thinks we need it now that we've got the baby coming."

"Well, his motives are good," said Noel.

"No, they're not. He's just being greedy."

"Maybe he's worried about finding a job once he gets out," Riley suggested. Mike was a nice guy. He would never cheat on his woman. Jo had no idea how lucky she was.

"He'd have no trouble getting a job. He'll be in high demand. That's why they're offering him such a big signing bonus. I told him it's either me or the navy. If he re-ups it's anchors aweigh. We're through."

Jo had dashed all over the emotional landscape during the last few months. Riley was sure this was simply one more case of whacked-out hormones. "You shouldn't make any big decision like that right now. And anyway, Mike loves you. And you're about to have a baby, for crying out loud."

Tears started leaking from Jo's eyes. "I don't want to raise this baby alone."

"You won't be," Riley assured her. "Yeah, Mike goes out to sea but he always comes back to you."

"He's gone for months at a time," Jo said, wiping her eyes.

"But we're all here."

"It's not the same. In the end it'll be me and Annabelle alone in this place. It'll be me up all night when she's sick, just me at the PTO meetings and the school plays. He'll be off…somewhere, keeping the world safe. Super Squid in a sub," Jo said bitterly.

"But think how noble—he's serving his country," Noel pointed out.

"I know, but he's been doing it for eight years. Isn't that enough? Can't he let someone else take a turn?"

This was obviously a rhetorical question, so Riley didn't respond. Instead she said, "You really need to think about this, sis. If you split with Mike you'll be even more alone."

"I'll replace him."

"You don't mean that," Riley said sternly.

Jo sighed. "I don't know what I mean. I'm just so…mad."

It was all Riley could do not to tell her to get over it. But that would be unkind and not very helpful. This was hormones talking. Had to be. So she decided to say, "Mike's a good man, and it's darn hard to find a good man." This was something she was now an expert on.

"Yeah, he's practically perfect," Noel added.

"There's no such thing as a perfect man," Jo said in disgust.

"I'll settle for *almost* perfect," Noel said.

"I'll settle for playing Farkle," Riley said. Sheesh. This was supposed to be a girlfriend party to cheer her up. At the rate they were going, they'd *all* be lying down in the middle of Pine Street waiting to get run over by a reindeer. "Come on, let's have fun. No more talk of men. Okay?"

Noel nodded. "I agree."

"Me, too," Jo said and fetched the game.

For the next two hours they played games. Then they turned on the Hallmark Channel and watched a Christmas movie. "The guys in these movies are all so great," Noel said with a sigh as the ending credits rolled.

"That's because they're not real," Jo said. "If you sit around waiting for the perfect man you'll be on your buttsky for a long time."

"Thanks," Noel muttered. "You sure know how to inspire a girl."

"Just sayin'." Jo heaved a sigh. "Oh, never mind me. I'm cranky. And I'm pooped. You guys feel free to stay up as long as you want, but my daughter and I are going to bed so we'll be ready to hit the mall tomorrow." She waddled off to her bedroom, calling over her shoulder, "Leave the mess. We can clean it up in the morning."

"I'm tired, too," Riley said. It had been a long day and she suddenly felt the weight of all her misery. She stacked the empty popcorn bowls and grabbed a couple of glasses.

"Me, too," Noel said, picking up the rest of the mess. "Do you think your sister's right?" she asked as they loaded the dishwasher.

"About what?" Not about Mike, that was for sure.

"About there being no such thing as a perfect man."

"Well, none of us is perfect, but I hope there's such a thing as the perfect man for me," said Riley. Maybe someday, somewhere, she'd find him.

Chapter Three

The problem with writing children's stories was that the only men you met were A) editors, who were either married or gay; B) happily married stay-at-home dads who brought their children to author appearances (where were the single dads these days?); and C) little boys who came to those author appearances (all those adorable little boys—where were the big ones?). Even Noel's landlord was a woman. Mrs. Bing was fifty-something and you'd think she'd have had a son but no. Actually, considering what Mrs. Bing looked like, that was probably just as well.

So, naturally, Noel had been thrilled when Donny Lockhart walked into Java Josie's one rainy fall morning. Noel had been seated at a table, working on her latest project with her gingersnap latte within easy reach. It was a Saturday, practically the only day of the week besides Sunday that she got out of her jammie bottoms and got out of the house. The coffee shop was packed with people. Tables were scarce. He'd asked if he could share hers. Donny was tall and cute with red hair and freckles and trendy glasses. Of course she'd said yes.

He'd taken out his tablet and gotten to work, typing away. There was no "Hey, we're both redheads." No "Crappy weather we're having, huh?" No "What are you drinking? It looks good." No "Wow, are you an artist?"

She could've asked him what he was working on, but she didn't have the nerve. All kinds of clever words poured out of her when she was working on her Marvella Monster books but when it came to picking up guys, she was more of a Timid Tillie Titmouse.

It wasn't that she was ugly. She was okay-looking. She just…well, all those years of wearing glasses before they became a fashion statement, coupled with braces and a few extra pounds (the kiss of death when you were in high school) had messed with her self-esteem. That, plus being a bit of a nerd. Who wanted a nerd when you could hook up with a cheerleader? That had become her belief and she'd kept it all through college, which left the shelves in the boyfriend department pretty bare. If a guy got things started, she was fine, but it was hard to put herself out there and make the first move, even though the glasses had been replaced with contacts and the extra pounds had long since disappeared.

So she'd sighed inwardly and gone back to sketching the illustrations for her latest Marvella book, *Marvella and the Monster Under Mary's Bed*.

She'd just finished sketching Marvella pulling a

protesting green gremlin out from under the hapless Mary's bed when someone spoke. "Are you an artist?"

Mr. Cute Glasses was talking to her? "Yes." Now, there was an area where she had complete confidence. "I'm a children's book author but I illustrate all my own books." That in itself was quite an accomplishment, if she did say so herself. Not many people could do both well.

"Yeah?" He'd leaned over and checked out Marvella, who was upside down. She'd turned her sketch tablet around so he could see her creation better.

"You're really good."

She'd smiled modestly and thanked him. Now that the conversational gate was open, she'd had no problem asking, "What about you? What do you do?"

His cheeks had turned a little pink. "I'm between jobs at the moment. What I want to do is be a writer."

A kindred soul! "Really? What do you want to write?"

"Legal thrillers. You know, like John Grisham."

"I love him." Something else they had in common. "So is that what you're working on right now?"

His cheeks had gone from pink to red. "Actually, no. I'm, uh, writing something different, along the lines of *Fifty Shades*."

She'd felt her own cheeks sizzling. She'd tried to watch the movie, but her eyes had started to melt five minutes in. Her life was more like fifty shades of white.

"I heard there's big money in romance novels," he'd said, "so I thought I'd start there."

"That sounds like a plan," she'd said, at a loss for anything better. She knew quite a few writers, and none of them were in it for the money. They wrote because they loved to write. Still, she supposed it was good to be practical.

Donny had introduced himself and they'd wound up talking for twenty minutes until he'd checked his cell phone and announced that he had to go. Writers group meeting.

But before he left, he'd gotten her phone number and promised to call.

Lo and behold, he had. They'd dated hot and heavy for six glorious months. Six months of foreign films at The Orpheum. Lunch at Lettuce Love, since lunch was cheaper than dinner and Donny was on a budget…so of course she always offered to pay and he always let her. (Very secure in who he was as a man.) Six months of open mike on Monday nights at Java Josie's, where aspiring writers read their work. (Donny always read. His stuff was… well, he was still a beginner. He had room to grow.)

Six months of Donny asking her if her agent represented romance novelists, if she could edit his latest chapter, what she thought of his new scene. Six months of Donny talking about Donny and his dreams and very little talking about Noel and hers. Six months of him looking for a job to support himself while he finished his novel and finding nothing and continuing to live in his parents' basement. Of him asking if he could borrow ten bucks and then forgetting to pay her back. Six months before she finally realized that Donny was cute and creative—and self-centered and a user. After six months, Donny was history. The last time she saw him at the coffee shop he was hitting on a blonde in a business suit. So much for true love.

But she wasn't going to think about that. There was more to life than men.

Like holiday sales. And the mall, which served both Whispering Pines and the nearby town of Salmon Run, definitely had that going now that Black Friday was here. Christmas decorations were up and oversize golden balls and swags hung everywhere. In the middle of the mall, right by the information booth, Santa's shack, a red plywood chalet with white gingerbread trim, was being erected. A sign at the corner of the fake snow lawn announced: Santa Arrives December 1.

Good thing he wasn't arriving this weekend, she thought. He'd never have found a place to park his sleigh. It looked as if everyone in Whispering Pines and their fishy neighbor seven miles to the east was here. They all seemed to be swarming the department stores, getting their cell phones upgraded or their ears pierced or buying cookies over at Carmen's Cookie House. And they were all ready to do battle for bargains, especially at Macy's. One woman beat her to the last black sweater in her size by all of two seconds.

Jo was currently using her belly as a lethal weapon, knocking competitors out of the way in the activewear department. "She's fierce," Noel observed to Riley.

"Yep. She always has been. Sometimes I feel sorry for poor Mike."

"You don't think they're going to split up, do you?"

"I hope not," Riley said. "His shipping out never bothered her when it was only the two of them, but now with the baby in the picture, she's been complaining a lot about him being gone so much. Of course, she's been complaining a lot about all kinds of stuff. It's really not like her. I'm not sure being pregnant agrees with her."

"It would with me," Noel said. Darn, but she wanted a baby. Here she wrote children's books and didn't have a child. What was wrong with that picture? "Maybe I'll adopt." Why wait for a man to come along? At the rate she was going, she could be waiting until she was fifty.

"I don't know," Riley said. "I think I'd rather have a dad in the picture, someone to take over when you've got cramps and just want to go to bed."

"Yeah, but what if I never find someone? What if…" *Oh, dear. Don't go there.* "But we're not going to think about that."

Riley frowned. "No, we're not. Instead we're going to try on dresses."

She hauled Noel over to a rack where evening outfits were thirty percent off. "I don't need an evening dress," Noel protested. Besides being on a tight budget, she wasn't exactly the fancy-dress kind of girl. Her pink sweats and Uggs said it all—*boring homebody who writes on her laptop in her jammies.* Besides, if they went out and she needed something fancy, she had the red bridesmaid dress she'd bought for Riley's wedding.

Except wearing that around her friend would be mean. And tacky. Anyway, where were they going to go with their love lives in the toilet?

"Well, I do," Riley said. "Let's buy some sexy dresses to wear on New Year's Eve."

"Uh, Riley, neither one of us has someone to go out with on New Year's Eve."

"This will be like thinking positive, putting it out there in the universe that we want someone to celebrate with. And if no one comes, we'll still go out. I'm not going to start the New Year feeling like an abysmal love failure."

"No one would ever call you that," Noel insisted.

Riley began furiously sorting through the dresses. She pulled out a black one with a sweetheart neckline, trimmed with fake pearls and gold beads and held it against her. "What do you think?"

"That Sean blew it."

Riley's lower lip wobbled and a tear slipped out of the corner of one eye. She dashed it away. "I can't become pitiful," she said in a low voice.

"You won't. You aren't," Noel assured her, and gave her a hug.

"Excuse me," said another woman, nudging them aside. "If you aren't going to look, could you please get out of the way?"

"Sorry," they said in unison and stepped aside.

Riley frowned. "You know what's wrong with us?" Noel wasn't sure she wanted to hear but Riley rushed on before she could say so. "We're too nice, that's what. We let people walk all over us."

"No, we don't."

"Yes, we do. I let Sean get away with sneaking out on me. I never made demands, never said, 'I'm sorry, you can't work late tonight because we have plans.' And you, you always let your publisher walk all over you."

"I do not!"

"Yeah, you do. You hated that last title they picked for your Marvella Monster book and you never said anything."

"That's because no one cares whether I like the title or not. Publishers want something that will sell, and they figure they know what works. Authors hardly ever get to keep their original title idea." Honestly, she should never have complained to Riley.

"Okay, what about Donny? How many times did he hit you up for loans before you finally got rid of him?"

She'd lost count. "I did get rid of him, though."

"Only after Jo threatened to call, pretending to be you, and break up with him."

Noel sighed. "Okay, maybe we are too nice."

"We are. I mean, how about what we did just now? Don't we have a right to stand at a rack and look at clothes?"

"We weren't really looking and we *were* kind of in the way."

"I was looking. Anyway, it's the principle of the thing," Riley said and stepped back over to the rack, giving the hangers a violent shove.

"Hey, watch it," the other woman snapped.

"Sorry," Riley mumbled. She grabbed a red dress and slinked away. "I guess it takes time to change your life. But I'm going to," she said with determination. "I'm going to be like Jo and take life by the horns. I'm going to buy a new dress and I'll go out on New Year's Eve. By myself if I have to. I'm not going to let Sean turn me into some pitiful reject who sits home all the time and feels sorry for herself."

Pitiful reject who sits home all the time—why did that have a familiar ring to it?

Jo was back with them now, carrying another bulging bag. She'd obviously succeeded in her quest for new workout pants.

She approved her sister's speech by saying, "All right, sis," and bumped knuckles with Riley. "I like this new you." She looked at the cocktail dresses in Riley's hands. "Oooh, pretty. Have you tried those on yet?"

"Not yet, but I will. Noel, how about you?" Riley challenged.

"Well…" A fancy dress so wasn't in the budget. She was trying desperately to save money for a down payment on the little house she was renting. She loved that place and when Noel had called to tell Mrs. Bing she wanted to rent for another year, Mrs. Bing had mentioned that she was thinking of selling it. Noel was determined to be the one she sold it to. In addition to saving for that worthy goal, Christmas was looming and she had more presents to buy.

Still, it would be fun to go out on New Year's Eve even if she didn't have a man. And since she could hardly go out with her friend and wear the bridesmaid's dress from the wedding that didn't happen…

"Thirty percent off," Jo reminded her.

Riley snagged a black dress in Noel's size. "Come on," she said. "Try it on."

"Okay."

Riley beamed. "Let's go."

Jo plopped onto a nearby chair. "There's no way we can all fit in a changing room. Come out and show me."

"If we ever get a changing room," Riley muttered. "This is like standing in line for the bathroom."

"I'll bet the bathroom line's shorter," said Noel.

But ten minutes later they were in a changing room, side by side and admiring themselves in the mirror, Riley in the red dress and Noel in the black one, accessorized with her Uggs. "Oh, we look hotter than cinnamon," Riley said with a smile. It was a big, wide smile, not one of the small, dull ones she'd been showing recently.

Noel smiled, too. "You look great."

"So do you," Riley said. "Except for the shoes," she added. "Come on, let's show Jo."

Jo approved. "Oh, yeah. You guys are crazy if you don't buy those." Then she grimaced at Noel's feet. "Shoe-shopping next."

Noel didn't want to be crazy, so she joined Riley at the cash register and bought the dress. Anyway, Riley had a point, and Noel decided she, too, needed to get a life, one that took place in the real world, not just inside her head with Marvella. She was going out and she'd be wearing this dress. And some sexy shoes, too!

"I'm starving," Jo said after they'd bought Noel a pair of red stiletto heels guaranteed to break her neck, as well as some rock-me-baby black boots. "Let's go to the food court and see if they have any chocolate chip cookies left at Carmen's Cookie House."

Chocolate chip cookies weren't as good as sex but they ran a close second. Noel followed the sisters out of the department store.

They all stopped for a moment to watch as Santa's Play Land came to life with mall employees setting out plastic elves and mechanical reindeer with heads that bobbed up and down. "Just think," Riley said to Jo, "this time next year you'll be taking your baby to see Santa."

"That was always so fun when we were kids," Jo said. "I can hardly wait to do it with mine." Then she grinned. "In fact, I'll start this year." She turned to

Riley and Noel. "You guys want to come with me to see Santa?"

Now Riley was grinning, too. "Like we all did when we were in high school."

Noel remembered that. Jo had been in her junior year, and she and Riley had been sophomores. Riley had asked for a car, which she didn't get. Noel had asked for straight As, and almost got there except for a B in algebra. And Jo had asked for a new boyfriend, which she did get. Jo had always been good at finding ways to get what she wanted. Sometimes Noel wished she was more like Jo. Considering all the time she and Riley had spent trailing her like puppies, you'd have thought more of her warrior princess attitude would've worn off on them.

"Let's do it," Riley was saying. "Let's come here on December first after I get done with school. We can see Santa and then go out for dinner."

"Twelfth Man Sports Bar," said Jo. "Who knows? There might be some cute guys there."

"I think we've met about every single man in Whispering Pines," Riley said, backing up Noel's theory about the shrinking male population. "But hey, you never know."

True. Maybe if Noel asked for a man, someone who was a step up from Donny (which would be just about anyone), Santa would come through.

They were buying their cookies when her cell phone rang. She looked at the caller ID and saw it was her landlady. What could Mrs. Bing want?

"Noel, I wanted to give you a heads-up. I'm

bringing someone to look at the house this afternoon. It's short notice, but I hope that's okay."

"The house?" Her house? "I don't understand."

"You remember I've been talking about selling
it."

Yes, to her! She'd told Mrs. Bing she'd love to buy
it. She'd hoped Mrs. Bing would be open to carrying a contract with her. Mrs. Bing hadn't been too
excited about that, so Noel had made her an offer.
It turned out to be an offer she could refuse. Still,
Noel had insisted she could come up with the money
Mrs. Bing wanted. Somehow. She'd been saving like
crazy for a down payment that would impress both
Mrs. Bing and the bank. All she needed was a few
more months. Okay, more like a year, but still.

"I have someone who's interested," Mrs. Bing
said.

"But *I'm* interested!"

"Yes, I know you are, dear, but this person actually has money and wants to make a cash offer, and
I'm a little strapped for cash right now."

"Oh, Mrs. Bing," Noel began miserably.

"I'm sorry, dear. I really am. Anyway, we'll be
coming by around four. Like I said, I should've
given you more notice, so I hope you don't mind."

Yes, she minded.

"You don't need to be home," Mrs. Bing continued. "In fact, I'm sure you're out enjoying the Black
Friday sales."

She had been until this.

"Now, don't worry. I'll see that you have plenty

of time to move out. A month's notice should do, shouldn't it? I heard they have vacancies in those new apartments over on East View."

Noel didn't want to live in the new apartments on East View, even if some of them did look out on Case Inlet. But before she could say that—or anything—Mrs. Bing said a cheery goodbye and ended the call.

"What's wrong?" asked Jo.

"Mrs. Bing's selling my house. Can she do that?"

"When's your rental contract up?"

Oh, boy. "End of this month. But I already told her I'd stay another year."

"Why's she bringing in someone else? I thought you told her you wanted to rent with an option to buy."

"Because she didn't want to do that," Noel said. "She wasn't exactly open to any of my ideas." She handed over her money and got a big cookie in exchange. Suddenly she wasn't in the mood for a cookie. She wasn't in the mood for anything except a good cry.

"She could have given you first dibs," Riley said, incensed on her behalf.

"She knows I don't have enough for a down payment yet." Now she wished she hadn't bought that fancy dress and boots. Or the stupid shoes. Even though the money she'd spent on them was only a drop in a very big bucket that seemed to have a hole in it.

"What if you went and talked to her, asked her

for a few days to see if you qualify for a loan?" Jo suggested.

Noel already knew the answer to that. She'd been to the bank. With her fluctuating earnings as a children's book author, Mr. Ridley, the loan officer at First Mutual, was nervous about giving her a loan, especially in light of how far short she was of what she'd need for a healthy down payment.

Her parents weren't currently in any financial shape to help her. Dad had been laid off, and he and Mom were trying to make ends meet on his unemployment and what Mom earned working part-time at the library. Plus, they now had a wedding to pay for.

If only Marvella was real. Noel would sic her on this would-be buyer and get him out of the way so she'd have time to pull together her finances.

But she didn't have a Marvella. All she had was herself.

"You should go over there and talk this potential buyer out of it. Don't let him or her swoop in and take your place away from you," Jo said.

Noel looked despondently at her cookie. "I have no idea how to talk somebody out of buying a house."

"Too bad it isn't falling down around your ears," said Riley.

"Too bad it doesn't have termites," Jo added. "Or rats." Then she grinned. "Rats, that's it!"

Riley stared at her as if she were nuts. "What are you talking about?"

"I'm talking about a strong deterrent," Jo said. "Come on, Purrfect Pets has got to be open today." She started waddling down the mall.

"What's she talking about?" Noel asked as they followed her.

"I think she's found a way to discourage your buyer," Riley said. "Would *you* fall in love with a house that was infested with rats?"

"You mean turn rats loose in the house?" *Eeew.*

"It's worth a try," Riley said as they caught up with Jo.

"But…rats?"

"You got a better idea?" Jo asked.

"No," Noel said with a sigh. "But I hate rats."

"They're kind of cute," Riley said. "Anyway, you'll probably only need a couple."

"What am I supposed to do with them after this potential buyer leaves?"

"Call me and I'll help you catch them. I could use some rats in my classroom."

"I guess," Noel said. Oh, but rats were so creepy with their little ratty paws and that long, ratty tail. *Eeew. Just. Eeew.*

Purrfect Pets was indeed open and filled with people hoping to buy puppies for Christmas. They passed a tank with snakes in it and Noel shuddered.

"Maybe we should get a snake, too," Riley suggested and Noel quickly vetoed it. The rats were bad enough.

Ten minutes later she was the proud owner of two gray rats. (Riley had fallen for a gray-and-white one, but Jo had vetoed him. Too domestic-looking. Noel wanted to veto the whole plan, but she'd been out-numbered.) She'd also shelled out for a cage, bedding for the cage and rat food.

"I can't believe I just spent all that on vermin," she muttered as they left the mall.

"Don't worry. I'll reimburse you," Riley told her.

Back in Jo's Honda Pilot, the two sisters took the front seats and left Noel in back with the rats, who kept making little scritchy-scratchy noises as they paced around their cage. "These things creep me out," she said, hugging the door.

"My kids will love them," Riley said.

"Let's hope the potential buyer hates 'em," Jo said then groaned. "Oh, my gosh, I swear this girl is going to be a boxer the way she keeps pushing me."

"A sure sign she's about ready to come out," Riley told her.

"The sooner, the better," Jo said as they turned into Noel's driveway.

"Want me to come in with you and set them free?" Riley offered as she took out the cage for Noel.

"No, I can do this," she said as much to herself as her friend. "But I will definitely call you to come back and help me catch them."

"Okay. Good luck in your mission," Riley said and hugged her. Then the sisters roared off down the road, leaving her alone with the rats.

She carried her new houseguests into the house, holding the cage as far away from her as possible.

This was too, too creepy. But she'd have brought home a boa constrictor if it would keep away the competition.

The house wasn't a mansion. In fact, it was small, with only two bedrooms. But it had a bay window in the living room and a brick fireplace that she loved using in the winter, with a mantel just right for hanging Christmas stockings, and a built-in china cabinet in the dining room. The lawn at the back of the house wasn't much, but it was the right size for a puppy...which she fully intended to get once she owned the place and was free of the no-pets rule. She loved sitting out on the patio in the summer, smelling the honeysuckle that grew on the side of the house and working on her books. The kitchen cabinets and floor vinyl were both as old as time. The windows tended to sweat in the winter and the hardwood floor was scratched up, but none of that bothered her. Someday, when she had money, she'd replace the windows and refinish the floor, refinish the kitchen cabinets, and this old place would sparkle like the gem it was. Meanwhile, though, she loved it, and she wasn't going to give it up.

She glanced around at her tidy living room with the apartment-size, cream-colored sofa and matching chair, the rocking chair that had been her grandma's, the fall candle arrangement on the coffee table. Ugh. It all looked way too inviting. She couldn't do anything to the house itself, but she could at least cut down on the cozy factor. She set down the cage and got to work messing up the room, putting away the candles and throwing some sofa pillows on the floor. In the kitchen she pulled dirty dishes out of the dishwasher and scattered them on the kitchen counter. There. That was better. Now, all she had to do was set loose the vermin.

Oh, wait. Did she want rats climbing on her sofa pillows? She put them back on the sofa. Okay, it was showtime.

She approached the cage as if it bore two ravenous tigers, reaching out a tentative hand to the latches on the little door. "You can do this," she told herself. Honestly, she was a huge, powerful human. They were only the size of her feet.

Rats the size of her feet running around the house!

She held her breath and opened the door, granting them freedom to pillage her place, then dashed for the sofa. Rats couldn't climb furniture, could they?

She huddled there and watched as the stupid things stood at the door of their cage and sniffed. "Come on, already, get out and do your duty." What was the problem here? Were they agoraphobic? She left the sofa and crept to the cage, giving it a wiggle. The rats planted their feet. Great. Just great. She'd brought home defective rats.

But no, now one was poking its nose out of the cage. Then, next thing she knew, he was out. With a screech she ran back to the sofa.

Brother rat came out, too, and she sat helplessly watching as they scuttled around her living room, sniffing and exploring. She was never going to be able to leave her sofa. And, oh, how dumb! Her cell phone was in her purse on the hall table. How would she ever be able to call Riley to come over and help her put them back in their cage? Doomed. She was doomed to stay on her sofa for the rest of her life like some poor flood victim camped on her roof, hoping for a helicopter.

The mantel clock told her she only had half an hour before the invaders arrived. Of course, *now* she had to go to the bathroom. Maybe she could wait until Mrs. Bing came. Maybe Mrs. Bing and the potential house thief would distract the rats long enough for her to dash to the bathroom. This had been such a stupid idea.

She nibbled her lip. She really had to go.

She was going to have to be brave. Time to make a break for the bathroom. The rats were over there, on their way to the kitchen. She was clear over here. She could do this. She put one tentative foot down and then the other. One of the little beasties lifted its gray head and looked at her. Looked right at her!

Eeeee! She dashed for the bathroom and shut herself in. She was never coming out.

She kept her vow until she heard her front door open, followed by the sound of voices, one feminine, the other masculine. Mrs. Bing and the interloper. Suddenly Noel had no idea what to do. Should she stay in the bathroom with the door locked? Ha! Not a bad plan. They'd both try the door and not be able to open it, yet another sign of a flawed house.

"This was my mother's home," Mrs. Bing said.

"She lived in it for fifty years. As you can see, it has a lot of charm."

Dear God, please let him be blind.

Footsteps moved from the hall into the living room and Noel opened the door and stuck her head out, trying to hear.

"Windows will have to be replaced," said the voice.

Yes, too expensive. You don't want a house where you have to replace the windows.

"What the hell?"

He must've seen the rats. *Hee, hee.*

"Oh, my!" cried Mrs. Bing. "We've never had rats in this house."

Noel crept down the hall and peered around the door frame into the living room. There was Mrs. Bing in all her glory, wearing a faux fur coat over a tentlike green dress that made her look like a Christmas tree. Atop that Christmas tree sat a face like a pumpkin with Chia Pet hair.

Next to her stood a tall, dark-haired man with a body to match his manly voice. He wore jeans and a black sweater and an old, leather jacket and had black stubble on his chin. His eyes were brown. And his mouth…it was lifted in a half smile.

"Those are domestic," he said, and pointed to the cage.

Darn. Why hadn't she hidden the stupid cage? Oh, yeah. Terror.

"That's impossible," Mrs. Bing said in shock. "Noel knows I have a no-pet policy."

Noel decided it was time to show herself. "I'm keeping them for a friend. She's a teacher. She's coming to get them tonight."

"Why are they out of the cage?" Mrs. Bing demanded.

Jailbreak? Noel had a very creative mind; why couldn't she think of something? "Um, the latch on their door must have jiggled loose." Did that sound lame to anyone besides her?

"Well, put them back," Mrs. Bing ordered.

"Now?" She'd have a heart attack right here.

"Don't worry," said the interloper. "I'll get 'em."

She watched as he chased down the first rat and bent to pick up the disgusting little squeaker. Nice butt. Oh, who cared?

"You didn't need to be home," Mrs. Bing told Noel as the unwanted visitor scooped up Useless Rat Number Two and stuck him back in the cage with Useless Rat Number One.

"I was done shopping," Noel said. "I wanted to come home and...check for leaks." Ha! Brilliant. No one would want to buy a house with leaks.

Mrs. Bing's eyes narrowed suspiciously. "When did you notice a leak, Noel?"

Noel's guilty conscience started a fire on her cheeks. "I thought I saw water the day before yesterday. In the kitchen."

"Really." Mrs. Bing was not fooled.

The rats were safely in the cage now. "Let's go look," said the interloper.

So they all trooped out to the kitchen to look.

The kitchen was as cheerful and warm as ever with its yellow walls. Noel and Riley had painted those walls last summer. She'd even sprung for the paint herself. All the love she'd been pouring into this house and Mrs. Bing was going to sell it out from under her just like that. Mrs. Bing was an ingrate.

"Where exactly was the leak?" asked Mrs. Bing.

"Uh, over by the window. I think."

The interloper gave the window and surrounding wall a checkup. "No signs of water damage. But the counters need replacing."

"The counters are fine," Noel informed him and he raised an eyebrow.

"Come on. I'll show you the rest of the house," Mrs. Bing said. "Noel, you can wait down here."

"That's okay. I'll come with you," Noel said. Her rent was paid up. She had every right to join the home tour.

They walked from room to room, the interloper seeing ways he could change every one.

"You know, this house is very nice just as it is," Noel informed him.

The interloper cocked his head. "Yeah? Then why don't you buy it?"

"I want to. Mrs. Bing knows that," Noel said and looked accusingly at her landlady.

Mrs. Bing's cheeks turned rosy. "Noel, if you had the money I'd sell it to you."

"Noel, pretty name," said the interloper. He thrust

out a hand for her to shake. "Mine's Ben, Ben Fordham."

Noel put her own hands behind her back. "What do you intend to do with this house, Ben Fordham?"

"I intend to fix it up."

"And then what? It needs a family, people to live in it and love it." Okay, she was lecturing now.

No, no. She wasn't lecturing. She was getting in touch with her inner Marvella Monster, chasing away a predator.

He held up his left hand. "Not married."

"Well, then…" Suddenly it dawned. "You don't want this house for yourself. You're going to flip it."

"I'm going to fix it up and sell it to a family who will love it."

Fix it up? Ha! He was going to destroy its character. Noel turned to Mrs. Bing. "Mrs. Bing, please don't sell the house to this…this…Scrooge. He only wants it so he can make a profit. *Please* let me rent to own or give me time to come up with a down payment. I love this place. I'll take care of it."

"I saw how you're taking care of it with the dirty dishes on the counter," Mrs. Bing said, pursing her lips.

"I never have dirty dishes on the counter, really. That was…" Noel was aware of Ben the Bad Man looking at her.

"Camouflage?" he guessed. "Like the rats and the so-called leak."

She wasn't too proud to beg. "I'm sure you can find other houses to buy."

"Of course I can," he said, and she breathed a sigh of relief. Until he added, "But not at this price point." He turned to Mrs. Bing. "Why don't we go back to your house and talk?"

Nodding, Mrs. Bing started down the hall.

Ben the Bad Man turned to follow her and Noel caught him by the arm. "Please don't buy this house."

He looked down at her pityingly. "This is nothing personal. It's just business." Then he gently disengaged his arm and trailed Mrs. Bing down the hall. "Nice meeting you, Noel."

"I wish I could say the same," she called after him then leaned against the wall and wished all manner of Christmas disasters on him. She hoped he fell off a ladder while hanging Christmas lights and broke his leg. No, make that both legs. She hoped his dog bit him. And if he didn't have a dog she hoped all the dogs in the neighborhood would poop on his lawn. She hoped Santa would drive right by his house or, better yet, drive over it and dump an entire load of coal down his chimney. She hoped…he'd have a change of heart. Maybe he'd have a dream and get visited by a bunch of ghosts showing him what a bad boy he was.

Or maybe, just maybe, she could find a way to win him over.

Chapter Four

Riley called Noel shortly after the invaders had left. "How'd it go?"

"He wasn't fooled. And he wants to buy the house and flip it. He's talking about taking down walls and ripping out counters and all kinds of things. He'll ruin its character."

"Too bad the rats didn't work."

"Please don't say that word," Noel begged, looking over at the useless rodents in their cage.

"Sorry. I'll come over and collect them for you."

"No need. The house thief already did that."

"He saw the cage?"

"What can I say? I screwed up. It's just that they had me so icked out I couldn't concentrate."

"We'll think of something," Riley said. "And I'll come and get them tomorrow, okay?"

"In the morning?" If she had to look at them all day...

"Yes, and don't worry. I'm sure this will all work out."

Perhaps, but meanwhile, she had to be proactive. She said goodbye to Riley then pulled out her laptop and did an internet search for Ben Fordham. She found him under Fordham Enterprises. *We Turn Nightmares into Dream Homes*, he promised on his website. And there was a picture of the dream-maker himself. He looked like an HGTV star in his jeans and T-shirt and tool belt, with his muscles and dark hair and trust-me smile. He was on the front porch of a pretty Victorian, sitting on the railing, one leg dangling casually. Underneath that was a before-and-after example of his work, two shots of the same house. In one it resembled something out of a Halloween movie, with peeling paint and a front lawn overrun by unruly shrubs; in the other, it had turned into a sweet, two-story charmer with a freshly mowed lawn and flowers blooming along its front walk. Very impressive.

But her house wasn't a nightmare. And she had her own plans for turning it into a dream home.

She poked around the site, checking out more examples of what he did. Various pages offered visitors a chance to sell a property (*You need out, we'll step in*) or buy property (*We did the work, you reap the benefits*), and his contact information gave not only his email address but the physical address and phone number of his business, as well. She knew that building. It was downtown, around the corner from the Wiltons' hardware store. It had once been a little on the derelict side, but now housed both his business and a real estate office, plus an escrow company and an interior decorator. Very handy. No doubt he worked hand in glove with the Realtor, and she supposed the home-decorating woman helped him stage his stolen homes.

Stolen was about what they were, she was sure. He probably never paid full market value, probably preyed on poor widows who were desperate for money. Like Mrs. Bing.

Except Mrs. Bing drove a new car and lived in a rambler in a nice neighborhood. Noel didn't believe she needed the money as badly as she claimed. Of course, in all fairness to Mrs. Bing, you never really knew about a person's personal finances.

Still, darn it all, she'd been providing the woman with a monthly income in the form of rent for two years now. Why couldn't Mrs. Bing have given her a chance? Greed. It came down to that.

Well, she wasn't going to let her house go without a fight.

That's the spirit, whispered Marvella, who sometimes hung around even when Noel wasn't working on a story.

She returned to the Fordham Enterprises home page and studied her nemesis. What a phony, insincere smile! She studied that naked ring finger on his left hand. The man was single, which might make him susceptible to female persuasion. A hot outfit, a plate of cookies...

Except, unlike Riley, she was a lousy baker. Okay, then, wine. Most people liked wine and that was more sophisticated, anyway. She knew nothing about it, but there was a new shop in town that sold wine. They could help her choose something classy.

That took care of the bribe. The hot outfit was another matter. The clothes in her closet fell into the lukewarm category.

But Jo the stylist had a whole closet full of clothes that didn't happen to fit at the moment. And she and Noel were the same size. Noel collected her cell phone and made the fashion equivalent of a 911 call.

"I need wardrobe assistance," she said, hardly giving Jo time to answer.

"The rats didn't work?"

"No. And he's over at Mrs. Bing's right now, making her an offer she probably can't refuse."

"That sucks. Hey, if you need a place to stay while you're looking for a new house, you can stay with me."

"That's really nice of you," Noel said, "but I intend to stay here. I'm going to talk him out of buying my house."

"Sounds like it's too late for that."

Deep down, Noel had the awful suspicion that her friend was right. "I've got to try. Maybe I can convince him to take back his offer."

"Ah, so when you say wardrobe assistance, you're thinking wardrobe malfunction."

"Nothing that extreme," Noel said. A vision of sexy Ben Fordham tugging at her top and setting a boob free à la Janet Jackson set her face (and other body parts) on fire. *Oh, no. We're on a mission. We're not going to think about costume malfunc-*

tions and sexy men with brown eyes and a black heart. And she certainly wasn't going to think about those big, strong-looking hands. He probably had big…everything.

Whew! Had Mrs. Bing turned up the thermostat? She walked over to check it. Nope, still set on sixty-eight. So the only thermostat getting turned up was hers. "I just want something sexy. I know you've got a lot of great stuff in your closet and we're the same size."

"We were, once upon a time, before I morphed into a whale," Jo said. "Yeah, come on over tomorrow morning. I can fix you up."

Fix you up, fixer-upper. Yes, she was the human equivalent of a fixer-upper. Her work wardrobe consisted of pajama bottoms and old sweaters, and even when she dressed up no one ever stopped her and asked where she got that cute…anything. No wonder Jo had suggested going to the mall.

"You just need some polishing," she told herself. Hopefully, Jo could get her good and polished. A hot look combined with a bribe…that might be enough to melt Ben Fordham's cold, cold heart.

Riley came over to pick up the rats the next morning, and when she learned about Noel's scheduled makeover, invited herself along. "I don't have anything else going on," she said, and her lower lip wobbled.

"It's okay. You will," Noel assured her. "We're going to have a great Christmas and a fabulous New

Year's no matter what." Even if they were manless and homeless. *Don't think about that!*

So, not thinking, Noel drove to Jo's place, Riley and the rats following behind.

Jo took in Noel's ancient coat, sweatpants and Uggs when she and Riley walked through the door and frowned. "Does your mommy know you're out looking like this?" she said, and hauled Noel inside and upstairs to her bedroom, where her bed was covered with all manner of sartorial delights— camisoles, Victoria's Secret bras and panties, jeans, leggings, blouses, jewelry, tops, sweaters, dresses.

"Better than Nordstrom, huh?" Riley cracked.

"I only need one outfit," Noel said.

"No, you need a wardrobe. Take off those disgusting clothes."

Noel obliged, and Jo began grabbing sweaters and blouses and holding them up to her. "No, no, not that… No, not sexy enough… Hmm, might be too small. Oh, yes!" she finally said after holding up a black, bell-sleeved winter top with a sweetheart neckline accented with crocheting around the neck. The crocheting also served as straps. Noel put it on and saw that it left her shoulders exposed and also allowed a peek at her cleavage. "That should do for starters." Jo handed Noel some tight jeans. "Now, try these on."

"Maybe we're not the same size, after all," Noel said, struggling into them.

"We are. You're just used to pajamas," she said, eyeing Noel's discarded sweatpants with revulsion.

"Honestly, I didn't know they even made those any-more."

They probably didn't. Noel had found hers at a thrift store a couple of years ago. "I don't wear them when we're out doing things," she protested.

"You shouldn't wear them at all. And the way you dress when we're all out doing things is barely a step above."

She'd heard that from Jo on more than one occasion.

"It's okay," Riley consoled her. "She says stuff like that to me, too."

"I only speak the truth," Jo said, frowning at her sister's jeans and tennis shoes.

As the oldest, Jo had tried to guide them. Maybe they were unguidable.

Noel zipped up the pants and Jo studied her care-fully. "Oh, yes," she said, nodding. "Now you're starting to look like something this goon might want for Christmas." She snatched up a pair of gold, chan-delier earrings. "Put these on."

Noel hesitated. "Isn't that a little, um…"

"No, it's not. Put them on," Jo commanded. Noel obliged and she smiled approvingly. "Oh, yeah. Siz-zle, sizzle."

"Sizzle, sizzle is right," Riley agreed. Jo turned Noel around so she could check herself out in the full-length mirror.

"Oh, my," Noel said with a smile.

"Just what every man wants on his tool belt," Jo murmured. "Now, your feet."

"I can wear those black boots we bought."

Jo nodded. "That'll do." She pointed at the Uggs. "No, wait. Put those back on. They might work. Anyway, you don't want to look like you're trying too hard."

Noel obliged, and Jo nodded again. "Actually, that's kind of buff and sexy. I think they'll be fine, for the first encounter, anyway. You can wear the boots another time. Now," she said, turning back to the pile of clothes on the bed, "what about the outfit for your second encounter?"

Noel wasn't sure there'd be a second encounter. She wasn't even sure she could pull off a first encounter. Jo handed her a simple white shirt.

"This," she said. "And leggings." She picked up a pair of patterned black leggings. "And the boots."

"How about this necklace?" Riley suggested, holding up a chunky stone number.

"Definitely. Third encounter wear the heels and this dress." She handed Noel a black dress with a scoop neck. "Redheads look great in black."

More jewelry, a Victoria's Secret bra, a black cashmere sweater, a white blouse—a wardrobe basic according to Jo—a little faux fur-trimmed jacket and Noel was in business. "Thanks," she said as they loaded her new wardrobe into the back of her car. "I really appreciate this."

"They're just hanging in my closet all sad and lonely," Jo said. "They may as well be out there doing some good. And I hope they do," she added and hugged Noel. "Wear the coat when you go see him, but make sure you shed it the second you're in his office. Got it?"

"Got it."

"And don't forget to wear makeup. And perfume."

Perfume. Oh, yeah. That. She had a bit of Viva La Juicy left.

So, she was going to look good, smell good, and bring something good as a bribe. Hopefully, by putting her best foot forward, she could impress him enough to convince him to reconsider buying her house.

She frowned, remembering his comment about price points. Bah, humbug!

Sunday afternoon she made her way to beautiful downtown Whispering Pines in search of the perfect wine for a house thief. Thanksgiving weekend kicked off the holiday shopping season, and it appeared that every business in town (including ones that often closed on Sundays) was open. She passed her favorite bakery, Hey, Cupcake, as quickly as possible, averting her gaze from the display of holiday treats. She'd indulged in eggnog at Jo's, and Riley, who was in a manic baking phase, had brought her M&M cookies when she came to collect the rats. If she didn't turn off the eating machine, she'd eat herself right out of Jo's wardrobe before she even had a chance to use it.

She did stop by Wilton's Hardware Store to pick up a few replacement bulbs for her Christmas lights. Mr. Wilton, Jo's father-in-law, was behind the counter and gave her a friendly hello as she ap-

proached. He had circles under his eyes and she noticed he took in a deep breath while ringing up her
sale, as if he was trying to draw in extra energy.
She knew the signs of overwork. She'd done that to
herself a few times, staying up late at night working on illustrations for her Marvella books, trying
to meet her deadline. She wondered how old he was.
Her dad's age? Older? He had some gray hairs and
wrinkles. Did he want to retire?

"Men never want to retire," Dad often said. Poor
Dad.

"Hey, Darrel, what are you doing still hanging
around?" called an older man as he entered the store.
"Thought you'd be in Hawaii."

"With a grandkid about to arrive? Are you kidding?" Mr. Wilton called back. "Anyway, who's got
time?" he added with a shrug and a wink for Noel.

"Looks like you're busy," she said. The place was
full of people, buying everything from chain saws
to mechanical reindeer.

"Always," he said. "And it looks like you're going
to be busy hanging Christmas lights, young lady."
He gave back her credit card.

Young lady, code for *I don't remember your
name.* Hardly surprising, considering how many
people came into the store. She'd been there with Jo
a couple of times, but other than that she only came
to buy seeds and fertilizer for her flowers from the
nursery section. And Christmas lights, of course.

"I like dressing my home for the holidays," she

said, and hoped this wouldn't be her last Christmas there.

"Be careful hanging them," he cautioned as he handed over her purchase. "Better yet, send your boyfriend up on that ladder."

She smiled and nodded as if she did, indeed, have a boyfriend to send up a ladder.

"Us guys are expendable."

Not as far as Noel was concerned. She thanked him and left with her purchases. Next stop, Cheese and Wine.

She entered the shop and was almost overwhelmed by the huge selection of wines for sale. One corner had a refrigerated case displaying a variety of cheeses, and boxes of crackers surrounded artfully displayed gift baskets on a table in the center of the shop.

Several customers were browsing. One woman was gobbling little cheese bits from a tray of samples. A large man in an overcoat, carrying his purchase in a tall bag, brushed past Noel. She walked over to a shelf and tried to pretend she knew what she was doing.

"May I help you?"

Noel gave a start and turned to see a pencil-thin middle-aged woman, all dressed in black, her dark hair pulled into an elegant upswept style. She looked like a transplant from Paris. Noel took in the cashmere sweater and wool slacks, the simple gold jewelry and black heels. Another Jo Wilton. And here she was in yoga pants, her favorite ratty sweater and an old coat. She hadn't wanted to waste any of her borrowed finery on a quick run downtown. Now she wished she had.

"I need a bottle of wine," she said, stating the obvious.

"Did you want a red or a white?"

"I'm not sure. I don't really drink it."

This brought a look of disdain from the woman, but she quickly covered it with a smile. "We have some very affordable ones over here," she said, moving Noel to the wine equivalent of a low-rent district. The way Noel was dressed, the woman probably thought she couldn't afford much of anything. The woman probably thought right.

"Can I get something decent for twenty dollars?" Noel asked. She preferred to spend ten, but that might look cheap. A cheap bribe wouldn't be good.

"I think so," said the woman.

"Never be afraid to seek advice when you need it," Mom always said.

"This is a gift. For a man. Would you recommend red or white?"

"You can't go wrong with a nice red. We have some lovely ones from Walla Walla as well as the Yakima Valley."

"Would you pick one for me?" Noel asked.

"Of course." The woman plucked a bottle from the shelf. "Here's a cab from Chateau Ste. Michelle, one of the oldest wineries in Washington. It has plenty of complexity and structure."

And it was in her price range. "I'll take it."

The woman rang up the wine and put it in a cheery red bag with the shop's gold logo. Perfect. Armed with wine and Jo's new clothes, Noel would be a force to reckon with.

She hoped.

Monday morning she showered, washed and straightened her hair, put on makeup, and donned her man-killer clothes. Then, with the wine in tow and sprayed with enough perfume that he'd be able to smell her coming for miles, she drove downtown to the office of Fordham Enterprises. A big red truck sat in front of the building, just the kind of vehicle a construction guy would drive. So Ben Fordham was in the building.

She took a deep breath, grabbed her red bag and went into the enemy camp. The first-floor offices were occupied by the Realtor and the escrow company. The second floor held two offices. The name on one door read Elegant Interiors. The other was Fordham Enterprises.

She entered Ben Fordham's domain and found that he had a guard on duty, a secretary. When Noel envisioned calling on Mr. House Thief, she hadn't taken into consideration that she'd have to go through a secretary to get to him. She should've, though. Now, what to do? The woman was smiling politely but her eyes said, *You look like competition, so I already don't like you.*

The secretary was only visible from the waist up, but Noel could tell that she'd also been to the Jo Wilton School of Fashion. She was wearing a very professional white blouse similar to the one Jo had lent Noel, and she'd gotten the memo about leaving it unbuttoned low enough to advertise. She wore a fancy gold necklace to fill in the gap and keep the professional vibe going. Her hair was an expensive shade of blond, complete with highlights and she, too, was wearing perfume. It wafted over to where Noel stood hesitating and smacked her in the face.

Was she a girlfriend or simply a girlfriend wannabe? More to the point, how was Noel going to get this wine to Ben the Bad Boy? If only Marvella would materialize and haul this fake blonde off her chair and out of the office.

"May I help you?" the secretary asked, her tone of voice adding, *Not.*

"I'm here to see Mr. Fordham."

A delicately penciled eyebrow shot up. "Do you have an appointment?"

Crud. She was sunk. Now what? *Get in touch with your inner Jo.* What would Jo do? Noel raised her chin. "No, I don't, but when I saw him last night he said to stop by."

She was lying! Mom always said nothing good ever came of lying. But this was just a half lie. She *had* seen him a couple of nights before, so why quibble over details? And what man, if he knew he was going to get a bottle of wine, wouldn't tell a woman to stop by?

The guard-secretary frowned. "Have a seat," she said. "May I tell him who's here?"

The woman whose house he's trying to take.

Marvella arrived on the scene. *Don't frown. She'll think you're competition and that'll set off her bitch alarm.*

The red bag was most likely already doing that, but Noel pasted a smile on her face. "Noel," she said and perched on the edge of a fake leather seat, part of a grouping of fake leather seats around a large coffee table strewn with magazines about home improvement. Would he remember her name? If he did, would he refuse to see her? "With his wine," she added. That might intrigue him enough to lure him out.

The guard called the inner sanctum. "There's a Noel here to see you."

"With wine," Noel prompted her.

"With wine," the blonde said and scowled.

A moment later the door to the inner sanctum opened and out stepped Ben Fordham himself. He wore jeans and boots and a casual plaid shirt, rolled up at the sleeves. He raised both eyebrows inquisitively at the sight of Noel. She probably had about one minute before he informed her that he had an important meeting or an appointment with the devil about interest payments on the soul he was selling.

Noel jumped up from her seat and quickly moved in Ben's direction. "I thought I might find you here," she said, keeping her voice light and friendly. Just one house-lover visiting another.

"Uh, yes," he said slowly. "But what are you doing here?"

She was very aware of the guard looking her up

and down through narrowed eyes. *Yes, what are you doing here, you and your borrowed clothes and your dangly earrings?*

"Maybe we could talk about that in your office," Noel said and swept past him on shaky legs.

"Hold my calls, Janelle," he said and followed her in.

Okay, she'd reached the inner sanctum and she had his full attention. Yay for her.

She glanced around. So this was where Ben Fordham plotted and schemed. A desk sat on the far wall, relatively uncluttered with only a laptop and a cell phone, a pad of paper and pencil. No pictures of a girlfriend. A couple of leather chairs sat in front of a wall lined with bookshelves, which were mostly empty except for a few books on finance, and some baseball trophies. Oh, and here were two framed photographs. One showed a house with a smiling family posed on the front porch, with writing over it. *Thanks for your help, Ben. Love our new digs!* Another was a picture of a Santa holding a hammer. Probably him, trying to disguise himself as a nice guy.

"Noel," he said as if trying her name on for size. "Didn't we meet Friday night?"

Yes, we did, you skunk. You know we did! "I think we might've gotten off on the wrong foot." Noel proffered the wine.

He took it. "That's, uh, nice of you. And about the other night, like I said, it's just business."

"Not to me. I love that house."

"It'll be even more lovable after I've fixed it up."

"Please don't buy it," she begged.

Now his expression was regretful. He shrugged. *What can I do?* "I'm sorry, but I already made your landlady an offer."

Noel sat down hard on the nearest chair. "Oh, no." Then she burst into tears. Her house, her sweet little house, had been snatched away from her. All her plans for it, all her dreams…

"Shit," he muttered. "Don't cry. Please don't cry."

"There are all kinds of houses in Whispering Pines. Why did you have to want mine?" she sobbed.

"Yours? Funny, I thought it belonged to Mrs. Bing."

Was that supposed to be funny? She glared at him.

"Lady, look—"

"Noel," she corrected him and took an angry swipe at her eyes. Good thing she was wearing waterproof mascara. She'd spent a lot of time on her makeup that morning. Big difference *that* had made.

"Noel. I'm not out to ruin your life."

"I'd say turning people out of their homes at Christmas is a good way to ruin their lives." What a heartless Scrooge.

He knelt in front of her. "I'm really sorry. I am. And nobody's turning you out of your house at Christmas. I'm not going to close on this until the end of January, so you'll have plenty of time to find a new house."

"Not a house, a home. That's my home and I love it."

He frowned. "Then you should've bought it."

"I was working on that!"

He sighed and sat back on his heels. "I don't understand what you want me to do."

"I want you to go away!"

He half smiled at that. "This is my office. I belong here."

"You know what I mean. You don't belong in my house."

"I'm not going to be in your house other than to fix it up. Listen, if you can come up with the money you can buy it after I've remodeled."

"As if I could afford it then. Anyway, it won't be the same. You'll come in and destroy the character."

The frown was back. "I assume you found me on the internet. So you've seen my website. Do the houses I've flipped look like I destroyed their character?"

Well, no.

"I promise I'm not going to wreck the place," he continued.

"You're going to pull up floors, take out counters and change the living room floor plan and…and who knows what else."

He studied her. "Okay, what would you do to improve the house?"

"I'd leave the built-in china closet, that's for sure. I bet you were going to take that out."

"I hadn't decided."

"It gives the house character. And you're probably going to modernize the fireplace. All those house people do it. I've watched *Flip or Flop*."

The frown was growing.

"Oh, never mind." She was doing this all wrong. She hadn't even taken off her jacket.

He laid a hand over hers and sent a jolt zipping along her nerve endings clear to her chest. "I promise I'll retain the character of the house."

Was it suddenly hot in here? She freed her hand and opened the jacket. His eyes slid to her cleavage. *Oh, Jo, you're so smart.*

"I'm in this business because I love houses and I love fixing them up," he said, returning his gaze to her face. He looked so sincere.

And maybe he was, but darn it all, why did he have to be sincere about *her* house?

"I've got an idea."

"What?" she asked.

"Why don't I stop by one night this week? You can share your vision for the place."

And show off Close Encounter Outfit Number Two. Perhaps she could convince him to sell to her on some kind of payment plan. Maybe he'd let her rent with an option to buy. Unlike Mrs. Bing, he could probably afford to carry her.

Financially. Not off to bed. *Get your mind out of the sheets!* "Okay," she said.

Don't leave it at that, scolded Marvella. *What are you thinking?*

That Ben Fordham has great eyes. Those brown eyes reminded her of chocolate. She loved chocolate.

Never mind his eyes! Promise him food. You can poison him.

Poisoning was not acceptable. But food… "I can make dinner," she suggested. Maybe he had a girl-friend. Maybe he'd think Noel was desperate for a man. Her cheeks began to heat up. "Unless you have, um, unless…"

"Dinner sounds good. How about Friday night?"

Friday night was a date night. He obviously didn't have a girlfriend.

Excellent, said Marvella. *Then you can sleep with him. That'll sweeten him up.*

I'm not pimping myself out for a house, she told both herself and Marvella.

A girl's gotta do what a girl's gotta do. Marvella said that a lot in her books, but never in this context.

Noel told her to butt out and stick to helping children in trouble. Then she smiled at Ben. "Thank you. You're being very considerate." *Even though you did buy my house out from under me.*

"I'm not out to make enemies," he said. "In fact, I've never found myself in a situation like this before."

He was looking at her so earnestly. He sure was… masculine. The sizzle on her face slipped way south. It was time to get out of this very hot office.

Noel stood. "Well, thanks. I guess you know where I live," she added.

He stood, too. Oh, he was…big. He smiled and all the hot spots got hotter. "I think I can find you."

She swallowed and nodded. "I'd better go," she said, backing up. She backed into the door and her face got even hotter. "Um, I'll see you Friday, then."

"What time?"

Anytime you want. "Six?"

"I'll be there."

She nodded again and then opened the door and hurried out.

Janelle, the secretary/guard, glared at her as she did her jacket back up. "Have a nice day." Translation: I'd like to poke out your eye with a candy cane.

"Thank you," Noel said with dignity and left.

Okay, mission accomplished. Sort of.

Sleep with him, urged Marvella. *It will help the cause.*

She was certainly not going to lower herself to that. But if she could convince him to sell the house to her, if he was willing to be creative and make a deal, maybe they could both end up with a happy New Year.

If not, poison him, Marvella advised.

Right.

Chapter Five

Monday meant a school day. Normally Riley was happy to get back to work after a holiday weekend. Not today. A woman shouldn't have to go to work and see the man-stealer who took her man. A woman shouldn't have to come into the teacher's lounge at lunch and find the man-stealer in there feeding her skinny, undernourished body with yogurt, passing up the pumpkin bread Marge Connor had brought in while mere mortals who had no power to resist snagged a piece and ate it to console themselves for their romantic loss.

Riley took her pumpkin bread and her sack lunch and seated herself at the far end of the table, determined to ignore the man-stealer. For her, Emily Dieb no longer existed.

"Hi, Riley," Marge said from where she stood at the counter, helping herself to a cup of coffee. "How was your Thanksgiving?"

Rotten, thanks to that woman who pretended to be my friend and then stole my fiancé. Riley shot a quick glance in Emily's direction. *Look at her over there, all remorseful and pleading, that sad expression in her eyes, like she really feels bad about what she did.*

"It was great," Riley lied, and then, before Marge could ask for any details on her wonderful weekend with Sean, she changed the subject. "I'm so glad you brought in some of your pumpkin bread."

"I had some left from the weekend with the kids and I had to get it out of the house." Marge patted one hefty hip. "There's been too much on the lips and now it's forever on the hips."

"You look fine," Riley told her. "There's nothing wrong with looking like a woman." Instead of a skinny, man-thieving stick.

"Well, that's kind of you to say," Marge said. "I really should go on a diet, but I'm not even going to attempt that until after the holidays. Speaking of, how are the wedding plans coming along?"

Riley's face suddenly burned. "Um, you'll be getting an email about that soon."

Marge's brows knit. "Trouble?"

"No trouble." Just no wedding. "You know, I've got some things I need to do in my room." With that, she gathered up her turkey sandwich and skedaddled. She was out the door and halfway down the hall when she heard Emily calling her.

"Riley, wait. Please wait."

She kept walking and now Emily was running. *No running in the halls.* Riley frowned and kept going.

A couple of little girls passed her. "Ms. Dieb's running in the hall," one of them reported.

I'll send her to the principal's office. Maybe she'd like to hit on him, add him to her man collection.

"Riley, wait," Emily said, catching up with her.

Did she really think Riley was going to stand there right in the middle of the hall and chat with her about their reality TV lives? Riley didn't wait.

Emily fell in step. "Are you ever going to be able to forgive me?"

"At some point, yes. But I'll never be able to stand being around you. Good luck and happy New Year," she finished and marched into her classroom and shut the door. Then she sat down at her desk and indulged in yet another good cry. Not that she had more than a few minutes to cry. Recess would soon be over and then she'd have to be on top of her game. The kids would be back in the room, and it would be time to go over math skills.

She looked around at her little kingdom of learning. It held eight tables, each with four chairs grouped around them so students could work together on projects. One side of the room was lined with a shelf of cubbyholes for students to store their coats and backpacks. Then there was the reading corner, with tubs of books and carpet squares for comfy kid seating. The table by the window housed science displays—a small aquarium, a terrarium and now Noel's rats. Computers sat at the back of the room, and the walls held everything from a white-board to a TV, along with posters promoting reading and math skills, plus her holiday decorations. Here in this room, thirty-two children adored her. Here her life was under control. Here was where Emily used to stop by after class and suggest they get a latte at Java Josie's.

Oh, no. No more thinking about Emily.

Here was where Sean had sent flowers for her birthday.

Especially no more thinking about Sean!

Thankfully, the bell rang, and within minutes rosy-cheeked children were pouring into the room, laughing and talking and still hyped up from chasing each other around the playground. The room smelled of sweaty little bodies and fresh air. She quickly took care of crowd control and got them settled down. It didn't take much because Monday after recess they always played Wise Old Owl, the trivia game she'd created from past assignments. Her students competed for such treasures as lip balm, glow bracelets, tentacle balls and stickers. She loved this game as much as the kids did, and soon they were deep into it, and thoughts of Sean the disloyal and Emily the Man-Stealer fell away. Thank God for work.

But then work ended and the orange school buses chugged off with her thirty-two distractions and Riley was left alone with her sad self. What would she ask Santa for when she and Jo and Noel went to the mall? How about a stocking full of happiness? She could use some.

You need to refocus, she told herself. *You still have lots of good things in your life.*

It was true. She did. She loved her job. She had a great family. She was about to become an aunt, for heaven's sake. And she had close friends. Faithful friends. Well, most of them were. The thought of Emily's betrayal left her needing a cookie. Maybe she'd bake some brownies. Yes, chocolate cured all ills. She'd barely gotten home when her mother called. "How are you doing?" Mom asked.

"Fine," Riley lied. Tears began to spill and she sniffed.

"It'll get better once you have a little distance from this. Would you like me to call the golf club?"

She was tempted to hand off the ugly chore of canceling her venue to her mom, but she resisted. "No. I reserved it. I'll cancel it."

"All right, if you're sure. I think we've gotten hold of all the family now."

Goody. All her relatives knew about the great Thanksgiving dumping. "Thanks, Mom," she managed.

"And your sister's got most of your friends covered. But you'll probably have to let your fellow teachers know."

Ugh. Telling the people she worked with every day was going to be the hardest.

"I'm really sorry this happened," Mom said.

That made two of them.

"But remember, all things work together for good."

Riley was sure this dilemma was the exception to the rule, but she said, "I know."

"Meanwhile, pamper yourself."

"I am. I'm going to make some brownies."

"Good idea," Mom said. "That can be your reward after you call The Pines."

Subtle. She'd call and cancel the venue, but first things first.

She ended the call with her mother and got out her ingredients and got busy. Soon her apartment was filled with the aroma of chocolate. She baked up half a batch of brownies (a girl had to have some self-control, after all) and then ate half the pan. *So, if Riley baked half a batch of brownies and only ate half, how many brownies did Riley eat? Too many!*

After she'd fortified herself, she sent out a group email to the Whispering Pines Elementary School faculty. Due to circumstances beyond my control... Scratch that. I hope you haven't bought a wedding gift yet. LOL. Ugh. Someone among us is a traitor, therefore... She hit delete again. She finally settled on:

Just a quick note to let you know Sean and I have called off our wedding. It would appear we're not a match, after all. Thank you for your understanding.

By the time she hit Send she was emotionally drained. She'd cancel the venue tomorrow. Or the day after. She'd get to it soon.

Riley didn't get around to canceling the venue,

but over the next few days she did create more story problems with new batches of cookies. *If Riley eats half the package of gumdrops before putting them in her gumdrop cookies how many pounds did she add to her thighs?* And… *If Riley makes a dozen sugar cookies and takes them to school tomorrow, how many would she have to force-feed Emily to put even an ounce on her thighs?*

When December 1 rolled around, she was sick of story problems, sick of cookies and sick of having to see Emily. And more than ready to pick up Jo and Noel, go to the mall and see Santa.

They'd all agreed to dress Christmassy for their holiday photo op, and Jo was looking chic in a cream-colored sweater accented with a red scarf and her maternity jeans. Her hair fell in a shimmering cascade to her shoulders, and she wore gold ballet slippers and a gold bracelet and earrings. Noel had donned a green sweater, a pair of Jo's pre-pregnancy black leggings and her new black boots.

Riley was in a red sweater, jeans and her favorite ankle boots. No shimmering highlights. Maybe if she'd highlighted her hair, gone more blond like Jo…

Okay, now you're just being stupid, she told herself. *You look fine.* Well, except for the extra cookie pounds she'd put on.

"We look good," Jo said, confirming it, and Riley smiled.

It was pushing six as they made their way to Santa's Play Land, and most people were home having dinner. The few left in the mall were down at the food court stuffing themselves with cheap Chinese food, hot wings, blended drinks and cookies, so there was no line of parents and offspring waiting to see Santa, who was sitting all by himself on his holiday throne in front of his red shack.

This year's version was sure authentic-looking, down to the nose like a cherry. Or berry. Or tomato. Whatever. His beard was full, but well-trimmed, and both that and the hair under his hat were white as new-fallen snow. The photographer wasn't your typical photo-snapping twenty-something. This year Mrs. Santa had come along for the ride. She appeared to be somewhere in her seventies and was as round as her famous spouse. Her hair was equally white and done up in tight little curls, like grandmas in the fifties used to sport. Wire-rimmed glasses perched on her nose and she wore a ruffled white blouse and a red skirt over which she'd tied a ruffled and beribboned candy-striped apron. The pair looked like they'd stepped right out of the poem that had made the modern Santa so popular.

Santa watched the three women approach with a cocked head and a grin. "I've been expecting you ladies," he greeted them.

"I think the only one expecting here is me," Jo cracked and patted her gigantic baby bulge.

"Ah, yes. You are about to experience a lot of Christmas joy, young lady," he told her.

They gathered around him. What kind of aftershave was the man wearing? It was great. He smelled like peppermint and balsam.

"So, Santa, can you guess what we want?" Jo asked.

"I have a pretty good idea. I keep a list of who's naughty and who's nice."

Jo snickered.

"You're the easiest of all," he told her. "I suspect you'd like that baby to come soon."

"You got that right."

"And you two ladies," he said, turning his benevolent gaze on Riley and Noel. "How about you? Old Santa knows what you want but you go ahead and tell him."

I'd like a man, Riley thought. *A perfect man.* "I'll just settle for having my picture taken."

Santa lifted a bushy, white eyebrow. "You're not going to come right out and ask for that perfect man?"

"What?" Riley stammered. Had she spoken out loud and not realized it?

"Ladies, it's time Santa brought you all what you deserve." He held out a hand, beckoning them to come closer. Then he settled Noel on his leg. "Tell me what you'd like, my dear."

"A house," she said. "I want to buy the house I'm living in."

"I think that can be arranged," he said. "And I bet you'll want to start a family in that house. How about a good man to go with it? There's nothing like going through life with someone who loves you," he added, smiling at Mrs. Claus, who was holding her camera and beaming back at him.

"That would be nice," Noel admitted. "But I'll settle for a house."

"You don't believe in love?" Santa asked. "Or maybe you don't believe in Santa."

Noel's face turned as red as the old guy's suit.

"That's fine," he said. "We'll make a believer out of you. I have the perfect man in mind."

"There's no such thing," Riley muttered.

"The one I have in mind for you will be," Santa said, drawing her onto his other leg. "You be on the lookout. You're going to find yours in quite a memorable way." He smiled at Noel. "You've already met yours."

Noel gaped and he chuckled.

"Oh, you're really good," said Jo.

"I try to be. Now, as for you, young lady."

She cut him off. "I already have a man."

"Yes, you do, and he's the perfect man for you. But you have another one who's going to arrive any minute."

Okay, this guy was creepy.

"Oooh," Jo wailed and Riley turned to see her looking down at her wet pants in disgust. "My water broke," she announced.

"What!" Riley jumped up.

"Get me out of here!" Jo demanded.

"Don't panic," Riley said. Where had she parked her car?

"We can be at the hospital in ten minutes." Noel took Jo's arm as if she was an invalid. Riley took her other arm and they rushed her off the platform.

"Ho, ho, ho," chuckled Santa. "Hope he waits that long."

"I'm having a girl," Jo snarled as they led her away.

"Not this time," Santa shot back. "You're going to have a merry Christmas, all of you. I'm going to make all your wishes come true."

"What kind of Santa is that?" Joe grumbled as they made their way across the mall. She looked down at her damp legs and groaned. "Oh, this is gross."

"But just think, the baby's finally coming!" Noel said, putting a positive spin on the situation.

"What if I have the baby here in the mall? Oh, please God, don't do that to me," Jo cried and started waddling faster.

"You're going to be fine," Riley told her. "We're *all* going to be fine." And she, too, picked up her pace. What if they had to deliver the baby right then and there? She didn't know anything about delivering babies beyond boiling water and telling the mother to pant during contractions. Wasn't that what the childbirth instructor had said when she'd gone to that class with Jo? She couldn't remember. She couldn't remember anything!

Jo stopped, her face contorted. "Ooooh."

Labor pains. Oh, no!

"Breathe," said Noel, who knew about as much about giving birth as Riley did.

"I *am* breathing," Jo snapped and started moving once more. "I'm never getting pregnant again. Never!"

As soon as they were out of the mall, Riley realized she'd taken the wrong exit.

"Wait, this isn't right," Noel said.

"You guys," cried Jo. "Come *on.*"

"Okay, we came in over by Kohl's," Riley said. *Duh.* What was wrong with her brain? Oh, yeah, they were having a baby.

Jo let out a groan and fell onto a little bench outside the door.

Yes! Sit down, rest. Stay CALM! "You wait here. I'll get the car," Riley said and took off at a run—in the wrong direction. A moment later she corrected herself and turned the other way. "I'll be right back," she called as her sister watched in panic.

"Hurry!" Noel urged.

Hurry, hurry, hurry. Yes, hurry. It had started snowing while they were in the mall and she found herself skidding as she raced across the parking lot. She hated driving in the snow.

You have snow tires. You'll be fine. Don't anybody panic!

Yes, yes, no panicking. Where the heck was her stupid car?

She pressed her key and it beeped at her. *Over here, stupid.*

Oh, yes. Over there. She skated toward it. *Walking in a Winter Wonderland.* More like running around like a crazy woman in a snowstorm. *Hurry!*

Get into the car, screech out of the parking slot,

*nearly hit two little old ladies, mutter, "Sorry," when
one of them flips you off. Hurry, hurry, HURRY!*

She pulled up in front of where Noel and Jo were
waiting, and Noel yanked open the passenger door
and literally shoved Jo inside, almost shutting her
foot in the door.

"Hey, watch it," Jo protested as Riley sped forward, leaving Noel at the curb.

"Wait!"

*Okay, back up, let Noel in. Breathe deep. Don't
anybody panic.*

Noel got in and Riley shot across the parking lot.

"Wait! My seat belt's not on," Noel protested.

Riley didn't slow down.

"We're all gonna die," Jo predicted. "Ooooh. I
don't feel good."

"Don't worry. We'll get you there," Riley promised.

"Alive. I want to get there *alive*. That's all I want
for Christmas. Just let me live to see this baby born,"
Jo pleaded.

"You know I'm a great driver," Riley said as she
ran a red light. Well, okay. She wasn't the world's
best driver, but this was no time to remind her sister of that.

"I don't think everyone in town agrees with you,"
Noel said.

Sure enough. There were the flashing red and
blue lights, a holiday greeting from the Whispering Pines police force.

Chapter Six

"I don't believe this," Jo wailed. Of all the times for the cops to actually appear. The Whispering Pines police force wasn't that large. (Not much needed in a town where the biggest crimes were mailbox-bashing and the occasional rash of teen shoplifting.) People joked that if you wanted a cop you had to go to Donut Delights. And now one of them had to show up and stop them. "I'm gonna have this kid right here!" In her sister's car. Without drugs! *Noooo.*

"Pleeease don't do that," Riley said.

Like she had any control over these contractions? "What am I supposed to do, cross my legs?"

The cop was at the car window now. Riley lowered it and before he could say anything, both she and Jo were talking at once. "This is an emergency," Riley said as Jo cried, "We have to get to the hospital!"

The guy's eyes bugged as if he'd just witnessed a zombie from *The Walking Dead* climbing out of the glove compartment.

"If you have to give me a ticket, can you please

wait and give it to me at the hospital?" Riley begged. "Her water broke and this baby's going to come out any second."

He looked slightly ill but nodded gamely. "I'll escort you there."

"That would be great," Riley gushed. "Thanks, Officer, uh…"

"Knight," he supplied.

"As in white knight," Noel said from the back-seat. "Or knight in shining armor."

Okay, so he was cute with those broad shoulders and brown eyes, but this was no time to be picking up men. "Let's go, you guys," Jo growled.

The officer touched the brim of his cap and returned to his patrol car. A moment later he was in front of them, lights flashing. Then he turned on the siren and they were off, racing down the street, cars hugging the curb to get out of their way, running more red lights, driving like crazy.

"I'm going to be sick," Noel groaned from the backseat.

"Don't barf in my car. We're almost there," Riley said.

"You're tailgating," Noel informed her. "And it's snowing."

"I'm just trying to keep up," Riley said. Her jaw was clenched and she had the steering wheel in a death grip.

Speaking of death grips, here came another contraction. "I'll never complain about cramps again," Jo vowed with a whimper. *You wanted this*, she reminded herself. She and Mike had been trying for the last three years. But…

Why didn't people tell you how painful childbirth was? Mom should have warned her. The childbirth instructor should have warned her. Yes, of course she'd had them practice their breathing and she'd talked about pain. But she hadn't talked about PAIN.

Mom. She needed Mom. She fished her cell phone from her purse and speed-dialed. Mom barely got as far as "Hi, sweetie," before Jo cut in with, "I'm having this baby now!"

"Where are you? Are you at the hospital?"

"Riley's driving me there. Oh, my God, don't hit that dog!"

Her sister swerved, rocking her against the car door and making Noel groan again.

"Why is Riley driving you? She's a terrible driver. You should have called me."

"There wasn't time."

"Well, don't worry. Grammy and I are on our way," Mom assured her. "Tell your sister to slow down. And what's that I hear?"

"Sirens."

"Why are there sirens? I thought you just said Riley's driving you."

"We've got a police escort. Hurry, Mom!"

"Sweetheart, don't worry. It's a first baby. You have plenty of time."

"My water broke."

"How far apart are your contractions?" Mom asked.

"I don't know," Jo groaned. "We haven't timed them." Of course they should've been doing that, but between the cop and her sister's crazy driving... another contraction rolled over her in a huge, sick wave. "Maybe three minutes," she said after the wave had crashed. "I don't feel good."

"We're leaving now. Meanwhile, don't push," Mom said and ended the call.

Another couple of blocks, and they pulled up in front of the emergency room. The cop ran inside and before you could say *episiotomy*, he was back with a hospital attendant pushing a wheelchair.

Jo doubled over halfway to the chair, her body anxious to launch her little girl into the world. "Oooh."

"Don't push," said the attendant.

"If one more person says that, I'm going to scream!" Oh, yeah. She *was* screaming.

Meanwhile, here was her sister talking to Mr. Cutie Cop as if they'd just met at a singles bar. There wasn't time for sweet-talking her way out of a ticket. They had to get going.

"Don't give her a ticket," Jo panted. "She probably saved you from having to deliver this baby."

"Just a warning," he said.

"Good. We've been warned. We can go," Jo said as the attendant wheeled her toward Labor and Delivery and an epidural. Oh, yes, the sooner, the better!

Since it was obvious her water had broken, she was admitted at the speed of light and a hasty birth plan was drawn up, since hers was at home, in the desk drawer in her office. Then she was taken to a room.

"I'll watch your purse," Noel offered, opting to stay behind. Big sissy. But she didn't blame Noel for not wanting to go any farther on this ride. That was nothing she'd signed up for. And frankly, Jo didn't want to go, either. She didn't want to be here at all. But childbirth was one of those things where there was no back exit, no other road. The only way was forward through the pain. And at the end of all of that was her baby, she reminded herself.

She was more than ready for her epidural, but first she had to change into her stylish hospital gown and provide a urine sample. *What if I have the baby in the toilet?*

Thankfully, she didn't. "Okay, time for drugs?" she suggested as she fell onto the bed.

"Almost," the nurse told her.

Almost. She said it to herself like a mantra. Almost, almost, almost. *You know how many women have babies? You can do this. Stop being such a wimp.* Where was the painkiller? Almost, almost, almost.

She was getting hooked up to monitors with Riley standing guard when Mom and Grammy arrived. "We're all here. Isn't this nice?" Grammy said after giving her a kiss on the forehead.

Nice. Was that what you called it?

"You know, back when I had you they wouldn't

let anybody but the father come in," Mom said to her as the nurse finished hooking her up.

"Yes, even I couldn't come in," Grammy added. "Can you imagine? Her own mother! Now it's a regular party. Give the hospital your guest list and the whole world can come."

"Times change," said Mom.

"Well, I'm glad we can be here," Grammy said. "But I don't think men should be allowed in to see… everything." She looked around the room with its monitors and screens and medical knickknacks. "All this equipment. We've certainly come a long way since the old days. You know your great-great-grandmother had all her children at home, on the farm." She shook her head. "The family sold that land for a song. If they'd only held on to it a little longer, we could all have been millionaires. Who would've thought they'd put in a mall there?" she finished as the nurse checked to see how things were progressing.

The story of the lost real estate fortune had been told many times and at the moment Jo couldn't have cared less. All she wanted was her epidural.

"You're six centimeters dilated, my dear," the nurse told Jo.

"Oh, my. Fast for a first baby," Mom said calmly as if the nurse had merely announced that it was still snowing.

"Six centimeters! Give me my epidural. Quick!"

Now Dad had arrived. "I came right from work. How's my girl?"

"Which one?" Jo managed to joke. Oooh, here was another contraction.

He smoothed her forehead. "You'll both be fine. Your brother's on his way. I'm going to go sit with him in the waiting room."

"You're on the list, Jay. You can stay here," Mom said.

"That's okay." Dad smiled weakly. "You've probably got enough people already."

That was true. Like Grammy said, they had a regular party going on and everyone was having fun except her.

The anesthesiologist finally showed up an eternity after her father left. "Oh, God bless you," Jo said when he'd introduced himself.

"I hear that a lot," he said then launched into a speech about the risks involved in numbing her pain.

"Just give it to me," she begged.

"Sorry," he said. "I have to tell you all this."

"Then speed it up, for crying out loud!"

The anesthesiologist hurried through his spiel. "Any questions?"

"Yes! Why are you waiting?"

"Okay, let's have you sign these papers."

Jo complied and then, finally, she got her drugs. "I'm going to need you to hold still," the anesthesiologist said as she crumpled around her large belly with a groan.

"Don't push," the nurse cautioned.

That was like asking a chicken not to lay an egg.

"Breathe," Riley said and started demonstrating.

Yes, breathe. Breathe, breathe, breathe. Pant, pant, pant. *Aaargh*.

"Focus," Riley commanded.

And she'd wanted her sister to be her coach because…? Oh, yeah. Because her husband, who should've been here, was out at sea playing Captain Nemo. She was going to kill him. No. First she was going to divorce him, then she'd kill him. *You did this to me!*

The process seemed endless with cycles of breathing and pushing.

"You're doing great," Mom assured her.

"You can do this, sis," Riley added.

Yes, she could. It was time to meet her daughter.

"We're crowning," the doctor said.

Crowning. Oh, yes. Annabelle Rose was about to make her entrance.

"Three more pushes."

With her final push Jo forgot about her pain and suffering, her indignity, her frustration over her absent husband—and brought her baby into the world. Oh, wow. There she was, Annabelle Rose, bloody and bawling, in the doctor's gentle hands, on her way to Jo's tummy. Joy. Amazement. New life. What suffering?

"It's a boy," Riley announced.

"No, it's a girl," Jo corrected her. The ultrasound had found no male appendages on this child. They were having a girl. She'd had the name picked out for ages, the nursery was pink, the drawers were full of girly pastel outfits.

"Guess you should've checked the sex of the baby," Grammy said. "Because this one has a Wee Willie Winkie on him."

A girl. She'd wanted a girl, planned on a girl. "But the ultrasound…"

"Doesn't always show everything," the doctor said.

"How lovely." Mom sighed. "Our first grandson."

And here he lay. Yes, he was definitely a he. Jo looked at her son and fell in love. Big eyes and a bloodied mat of brown hair the same color as his daddy's, a sweet little mouth. That was making a lot of noise.

"Good, healthy lungs," said the doctor.

Jo touched a finger to his cheek. He was beautiful. No, he was more than that. He was a miracle. To think this new little person had grown inside her.

"Who would like to cut the cord?" the doctor offered.

"That should be you, Rose," Grammy said to Mom.

So, with tears in her eyes Mom did the honors and they all wiped at their eyes and hugged each other as the nurse took the baby to clean him up and put him in the warmer.

"I'm so proud of you," Mom said to Jo as she hugged her.

Jo hugged her mother back, tears still flowing down her cheeks. She had just gone through hell but now she felt as if she was dancing at the very gates of heaven. She'd experienced the mystical wonder of the cycle of life. Like Eve and billions of other women down through time, she'd grown a living being inside her, started a whole new person. This baby that had begun as a speck would grow up to play baseball like his daddy, would trick-or-treat wearing little superhero costumes, would make her plaster handprints for Mother's Day. Maybe he'd become a track star or a rock singer. Maybe he'd go to law school or medical school. Maybe someday he'd deliver babies himself. Oh, yes, this baby was going to grow up to do something wonderful.

No, there was no *going to* about it. He already was wonderful, more than wonderful. "He's perfect."

"Santa," Riley said suddenly.

"Yes, Santa brought you the perfect Christmas present," Mom said to Jo, beaming.

"No, the mall Santa. Remember what he said?" Riley asked Jo.

"This night's a blur," Jo replied.

"What did the Santa say?" Mom asked.

"He predicted this when we went to see him," Riley explained.

Mom gave her an indulgent smile and patted her on the arm. "It wasn't too hard to predict."

"No, I mean he predicted everything. He told Jo she was going to have a boy. How could he have known that?"

"Lucky guess. He had a fifty-fifty chance of being correct."

"He said the baby would come right away and

then my water broke," Jo remembered. "Actually, that kind of creeps me out."

"It was time," Mom said, not getting it.

"You had to be there," Riley said. "We were talking about perfect men and he told Jo she had the perfect man and that another was going to arrive any minute."

Mom raised an eyebrow and smiled. "So you got a Santa who moonlights as a fortune-teller?"

"Okay, that does sound weird," Riley admitted.

"Anyway, who cares? All that matters is that our little guy is here, safe and sound," Jo said.

"Amen to that," Grammy said heartily. "You done good, kiddo."

Yes, she had. And she was on such a high she was sure she'd never come down.

Later, after she'd been installed in her room, after the in-laws had showered her with chocolates and her family had all congratulated her, and finally, at Mom's insistence, left her to get some rest—when it was just her and her son cuddling in that hospital bed in their postpartum room—she looked down at the little guy. She held his tiny hand and decided there was no gift on the planet, no gift in the history of gifts, as great as motherhood.

And then it was time to attempt nursing. Oh, dear Lord. Here was more pain nobody had told her about. Where was her husband right now?

Chapter Seven

The next evening Riley drove to the hospital to visit her sister. As she swished along on slushy streets she couldn't help thinking that normally on a Friday night she'd be going out with Sean. What was he doing tonight? Probably taking Emily to dinner and a movie. Emily would be on her way home via the gym, where she'd run six hundred miles. After that she'd go home and get into something sexy. Sean would come over, take one look at her and say, "Let's stay in tonight." And then she'd take off her something sexy...

Riley ground her teeth. Maybe when she was done visiting her sister she'd go home and make some more cookies. *Riley has doubled her recipe for snowball cookies. If she eats the whole batch how many calories has Riley consumed?*

No cookie-baking. She'd stream a movie. Or she'd just spend the whole evening at the hospital with Jo and her new nephew. Yes, that was a much better option. Mom and Dad and Grammy would be there—all the people who loved her.

Okay, that took care of tonight. But what about tomorrow night? *If Riley bakes a red velvet cake…*

Sigh. The holidays were going to be tough. There was no getting around it.

She got to her sister's room while a feeding lesson was taking place. Although from the grim expression on Jo's face it looked more like a torture session. Mom and Grammy and Jo's mother-in-law, Georgia, were all by the bedside. So was a woman with long dark hair and the face of those Madonnas you saw on stamps at Christmas.

"You're doing great," said the imitation Madonna. "He's latching on beautifully."

"There you have it," Grammy said. "You'll be a pro at this in no time."

"If my nipples don't fall off," Jo said through gritted teeth.

"Gross," Riley muttered as she entered the room.

"You'll toughen up," Georgia assured Jo.

Jo grimaced. But then she looked down at the baby in her arms and smiled. "He is perfect, isn't he?"

"Just like Santa predicted," Riley said. She greeted Georgia, kissed her mother and grandmother then squeezed in to get a closer view of her beautiful nephew. Those tiny hands, that cute little button nose. Jo was so lucky.

"I think you have everything under control," the woman said. She produced a business card. "Feel free to call if you have any more questions."

Jo murmured her thanks and the woman left.

"Who was that?" Riley asked.

"She's a lactation consultant," Jo said. "They're experts in nursing."

"In my day you didn't need an expert," Grammy said.

"That's because you bottle-fed us," Mom reminded her and Grammy shut her mouth and pouted.

"Have you let Mike know yet?" Riley asked.

Jo nodded, then frowned, and this frown had nothing to do with the little guy in her arms. "It has to go through the Red Cross."

"Strange, if you ask me," Grammy said.

"They do things differently when the men are on a sub," Georgia explained. "Secrecy."

Jo sighed. "Frustrating," she said.

"He'll be home soon." Georgia smiled, encouraging her to look on the bright side.

Jo didn't appear inclined to look in that direction.

"It does kind of suck not to have her husband here," Riley said.

"Of course it does," Grammy agreed. "But he's a sailor. Sailors go to sea."

"He's been going to sea for eight years. He needs to be done," Jo growled. "I'm not going to raise this child alone."

Her mother-in-law squirmed in her seat and her mother patted her hand and said, "Don't upset yourself, honey."

"Yes, you'll sour your milk," put in Grammy, the faux expert.

Jo's jaw was now clenched so tight Riley was

sure they wouldn't be able to pry it open even with the Jaws of Life. Time to change the subject. "Have you picked a name?"

Jo's jaw relaxed somewhat. "We didn't talk much about boy names, but I'm thinking Michael Brandon."

Naming their son after her husband—that was a nice gesture, and surely a sign that there was hope for Jo and Mike.

"Mike will love that," Georgia said.

Jo's jaws clenched again. This time in pain. "Lord, help me. I recant."

Oh, the things women endured for love. Riley thought of Sean and she grimaced, too.

"I guess I owe that crazy Santa a big thank-you." Jo ran a finger over the baby's downy head. She glanced up at Riley, her brows drawn. "Darn. I just realized we never got our picture."

"You're right. I wonder if it's too late."

"Considering the circumstances under which you left, the photographer probably saved it in her camera," Mom said.

"I can go check," Riley offered. It would give her something to do.

"That's a great idea. Bring it back here and we can all see it," Grammy said. "And while you're out, pick up some burgers. The food here is awful."

With two grandmothers and a great-grandmother all hovering by the bed, Riley knew it would be an age and a half before she got to hold the baby, so she touched his little hand and then departed on her mission.

There was a line of parents and children waiting at Santa's Play Land to see him. This was a new Santa, with a long face and tired eyes and an equally tired-looking costume. And where was Mrs. Claus?

Riley skirted the line and went to where a college-age girl in an elf suit stood, snapping pictures while Santa said, "Ho, ho, ho," and waved goodbye to a tearful toddler.

"Hi," Riley began.

The elf gave her a distracted hello and fiddled with her digital camera while another supplicant approached Santa's throne.

"Ho, ho, ho! Who have we got here?" Santa asked the boy in the Christmas suit and red bow tie. Not quite as prescient as her Santa had been.

"I was here yesterday," she said to the elf.

The elf looked at her warily. "Is there a problem?"

"No, no problem. Well, just a small one. About our picture."

"If you didn't like your picture you should've said so yesterday." The elf studied her. "I don't remember you."

"Ho, ho, ho," Santa said.

"That's my cue," said the elf, and raised her camera.

"You weren't here yesterday."

The elf frowned. "Yeah, I was. The whole night except for when we went on break."

So theirs must have been a substitute Santa. "I

guess you were on break when we came." The elf continued to frown and Riley hurried on. "Anyway, we left without getting pictures because my sister was pregnant and her water broke when we were talking to him."

The elf made a face. "Yuck."

"Is there some way I can get a copy of the picture now? I was hoping the Mrs. Claus who took it saved it in the camera."

"We don't have a Mrs. Claus."

"She was here. Last night. Around six. Taking pictures for Santa."

"Santa was on break then. So was I. There wasn't anybody here."

That couldn't be right. "There was a Santa here," Riley insisted, pointing to the plywood chalet. "Over there."

"Trust me. He wasn't. He was eating a burger and fries at the Dairy Queen drive-through and I was with him."

"Then who?" The hairs on the back of Riley's neck snapped to attention.

The elf looked at her as if she was crazy and shook her head. "Sorry. I don't know who took your picture but it wasn't us." Santa ho-ho-hoed again and she got back to work with her camera, leaving Riley to go away and puzzle out her close Christmas encounter on her own.

She was still puzzling as she drove down the street toward the fast-food drive-in. Who was that guy? Should she tell security that they had someone with a red-suit fetish running around impersonating Mr. Claus? And what about his accomplice? She'd seemed like such a sweet old lady. What was their racket, anyway? Maybe they were kidnappers out to make contact with trusting little kids.

No, that was silly. What were they going to do there in the mall, tuck kids under their arms like two-legged footballs and run for it? Hop on a reindeer and gallop out of town? And what about all those strange predictions? Once more, the hairs on Riley's neck stood at attention, like soldiers in *The Nutcracker* ballet. This was so…weird.

With her brain fully occupied by the mystery of the phony mall Santa, she wasn't paying proper attention to traffic. The red light and the red taillights in front of her didn't register until… Yikes! She slammed on the brakes and skidded right into the car in front of her.

Oh, no. She'd never been in a traffic accident. Never even had a ticket. Well, okay, three warnings, counting last night. But those weren't the same as tickets.

She hopped out of her car and started to run up to the dented compact. Wait a minute. She knew this car… The driver got out. "Emily!"

Emily's sweet expression morphed into something Ebenezer Scrooge would've been proud of. "Riley."

"Are you okay?"

Emily ignored the question. "You hit me."

That was stating the obvious. "I'm so sorry."

"You did it on purpose."

"What? Why would I do that?"

Emily gave a snort of disgust. "Because you're passive-aggressive. Who knew?"

"I am not!" Riley protested. "You might've stolen my fiancé, but that doesn't make me passive-aggressive."

"See? Listen to you."

Two other drivers had pulled up. An old woman in a red wool cape and black stretch pants joined them. "I saw it all. I'll be a witness."

"There's nothing to witness," Riley said. "All we have to do is exchange—"

She didn't get a chance to finish. Emily pointed a finger at her. "What did you tell everyone?"

"What do you mean?"

"Don't play dumb. Everyone at school knows I'm the reason you and Sean broke up. I can tell by the way they all look at me."

"I didn't say anything about you. Marge asked what happened and I said he'd found someone else."

"It wasn't all that hard to figure out who the someone else is, since you're not speaking to me anymore," Emily snapped.

Wait a minute. How did *she* become the evil witch in this story? "Well, excuse me if I don't want to talk about how things are going with you and my ex or ask about your plans for the weekend."

Emily whipped her cell phone out of her jacket pocket. "I'm calling 911."

"For a fender bender?"

"No, for a personal attack."

Now here was the woman from the second car. She was raising her cell phone in Riley's direction, taking pictures. She had a tall guy in a parka with her and he, too, had a camera—a big fancy one that probably took great night shots.

"I'm Lizbeth Parker from the *Whispering Pines Chronicle*," the woman said to Riley. "Do you have a comment?"

"What?"

"She attacked me with her car," Emily insisted.

"I did not!" Riley cried. But boy, she'd like to do exactly that right about now. "And there ought to be a number you can call when women steal their friends' fiancés," she added, glaring at Emily. Oh, no. Had she just said that in front of a reporter?

The old woman in the red cape looked at Emily aghast. "You stole her fiancé?"

"Not on purpose," Emily said.

Accidental man theft—there was no such thing.

"I don't blame you for rear-ending her," the old woman told Riley.

"I didn't do it on purpose." She realized she'd echoed Emily's words. How ironic. "I was... My mind was somewhere else."

"Then you shouldn't be driving." The old woman leaned forward and sniffed Riley's breath. "Have you been drinking, young woman?"

"No! And turn off your phone and that...camera," Riley said to the reporter.

"Sorry. This is news."

"Since when is a fender bender news?"

"Since the woman whose fender you're bending took your man," replied Lizbeth Parker.

This couldn't be happening.

Now here came a patrol car, his red and blue lights flashing. And out of the car stepped… Oh, no. Riley's escort from the night before. First he caught her running a red light and now this.

"Is there a problem?" he asked.

Emily pointed a finger at Riley. "She rear-ended me. It was an assault! With a car."

"I did not!" Riley shot back, her cheeks hot. Oh, boy. This was probably going to be in tomorrow's paper.

"I saw it all," said the old woman. "She did."

"It was an accident," Riley explained. "I was…" *Thinking about the mystery mall Santa.* No way was she saying that in front of a reporter. "Never mind. Just give me my ticket."

"You need to arrest her," Emily insisted. "Wait till I tell Sean what you did."

Tattletale.

"He'll be glad you broke up," Emily added.

"I can't believe I once thought you were my friend. I even asked you to be my bridesmaid!" There was no stopping her runaway mouth. *Tell the reporter what you weigh while you're at it, why don't you?*

"Ma'am," the officer said to Emily, "we don't arrest people for rear-ending someone."

"I was just sitting here waiting for the light to

turn and she plowed right into me," Emily said. "That's assault. She's out to get me."

"I am not! I don't ever want to see you again. Why don't you…find a new school and go corrupt some other young minds?" Oh, Lord. She had to shut up. That would probably make the news, too. Would she and Emily both get fired? "Don't print that," she warned the reporter. "Or I'll…sue you."

Her cell phone rang. It was Grammy. "We're all starving. What's taking you so long?"

"I've been unavoidably detained," Riley said. "You might want to order that hospital food."

"What? What's happened?"

"I was in an accident."

"An accident!" Grammy cried.

"It was an assault," Emily corrected.

Mom was on the phone now. "What's going on?"

"I ran into someone." *Guess who I ran into on my way to the hospital.*

"Are you okay?"

"Yes, I'm fine. I'll see you all later," Riley said and ended the call. Meanwhile, Emily was glaring at her.

The officer took out his handy-dandy ticket tablet. "I'll have to cite you for following too closely," he said to Riley. He sounded almost regretful.

Tears spilled out of her eyes and started down her cheeks. She nodded.

"I'll need your driver's license and registration."

Riley sniffed and produced the necessary information.

Meanwhile Emily was still sputtering. "I'm going to get a restraining order."

The policeman turned to her. The look on his face was enough to make Riley want to confess to something, anything. *I stole half my sister's Halloween candy when I was seven. I cheated on a math test in eighth grade. I ate half a batch of brownies single-handedly.*

I hate Emily Dieb. Riley pressed her lips firmly together.

"You need to get hold of yourself," the officer said to Emily.

For sure. "Emily, I think you're sneaky and pathetic and I don't want to be your friend anymore but I have better things to do than run around trying to take you out with my car," Riley told her. "I mean, look at my front bumper. My insurance is going to go up."

"Yeah? Well, I've got whiplash," Emily retorted.

Good. "I'm sorry. My insurance will pay for whatever you need. And meanwhile, maybe Sean will give you a back rub." Oh, dear. Where was her brain when her mouth needed help?

"See? She *is* out to get me."

"You are not worth getting," Riley informed her. "And you can have Sean. Any man who'd cheat on his fiancée can't be trusted. Just remember, if he'll do it with you, he'll do it to you."

"Okay, ladies, that's enough," the officer said firmly. Jeez, he was cute. And disgusted. "One more word out of either of you and I'm going to haul you both down to the station."

"And what would be the charge, Officer?" asked Lizbeth Parker, girl reporter.

"Lizbeth, go home," the cop said wearily.

"I have to report the news."

"This isn't news. It's a fender bender. Now get out of here."

"Do you need my statement?" the older woman asked eagerly. "I saw it all. My name is Willa Parsons." She proceeded to give the officer her phone number and he dutifully wrote it down. "You can call me anytime," she added.

Same here, thought Riley. Except now she looked like a whack job.

Another few minutes, and insurance information had been exchanged and Emily had settled down and promised not to press charges. Then she climbed in her car and drove off into the night.

Lizbeth and Willa had taken off by now, so that left Riley and the handsome Officer Knight. "I really didn't hit her on purpose," she said.

He nodded. "I know." Then he tipped his cap, told her to have a pleasant night and got back in his patrol car.

"Thanks for being so nice," she called after him and he raised his hand in a wave. *Do you have a girlfriend? Do you like cookies?*

If Riley baked a batch of gumdrop cookies and invited Officer Knight over to help her eat them,

*how many cookies would they eat before they got
around to kissing under the mistletoe?*

Sigh. Who was she kidding? Policemen didn't
hang out with crazy women who rear-ended man-
stealing former friends. Although he'd seemed…
sympathetic. Sympathy, attraction—surely those
two were related somehow.

She continued on her way to the hospital…driv-
ing oh, so carefully, and got to Jo's room in time to
find her sister, mother and grandmother all enjoying hamburgers from the hospital cafeteria. Georgia had gone home to make dinner for her husband.

"These aren't half-bad," Grammy told her.

"Did you have one sent up for me?" Riley asked.
Nothing like a close encounter with a former friend
to work up a girl's appetite.

Grammy and Mom both looked guilty. "We'll
call right now," Mom said and picked up the phone.

"Meanwhile, tell us about this accident. You don't
have whiplash or anything, do you?" Grammy took
another chomp of her burger.

Riley shook her head and fell onto a chair. "No,
but Emily claims she's got it."

"Emily?" Jo stared at her. "What are you talking about?"

"I rear-ended her," Riley confessed.

"Why on earth did you do that?" Mom asked,
taking a moment from her conversation with the
cafeteria. "And ice cream for dessert," she finished.

"No ice cream for me," Riley said. The last thing
she needed was more calories.

"I'll eat it," Grammy said. How her grandmother stayed so slim when she ate so much was a mystery. Maybe she had a tapeworm.

Mom hung up the phone and turned to Riley. "So, sweetie, what exactly happened with Emily?"

Public humiliation, that was what. "It was awful," Riley said miserably. "She started ranting about how I've turned all the teachers against her. Then the police came. And then there was this woman from the newspaper. I swear, if I end up in the paper as a crazy ex-bride stalker, I'm going to sue…someone."

"Don't worry. The paper has bigger stories than that to print."

"In Whispering Pines? Right," Jo said cynically.

Mom frowned at her. "You're not helping."

"Our poor girl." Grammy leaned over and gave Riley a hug. She smelled like onions.

"Did the awful woman back into you?" Mom wanted to know.

"No. I did rear-end her, but not on purpose."

"Of course not," Grammy said.

"Although that might've been fun," Jo cracked and kissed her baby's head.

"Don't listen to your mother, little Mikey," Mom said, giving Jo another disciplinary frown. "Violence is never a solution."

Jo rolled her eyes, and Mom returned her attention to Riley. "How did you happen to rear-end her? Did she stop suddenly?"

Riley shook her head and sighed. "No. She was

already stopped for a red light. Which probably explains why she thought I was out to get her."

"And you didn't see the red light?" Grammy asked in shock. "Or recognize her car?"

"I'm afraid I was, um, thinking."

"Thinking!" Grammy exclaimed. "You're not supposed to think when you drive. You're supposed to pay attention."

"Oh, sweetie," said Mom, "were you thinking about Sean?"

"No, I was thinking about Santa."

Her mother and grandmother frowned in unison.

"What about Santa?" Jo asked.

"He wasn't at the mall. Neither was Mrs. Claus."

Jo looked puzzled. "What do you mean, he wasn't at the mall?"

"I mean there was a Santa, but he wasn't ours."

"How would you know?" Mom scoffed. "All those shopping mall Santas look the same."

"I could tell," Riley insisted. "And there was an elf taking pictures and she said they didn't have a Mrs. Claus. And get this. The guy who's at the mall now was on duty last night, except he and the elf were taking a break when we were there."

"So what did we see, the Ghost of Santa Past?"

"I don't know what we saw, but he wasn't the mall Santa."

"Not this again," Mom groaned.

Jo ran a hand over her baby's head and frowned. "That's kind of woo-woo."

"Oh, you girls," Grammy said. "I'm sure there's a logical explanation."

"I'd like to know what it is." Riley looked at Jo. "What if he really was...?"

Jo gave a cynical snort.

Yeah, it was downright silly to think they'd met the real Santa, since Santa was nothing more than a work of fiction in a red suit.

"I guess the only way we'll find out if he was who he said he was will be if his predictions come true for you and Noel," Jo teased. "You were certainly doing your part with all that flirting last night. While I was about to drop this baby on the pavement, I might add."

Riley felt a holiday glow spread across her cheeks.

"Flirting?" Mom asked. "With whom? Have you met someone?"

"Of course she hasn't met someone," Grammy said. "She just got rid of someone."

"You don't want to rush into anything so soon after... I mean, so soon," Mom cautioned.

"I'm not." But that was one sexy cop. And he'd seemed really nice. Still, it was ridiculous to think that a random meeting with a policeman had anything to do with a crazy prediction by a fake Santa.

"What did Santa say about you? Oh, yeah. You were going to meet your perfect man in a memorable way." Jo smiled and cocked an eyebrow. "I'd say last night was pretty memorable."

"You met someone last night?" Mom asked again.

"The cop who gave us a police escort," Jo replied. "I think he was into Riles."

"I saw him again just now," Riley said. "Although I'm sure he's decided I'm a complete psycho."

"Twice in twenty-four hours. That's got to mean something," Jo said with a grin.

"Yes, it means she shouldn't drive," said Grammy.

"This is all a lot of nonsense," Mom told her, "and I forbid you to get in any more accidents."

"I didn't do it on purpose," Riley said—not for the first time. Except it did seem to be a good way to meet Officer Knight.

Hmm. Maybe she should try for another traffic violation (a minor one, of course, where no one got injured) and see what happened.

Chapter Eight

Wﾠhat should you serve someone you wanted to impress? It had to be good, because Noel needed to butter Ben Fordham up like a Thanksgiving dinner roll, convince him that he had to cut her a deal and let her have her house. That was a tall order since the man was in the business of flipping houses. That meant he wanted to make a profit. And that meant…

She was in deep doo-doo. Noel stood at the meat counter in the Pineland Supermarket and considered her options. Certainly not hamburger. She loved hamburger, but nothing she could make with that would be impressive. Pork chops? What if he didn't like pork? Chicken? No. Chicken was so…common. What about goulash? What man didn't like goulash? Maybe Ben Fordham. Anyway, the last time she'd attempted to make Mom's goulash, she'd burned the meat and forgotten the paprika.

She could broil steaks. That was it! Every man liked steak, right? She picked up a package with two filet mignons. She'd never cooked filet mignon.

Well, there was a first time for everything. Anyway, all you had to do was stick it under the broiler. No paprika necessary. She could handle that. She'd bake some potatoes and put together a salad and… what for dessert?

Cheesecake, she decided. Everyone liked cheese-cake. She swept through the bakery department and picked up an eggnog cheesecake. After that she re-turned to the wine shop and splurged on another bottle of red wine, and then she was good to go.

Back home again, she cleaned the house—no point leaving it messy now—then took a shower and shaved her legs and slathered herself with lotion. After that, she put on Borrowed Outfit Number Two.

Hmm. The boots Jo had suggested were a bit much for indoors. But if she didn't wear those, what would she wear? Not her Hello Kitty slippers. They were cute but they weren't exactly sexy. *WWJWD?* What would Jo Wilton do?

The red stiletto heels called from a corner of her closet. *Pick us. We're ready to party.*

The shoes might have been ready but she wasn't sure she was ready for them. Just tottering around in them at the store to check their fit had been a challenge. Probably not the best purchase she'd ever made. These babies were higher than anything she normally wore, which consisted primarily of flats and tennis shoes. But both Jo and Riley had con-vinced her that the power in a pair of red stilettos was matched only by Dorothy's red slippers. If she wanted to make something happen in the romance department, these were the ticket to Orgasmo Land. No man could resist red heels.

Not that she was planning on traveling there. No, she simply wanted to make a good impression.

Yeah, right, sneered Marvella.

All showered and lotioned up, and dressed in the white shirt, leggings and necklace, she then topped off her ensemble with a generous spritz of perfume. The shoes she would put on at the last minute. She didn't need to be tottering around her kitchen in them, cramping her arches.

While the potatoes were baking, she set the table using her plain white plates, accented with red napkins. Red taper candles on either side of a small vase of red silk roses looked festive and romantic.

Romantic. Was she laying it on too thick? After all, this was just dinner and a conversation about home improvement.

On the house that should've been hers. She frowned. Maybe Marvella had a point. She should just poison the house-flipper and be done with it.

Another of her mother's sayings came to mind— you can catch more flies with honey than with vinegar. She hoped Mom was right.

It didn't take her long to prepare the salad, which was a good thing because she'd wanted to leave her makeup till the last minute. She was just finishing up with her mascara when the doorbell rang. Okay. Showtime.

She started to hurry to the door then realized she was still wearing her Hello Kitty slippers. She kicked them off, grabbed her stilettos, raced down the stairs then put them on, hopping for the door... and turned her ankle in the process, falling in a heap in the hallway. *Ow. Pain. Ow.*

"Coming!" she called through gritted teeth and scrambled back onto her feet. Telling herself to slow down, she hobbled the rest of the way to the door and opened it.

There stood Ben Fordham. Shocking how good a human wrecking ball could look. He wore jeans and a black sweater over that hard, muscled, put-him-on-a-calendar body and the same jacket he'd worn when she first saw him.

When he came to take your house, Marvella reminded her, pulling her out of her lust-induced fog.

Yes, she was on a mission. No getting sidetracked by sexual attraction. She was in charge here and she was calling the shots. And...oh, he'd brought flowers.

Heaven help us, groaned Marvella.

"You shouldn't have," she said as he handed over a bouquet of red and white carnations.

You got that right, Marvella sneered. *We're not swayed by a bunch of carnations. He was too cheap to buy roses.*

Still, it was a nice thought.

"I wanted to," he said as he stepped inside. "I don't want you to think of me as the enemy."

He is. And don't you forget it.

Marvella was right. But now they were in the middle of peace negotiations. It wouldn't help Noel's cause to be adversarial. "Come on in," she said. "I hope you like steak."

"Love it," he said.

She offered to take his coat, but since her hands were full of flowers he hung it up himself. Of course, he knew where the coat closet was. He knew where everything in this house was. This house that would soon be his.

Don't get bitter and cranky, she warned herself as he followed her to the kitchen.

"Doesn't look like you needed flowers," he said as they walked past the arrangement on her dining room table.

"I always need flowers. They're good for the soul," she said and got busy putting his in water.

"Did you put that arrangement together?" he asked.

She nodded.

"It's pretty."

"There's not much to it."

"Sometimes keeping things simple is the best."

"*We* could keep things simple," she said. "How about you let me rent from you with an option to buy?" Uh-oh. There went the smile.

"I don't usually do that."

"You could make an exception."

He jammed his hands in his pockets. "Maybe coming over was a bad idea."

Okay, misstep. "No, it was a great idea. I'm sure we can find a way to work something out." And now it was time to retreat and try an attack from a different direction.

You'd better sleep with him, Marvella advised. *That's your only hope now.*

Would that be so awful? Just looking at the man revved up her hormones. Still, sex without love was never smart, Noel was certain of that.

"Let's call a truce," she said.

Marvella approved. *Hee hee. Lull him into a false sense of security.*

His smile returned. "Okay."

So then, if they weren't going to talk about the future of her house, what *were* they going to talk about? What to say, what to say?

She set the flowers on the kitchen counter with hands that were suddenly sweaty. "Would you like a drink? I have wine." And a brand-new corkscrew.

"That sounds good," he said. "You gonna join me?"

"I'm not much of a drinker." But… "I'll try some wine if you'll open the bottle," she said, handing over the corkscrew.

He obliged and she poured them each a glass, a nice big glassful for him, a small amount for her. Some wine might steady her nerves. She tried not to make a face but oh, that stuff was yucky. Why did people drink it?

He was smiling. "Not into wine?"

She shook her head. "Not really." The wildest she ever got was a piña colada or some other fun drink loaded with sugar and cream when she went out with the girls.

"That was a pretty nice one you brought me."

"I had help selecting it."

"So, what do you drink? Beer?"

She wrinkled her nose. "I tried it a few times but it's just so…yeasty-tasting."

He smiled at that. "It's an acquired taste."

"I think I'll stick with soda and tea and hot chocolate."

"All excellent choices. I like tea."

"You do?"

He nodded. "Rooibos. Very healthy, full of antioxidants." He held up his glass. "I like wine, too, though. Thanks for getting me some."

"I like to be a good hostess." Okay, that sounded stupid.

"You like to entertain?"

She enjoyed having girlfriends over to watch movies and binge on TV series. She'd bought pizza for her friends when they helped her move. Not exactly HGTV-level entertaining. "Yes. I'd like to do more." Someday, when this house was hers and she had a man in her life, then she'd beef up her kitchen skills and have dinner parties complete with place cards and…whatever.

"Why don't you?"

She shrugged. "I'm busy." *Sitting around in my jammies writing, leading a life as exciting as stale bread.*

"Yeah?" He took a sip of his wine. "Busy doing what?"

"I'm a writer."

"Yeah?" The level of interest had risen. He probably thought she wrote something exciting like mysteries or sexy romance novels. She got busy putting the steaks on a broiling sheet.

Hey, there's nothing wrong with writing children's books, Marvella said.

Marvella was right. Noel was proud of what she did. "I write children's books," she said and shoved the steaks under the broiler.

"Cool," he said and took another drink of wine. "You must like kids."

"I do." And at some point before menopause, she hoped to have one. But at the rate she was going, with no man in her life… "I might adopt."

A brochure for an organization that helped children in third-world countries was sitting on her counter by the phone, and it caught his eye. He picked it up. "Is that what this is?"

All of a sudden, she felt self-conscious. She liked to keep her good deeds a secret. She plucked it out of his hand and stuffed it in a drawer. "No, that's just something I donate to. But I would like to adopt a child. Sometime. Down the road." She almost added, "When I have money," but stopped herself. Reminding him about her not-so-plump pockets would hardly impress him .

He nodded, taking that all in. "No guy in your life who wants to adopt with you?"

No guy in her life who wanted to do anything with her. "Not now." There had been. She should tell him that so he wouldn't think she was some desperate, love-starved caricature. "There was." Then, before he could ask about that man, she hurried on. "What about you?"

"No one special," he said with a shrug.

"I thought maybe your secretary," Noel ventured.

"We've gone out a few times. We're just buds."

He was buds. The secretary obviously wanted more.

"Not sure I'm in the market," he said.

So the flowers were simply a polite gesture and he was only here because he felt bad that she was so upset. She was wearing these dangerous shoes for nothing. Well, darn him, anyway. Arriving with flowers. Flowers! And all when he wasn't *in the market*, anyway.

"Sometimes it gets awkward when things don't work out," he added.

That was his reason? What a coward. "Hmm."

"Hmm. What does that mean?"

"Nothing. Just that…" She stopped herself and shook her head. Tried another sip of wine. *Ugh.*

"Go on," he said. "What were you going to say?"

"Only that, well, it seems funny that somebody who's willing to put so much work into restoring houses would be afraid of working on a relationship."

"Houses are easier, believe me."

"Relationships can be complicated," she admitted. "But if one's worth working on…" *If the man turns out to be nicer than you thought when you first met him. If it looks like maybe he has a heart, after all. If he brings you flowers…*

"Your oven's smoking."

She whirled around—not too smart when you were wearing shoes with heels the size of stilts—lost her balance and went down. He bent to help her just as she was reaching to pull a hot pad off the counter and she socked him in the nose. Hard.

"Oh, no. I'm so sorry," she said, scrambling to her feet.

"It's okay," he said, stepping away and coughing.

The kitchen started to fill with smoke. Noel grabbed her hot pad, yanked open the oven door and jerked out the meat. More smoke. Now the smoke detector was going off.

"A broom," she cried and rushed for the water heater closet where she kept hers, twisted her ankle. Again. Yelped. Grabbed the broom, waved it around and whacked her guest upside the head. "I'm sorry!" she said. Again.

He was holding his nose, but he held out his free hand. "No worries. Let me do this for you."

Please! She was dangerous.

He fanned the broom in front of the screaming smoke detector while she turned off the oven. Once the smoke detector shut up, it was time to set aside the broom and peer through the haze at dinner. It looked great if you liked burnt offerings.

"Oh, no." All that money she'd spent, down the drain.

"That's okay." Cough, cough. "I like it well-done."

"Do you really?" Cough, cough.

"No. But I thought it would make you feel better if I said that."

Aww, how sweet was that?

He didn't care how you felt when he bought your house out from under you, Marvella reminded her.

Well, she'd had her petty revenge. She'd whacked the poor guy on the head and probably broken his nose. Which was bleeding. "Your nose." She got a dish towel and offered it to him. "It's bleeding." Cough, cough.

"I don't want to bleed on your dish towel," he protested. "Do you have a paper towel?" Cough, cough, cough.

"Oh, yes, of course." She pulled a handful off the paper towel dispenser, but she pulled so hard it came right out of the wall." Could this dinner get any worse?

"Don't worry," he said, putting the towel to his nose. "I can fix that."

"I hope I haven't broken your nose," she said.

"It's fine," he assured her. "No worries."

She opened the back door to let out some of the smoke. Then, as both she and her guest were about to suffocate, she suggested they repair to the dining room.

"This meal isn't exactly going well, is it?" she said once her lungs were working again.

He smiled at that and let out a final cough. "How about we order pizza?"

"Sure," she said and started for her purse. Carefully. No more ankle-twisting.

"I've got this," he said. "I'll call That's a Some Pizza. They make a great pizza supreme. Is that okay?"

She nodded. *At this point, anything.*

With their order called in, there was nothing left to do but settle on the living room sofa with their drinks. Which she fetched, bravely entering the smoky kitchen. "I smell like a fireman," she said when she returned. So much for the perfume she'd put on.

"At least we didn't have to call the firemen," he said. "And you look great."

She could feel herself blushing.

Oh, brother, Marvella said in disgust. *Who's buttering up whom?* Marvella needed to go away.

"So, your landlady never told me your last name. What is it?"

"Bijou. It's French. My great-great-grandparents were from France."

Ooh, la, la, mocked Marvella.

Scram or I'm going to find a new heroine for my next book.

That silenced her.

"Sexy name you've got," said Ben Fordham.

She shrugged. "What's in a name?" The name itself meant jewel, but as far as she knew, none of her ancestors had owned much in the way of jewels. Or anything else, for that matter.

"A rose by any other name?"

"You know Shakespeare?"

"That's a pretty famous quote. Anyway, just because I like to swing a hammer it doesn't mean I don't have an education," Ben said. "Or a brain."

How about a heart? She bit her lip. This was not the time to plead her case. She hadn't had a chance to butter him up yet. Butter him up, ha! So far she'd ruined dinner and almost killed him from smoke inhalation.

Okay, she needed to start buttering. "I like your name. It's...solid, dependable."

"That's what my mom says."

"Do your parents live around here?"

"My mom lives in town. My dad's not in the picture."

She'd grown up with the security of happily married parents. She hated to think what it would be like not having that. "I'm sorry."

He set his empty glass on the coffee table. "Don't be. We've been okay. I had an uncle who stepped in. What about you? Wait. Don't tell me. Your parents are happily married."

"For thirty-four years."

He nodded thoughtfully. "I guess it can be done. I've never found anyone I thought I could do it with."

"Maybe you've looked in the wrong places."

"Maybe," he conceded.

She was about to suggest that surely there were lots of women who wouldn't mind spending their lives with him—something she'd say just to flatter him, of course—when the doorbell rang.

"Looks like our pizza's here," he said and started for the door.

"Let me pay," she said, trying to hurry across the room on the shoes of death.

"I've got it."

So she stood in the middle of the living room and watched as he paid for dinner. So much for softening him up with a great meal. But hey, she had salad. And there was still dessert.

They ate at the dining room table and she got him talking about all the houses he'd restored and flipped. He obviously loved what he did. "And I promise I'll make this one nice," he finished.

"Please don't get rid of the brick around the fireplace," she begged. "I hate those modern fireplaces and it wouldn't fit the house."

"Agreed," he said. Then smiled. Wow, what a smile.

Never mind his smile. Get him to promise to sell it to you.

Oh, yeah. That. "And you *are* going to sell it to me, right?"

He suddenly became very fixed on the last of the salad on his plate. "Your landlady said you were having trouble getting the money together."

"She didn't give me enough time. I can."

"It's not that I don't want to help you out," he said.

"Well, then, there you go," she said cheerily.

"I can't afford to give the house away once I've made the improvements. I have business expenses, obligations."

What kind of obligations? None of her business. "I'm sure we can figure something out," she said.

Now would be a good time for dessert. Mom was a big believer in the power of sugar. "Always leave a good taste in their mouths," she liked to say.

"How about some dessert?" Noel asked.

"Thanks."

She went into the kitchen and took a deep, restorative breath. This was going well now. He was softening. Sort of. Some cheesecake, some more flattery.

The kitchen was feeling downright arctic. She shut the back door and cut two pieces of cheesecake, a small one for her and a generous slice for him. Then she went back to the dining room, caught the heel of her killer shoes on the area rug and began the dance of the dodo. He jumped up to steady her just as she pitched forward, smearing his shirt with eggnog cheesecake. Two plates' worth.

"Oh, no. I'm so sorry." That was the third time… She grabbed a napkin and tried to help him wipe it off.

"Don't worry. It could happen to anyone."

"Things like this never happened to me before," she said. "It's the shoes." The shoes from hell. Sexy as they were, they'd done nothing for her image tonight. Or her sense of balance.

He nodded and smiled at her as if she was deranged. "You know, it's getting late. I should get going."

"We haven't even talked about improvements," she protested. Like he wanted to stroll around the house with cheesecake on his shirt! Could this evening have gone any worse?

"Next time."

Would there even be a next time? She doubted it. She kicked off the stupid shoes. It was all she could do not to pick them up and hurl them across the room. "I could wash your shirt for you," she said.

"That's okay. Really."

She couldn't blame him for turning down her offer. The way the evening had gone, he probably figured she'd shrink it. "My life is never like this." In fact, it had been going great until Ben Fordham came along. Sort of great, anyway. Well, not *that* great. But he'd definitely made it worse.

"We all have bad days," he said. And then he smiled. A genuine, I-could-learn-to-like-you smile. "You've got a good heart, Noel Bijou."

So she had managed to butter him up a little. "How about you, Ben Fordham? Have you got a good heart?"

The smile switched from easy to uncomfortable. "I like to think so."

"I hope so," she said softly.

Now things were feeling distinctly uncomfortable here in her little living room. She'd had such plans for this night: a nice dinner, a fire in the fireplace…

Yeah, well, you had a fire in the kitchen.

Great. Marvella was back. *Get lost,* Noel told her.

Ben walked to the door and she walked with him—so much easier without the red stilettos. She took his coat out of the closet and handed it to him. "This wasn't quite how I envisioned the evening," she confessed as he put it on.

Now the genuine smile was back. "It's been… interesting."

"I'd offer to send some cheesecake home with you, but so far your pants are still clean."

That made him chuckle. "We'll try again."

Would they? Okay, that had to mean she'd made some sort of progress. She nodded.

"Thanks for, uh, everything," he said then slipped out the door.

She watched from the living room window as he went down the front walk to his truck. Maybe the evening hadn't been a total bust.

Yes, it was, Marvella whispered. *He's going to gouge you. You'd better write like the wind and hope you get a new contract or we're going to be homeless.*

No, they weren't. Of course she'd get a new contract. And she and Ben Fordham would find a way to make a deal.

All brave talk. She went back to the kitchen and cut herself a very large wedge of cheesecake. It didn't help.

Riley called the next morning to check in on her. "How'd it go last night?"

"I set off the smoke alarm, socked him in the nose, hit him with a broom and dumped cheese-cake on him."

There was a long moment of silence while her friend took in the whopping disaster that had been her night. "Uh, how did you set off the smoke alarm?"

"Broiling steaks."

"And the nose?"

"Reaching for a hot pad."

Riley moved on to Disaster Number Three. "The broom?"

"Trying to shut up the smoke detector. Then I got him later with the cheesecake when I tripped. It was awful."

"I'm sorry your evening sucked."

"There's an understatement. He said we'd get to-gether again, but he was probably just being polite."

"Maybe not. Maybe he really likes you."

Good old Riley, always trying to be positive. "And maybe he's a masochist, although I doubt it. I should give up on getting the house."

"Don't do that. Remember what Santa said," Riley urged her in a lame effort to cheer her up.

"If I ever see him again I'm going to rip off his beard and burn it," Noel muttered. Okay, she'd been spending way too much time with Marvella. She was starting to get violent. Anyway, she'd burned enough stuff.

"Things will work out," Riley said.

Noel was beginning to have serious doubts about

that so she changed the subject. "That's enough about me. How's Jo doing?"

"Coming home from the hospital today. I'm going to go see her later. Want to come?"

"Sure." Focusing on her friend's happiness beat focusing on her own unhappiness.

Riley picked her up later that afternoon and on their way to Jo's house filled Noel in on her Friday-night adventure. "My only consolation is that it wasn't in the paper today so I think I dodged *that* bullet."

"There you go. Every cloud has a silver lining," Noel said.

Riley sighed. "I guess."

At least Jo was happy. And the baby was beautiful. Holding the precious bundle, Noel felt a twinge of jealousy—yes, she wanted one of these—but she suppressed it with a reminder that Jo had waited a long time for her happy ending. After three years of trying, which included a miscarriage, she finally had her perfect little man.

Santa had gotten it right for one of them, anyway, Noel concluded later that night when she settled in with a holiday romance novel and a mug of tea. However, she wasn't holding out much hope that he'd come through for her.

You should never listen to fictional characters, Marvella said.

"Oh, shut up," Noel growled.

What she needed was a plan B. She was creative. She should be able to search around in her brain and find one somewhere. Where was that pesky plan B hiding?

Who knew? She went in search of more cheese-cake.

Chapter Nine

"Jo, I know you're on maternity leave but this is an emergency."

Every event that required a nice outfit was an emergency with Alisha Walsh. Jo had seen the caller ID and known she shouldn't take the call. Why didn't she ever listen to herself?

"Alisha, I just gave birth four days ago. I'm a little busy." What time was it, anyway? Good Lord. 7:00 a.m. on a Monday. Alisha should be put on phone restriction.

"Oh, you had your girl?"

Jo flopped over on her back and covered her eyes. "Actually, we had a boy."

"Boys," Alisha said with a snort. "They just grow up to be men."

Alisha was recently divorced and somewhat prejudiced at the moment. "Well, mine's going to grow up to be wonderful."

"He'll be a good dresser, that's for sure. And speaking of dressing…"

Here they went again. Jo liked Alisha. She was

one of her top customers and fun to shop with. But honestly, Alisha had no boundaries. The fact that she was calling on a Monday morning before the stores were even open and half the town hadn't had their morning coffee yet was proof. "Unless you're meeting the president—"

"I am," Alisha interrupted.

"What?"

"I'm going to a dinner party at La Rive Gauche Paris this weekend and the president of the company will be there. I have nothing to wear."

Jo *knew* that wasn't true. Alisha's closet was packed with clothes. She'd picked out half of them.

"You have to come help me. Can't you get away for a couple of hours today?"

"Today?"

Alisha obviously sensed the raised eyebrow. "Okay, later this week, after you've had time to recover."

Jo had been up twice in the night with the baby. She was exhausted, cranky and her nipples were raw meat. Recovery was a ways off. And not for a thousand bucks would she take her newborn to that germy mall.

Of course, Mom would be happy to watch little Mikey, but she and Grammy had been over all day Sunday, cleaning and cooking and changing diapers. Mom needed a break, too. Anyway, Jo didn't want to leave her sweet new baby and she didn't want to miss out on the possible opportunity for an afternoon nap just so Alisha could look hot at her company's office party.

"Sorry, but you're on your own. And you should be fine. We found you that great black dress last month."

"Black is so boring," Alisha whined.

"Okay then, wear the dress with the silver sequined skirt. You can pair it with the black tuxedo jacket from last year and some rhinestone earrings and you'll look a thousand percent hot."

"The jacket, I didn't think of that. Thanks, Jo."

"You're welcome," Jo said and rolled over to catch a few more Zs.

That lasted about two minutes. The phone rang again. This time it was Riley. "This better be good," Jo groaned. "I'm sleep-deprived."

"Did I wake you up? I'm sorry. It's just that…I'm in the paper," she finished on a wail.

Jo rubbed her gritty eyes and sat up. "Why are you in the paper?"

"Remember the reporter who showed up when I ran into Emily?"

"Uh-oh."

"Uh-oh is right. There are pictures and everything and it's captioned Ex-Bride Runs into Bride-to-be."

Pretty clever. Jo wisely kept that thought to herself. "It's not on the first page, is it? If it's not on the first page, hardly anyone will notice."

"It might as well be. It's in the Whispers section. Everyone reads that."

All the soft news and gossip about what had happened over the weekend went in that section. Riley wasn't kidding. Everyone in town read it.

Jo tried a new tack. "Nobody'll care. Who reads the paper anymore, anyway?" Except the Whispers section. Poor Riles.

"It's on the *Chronicle*'s website, too. I checked."

"As long as it's not plastered all over Facebook and Twitter you'll be fine." But it was only a matter of time until that happened. Ugh.

"I can't believe this," Riley continued. "Things were already bad enough. I don't need to be the joke of Whispering Pines."

"You're not a joke," Jo said firmly. "Sean's the joke."

"No one's laughing at him," Riley said in a small voice.

"No one's laughing at you, either, sis." And if anyone did, she and Harold would beat 'em up. "Trust me. You're going to be fine."

"It's just that this is the cherry on the poop cupcake." Riley began wailing again. "Everyone's going to know."

"Everyone already knew."

"Not about this. It's all there, Emily accusing me of trying to take her out because Sean dumped me for her, the fact that she was going to be my bridesmaid..."

"This will blow over. Laugh it off."

"Ha, ha, ha," Riley said bitterly.

"You're going to be okay, Riles. You really are. This is a bump in the road."

"A big bump."

"Nothing you can't get over."

Riley heaved a sigh. "Thanks, sis."

"You're welcome. Now, go to work and let me go to sleep. Okay?"

"Gotcha. Pleasant dreams."

In the bassinet next to her she heard the little snufflings and stirrings of the new man in her life. *Here it comes. Brace for it, boobs.*

Sure enough, a moment later Mikey was exercising those healthy lungs of his. Sleep would have to wait. Jo stumbled out of bed and looked through sleepy eyes at her beautiful infant. She'd known babies took work but she hadn't known as much as she thought she did.

"It's okay," she crooned as she picked him up. "You're worth it." She continued to talk to him as she changed his diaper. "I'm sorry your daddy isn't here to hold you. Or help with diaper changes. Or maybe do the dishes. Or anything. But, you see, he's off saving the world."

Once upon a time he'd told Jo *she* was his world. That had been eight years ago, when they first got married. They'd been really young. She'd believed him.

Actually, she hadn't minded being a navy wife. At first. She'd been proud of his service, and when he was gone she'd filled the lonely months hanging out with her family and friends. Over the last few years she'd finished up school at Olympic College and started her business as a style consultant. She'd had more than enough to do. But usually about two weeks before it was time for Mike to return home, the days and hours of missing him would start weighing on her and she'd get antsy. And, yes, a little resentful. During this last tour of duty, she'd been more than a little resentful. They were finally starting a family and where was he? Who knew? Certainly not a lowly navy wife.

"What he does is important," she explained to both herself and Mikey. "But he has you now. And if he wants to keep me…well, we won't bother you with grown-up worries." That would be a bad habit to begin. "Your daddy and I will work things out. Not to worry, little one."

The only thing Little One was worried about was his next meal and he was getting very angry about the amount of time his mother was taking to deliver it. She settled back on the bed with him and he latched on, making Jo clench her teeth.

She blew out a breath. "Don't worry. We'll get the hang of this. I won't let you down."

Would it be letting him down to divorce his daddy? If Mike kept shipping out, the poor kid wouldn't see much of him even if they were married. Still, what would it solve to divorce Mike? She'd be just as alone. Or even more so…

She didn't know why she was entertaining such thoughts. She didn't want to dump her husband.

But she didn't want to go on like this, either. She

picked up her cell phone and checked her email. Something had come in from Mike.

Can hardly wait to see you and our son! Love you both more than I can say.

"Prove it," she muttered, then typed,

Enough not to leave us again?

Wait a minute. The navy screened stuff, didn't they? She decided to be more cryptic. She deleted her question and wrote,

You know what you need to do to prove it.

There. That said it all. Talk was cheap. The best way to show he loved her and the baby would be to commit to them. She looked down at her son. Perfect skin, beautiful little face. Mike was going to fall in love with him just as she had.

The baby finished nursing and now he was gazing up at her intently, like a newcomer to the planet trying to figure out the customs and language of the natives. "You'll catch on," she assured him. "We'll all figure this out."

His eyes were drifting shut. So were hers. She put him back in his bassinet and climbed under the covers. Sleep. All she wanted was to sleep.

An hour later the phone rang again. "Hi, sweetie, it's Mom. Were you awake?"

"Barely." What was with everyone calling her at the crack of dawn? Okay, so it wasn't the crack of dawn anymore but close enough.

"I figured you'd be up by now. Would you like some help with the baby today?"

Jo had to smile. So much for worrying about overloading her mother. Mom couldn't get enough of her first grandson. "Sure."

"All right. I'll come over around eleven thirty. I made some goodies for you to stick in the freezer."

She'd really lucked out in the mother department. "Thanks. You're the best."

"I know," Mom joked. "Meanwhile, see if you can get some rest."

"I will," Jo said, and the minute she ended the call, she turned off her phone. There. If anyone was having a clothing emergency or a meltdown, she'd be having it without Jo.

She looked at her baby, who was lying on his back with his eyes shut. "Someone needs to put your picture on a baby food jar," she murmured. He was so beautiful. Just like his daddy.

She'd met Mike at Christmas. His parents were new in town back then. They'd recently bought the hardware store and he'd come home from college for the holidays to help out. He'd found her in the grocery store, in the Christmas goodies section. She'd decided to decorate her presents with candy canes and had picked up a box. She'd also been hovering over the Andes Mints, thinking about buying some

of those, too, so she and Mom could bake chocolate mint cookies.

"Go ahead, get 'em," had said a low voice behind her.

She'd turned around and there he was, six feet
of gorgeous with dark brown hair and brown eyes
and a killer smile. The Sugar Plum Fairy had started
fluttering around in her tummy.

"Live it up, it's Christmas," he'd added.

"I think I will," she'd said and grabbed a couple of boxes. "These make great icing for chocolate cookies."

"Yeah?"

"My mom and I make them every year at Christmas."

"Sounds good. Maybe I should come by your
house and sample some. Unless you've got a boyfriend who'd beat me up," he'd said with a cocky
grin. As if he had to worry about anyone beating
him up. The guy looked like he could be on the cover
of a fitness magazine.

She'd had a boyfriend. But she'd known the minute she saw Mike that the other guy was going to be
history. She'd felt this crazy connection. It was as
if the Ghost of Christmas Future was whispering,
"This is the one."

He had been the one. They'd chatted in the store
and then gone to Java Josie's for peppermint lattes.
She'd not only canceled her date, she'd canceled the
boyfriend. Then she'd invited Mike to her house that
very night. He'd hung out with her family, suffering

through card games and a third degree from her dad. After he'd left, Dad had given him the thumbs-up and so had Harold. The women in the family had all been pushovers. Like Jo.

Well, she wasn't a pushover anymore. She had a child to raise, and Mike would have to be around to help. "Call me demanding," she said, "but that's how it's got to be."

She burrowed under the blankets and went to sleep. Mr. Sandman must have been a navy guy because he decided to make her pay for her unpatriotic attitude. Suddenly she found herself on an island somewhere in the Pacific, hugging two terrified children to her legs. One was a boy, who looked a lot like pictures she'd seen of her husband as a child. The other was a little girl with the same blond hair she'd had when she was five. And they were being bombed. With giant chocolate Santas.

A woman who looked suspiciously like her mom raced past her, crying, "Run for your life! The North Pole is attacking!"

And there went her mother-in-law, crying, "Where's my son in this hour of need? If only he hadn't listened to that awful wife of his."

"I'm not awful!" Jo hollered. But her voice was lost in the noise of exploding Santas.

Here came her sister, wearing an ugly Christmas sweater and fleecy pajama bottoms with penguins on them. She was covered in chocolate and staggering. "We're unprotected!"

"What do you mean we're unprotected? Where's Mike?"

"He's at the local bar getting drunk on peppermint Schnapps, same place he's been every day since you messed up his life."

"I didn't mess up his life."

"Yeah, you did. You made him quit the navy."

"He needed to! He needed to be with his family."

"Duck," hollered Riley and pulled Jo and the kids into a huddle just as an enormous chocolate Santa fell and exploded next to them, pelting chocolate all over them.

"This is ridiculous. I'm dreaming," Jo insisted as a shower of miniature candy canes rained down on them.

"Mama, I'm scared," cried her son.

"I want my daddy," the little girl wailed.

"You don't have a daddy anymore," Riley snarled. (Riley never snarled!) "Your coldhearted mother divorced him because he wouldn't stick around and change diapers."

Jo pulled away from Riley. "You're not my sister. My sister would never wear pajama bottoms out in public. I taught her better."

"You're right, I'm not." And with an evil grin Riley morphed into a seven-foot-tall chocolate Santa. "Would you like your picture taken with Santa? Before I...EAT YOU!"

The children shrieked and ran away in opposite directions.

"Ha! Even your children don't want to be with

you now. You've ruined their lives," chortled Chocolate Riley.

Jo scooped a candy cane off the ground and hurled it like a giant sword.

"Ha, ha, missed me," Chocolate Riley taunted. "And now, you ungrateful, selfish bitch, I'm going to smother you." With that, she melted into a river of chocolate lava and poured herself over Jo.

"Noooo!"

Jo awoke tangled in her blankets and sweating. Okay, that was nothing more than her subconscious wanting her to feel guilty. Well, she wasn't going to, darn it all.

Suddenly she didn't have much of a craving for chocolate. She sure hoped Mom wasn't bringing over those chocolate mint cookies.

Sadly, she did. Jo took one look at them and shuddered.

"Aren't you feeling well, honey?" Mom asked.

"I'm fine," Jo insisted. "Just…tired."

"That's to be expected."

"And stressed."

"That's hardly surprising, either," Mom said. "You've just had a baby. You have a lot to adjust to."

"Alone," Jo added, in the mood for a pity party.

"You won't be alone much longer." Mom gave her a hug. "Mike will come back and everything will be wonderful."

Would it? Jo didn't know. One thing she knew for sure. She didn't want to go to sleep again for a long time.

Chapter Ten

"*I'm afraid*," *whispered Little Jenny.*

"*That's right*," *cackled the Creepy Crumbly Confidence Stealer.* "*Be afraid. Don't raise your hand in class.*"

Marvella Monster hated it when the Creepy Crumbly Confidence Stealer stole girls' and boys' confidence. She stomped across the classroom and gave Creepy a whack with her big, blue tail. "*That's enough out of you.*"

Creepy rubbed his crumbly ugly face and took a step back, but not before whispering to Jenny, "*You don't really know the answer. You just think you do. And you don't know that Ben Fordham will call. In fact, he probably won't.*"

"*What?*" *Little Jenny looked confused.*

The Creepy Crumbly Confidence Stealer lowered his crumbly brows. "*Wait a minute. Who's Ben Fordham?*"

Do you mind? Marvella snapped. *We're working here.*

Yikes! When had Ben Fordham sneaked into her

story? This was no time to be thinking about him, especially with such a defeatist attitude. Noel gave herself a mental shake and went back to work.

"You can do anything you set your mind to," Marvella told Jenny.

How does that apply to Ben Fordham?

Marvella threw up her blue hands. *I can't work like this. Go...do something. Come back when you're ready to be useful.*

Marvella was getting awfully bossy lately. But she had a point. Noel shut her laptop and returned to the real world. Since no plan B had presented itself yet, she needed to get back to flattering Ben Fordham some more.

She wasn't exactly dressed to see anyone. She was in her usual work attire—fuzzy pajama bottoms, an Old Navy top and her Hello Kitty slippers, so she decided to give him a call and see if he'd like to try dinner again. This time she'd take him out. She hoped he liked burgers, since that was all she could afford.

She picked up her cell and called his office.

His secretary answered. "Fordham Enterprises."

"Is Ben Fordham in?"

"He's in a meeting. May I take a message?"

"Just tell him Noel called."

"All right."

The woman didn't sound very sincere. Maybe she recognized Noel's voice. Still, short of saying, "Promise?" there was nothing Noel could do to guarantee that his secretary would give him her message.

"Thanks," she said and did the phone call equivalent of slinking away. The minute she disconnected, she realized she hadn't left her phone number. That wouldn't do. He knew where she lived but he didn't have her number. She called back.

"Fordham Enterprises."

"This is Noel again."

"He's still in a meeting," his secretary said, her tone of voice adding, *pest*.

"I forgot to leave my phone number."

"What is this regarding?"

Okay, somebody was definitely sounding a little adversarial now.

You shouldn't have called back, said the Creepy Crumbly Confidence Stealer.

Great. Bad enough that she had Marvella constantly whispering in her ear lately. Now she was hearing from the villains in her stories? But old Creepy Crumbly had a point. She looked like an idiot.

For heaven's sake, she's just an employee, cried Marvella. *Tell her to shape up or you'll have her fired*.

Marvella talked to people like that, but Noel didn't. *I certainly won't*, she informed Marvella. But what should she say? "It's personal."

There was a long silence on the other end of the line followed by an abrupt, "All right."

Noel recited her number and hoped the message

would get delivered. She had her doubts. The secretary ended the call, leaving Noel to sit there, drumming her fingers on the table. She picked up her cell again and checked the time. Ten thirty. Everyone deserved a midmorning coffee break. She'd go out, after all. She'd swing by Java Josie's and pick up some coffee for Ben Fordham. Maybe Ginger the barista knew how he liked his coffee. Yes, that was a good plan. She needed to get out more, and this was much better than sitting around hoping his secretary would give him her message.

She showered and dressed in the skinny jeans she'd borrowed from Jo, along with a black sweater. Oh, yes. Jewelry. On went the borrowed necklace. She pulled on her boots, grabbed her loaner coat and went out to do some serious buttering up.

The day was clear and the skies were blue. She had a perfect view of the Olympic Mountains as she drove from her quiet neighborhood of older homes down the hill toward downtown. Whispering Pines was one of many small, picturesque towns on Washington's Olympic Peninsula, situated along Case Inlet. Travelers often stopped on their way to the beach towns on Washington's coast to get a bite to eat at the Olympic View Café or The Rusty Saw. Sometimes people would stay at Waterside House, the town's one B & B, to enjoy the scenery or play a round of golf at The Pines Golf Course.

In spite of that, it remained a quiet burg. Most of the people who lived there owned a local business, worked remotely with an occasional foray into the city, or enjoyed retirement. Traffic jams were rare and townspeople never got their grocery-shopping done without running into one or two acquaintances or fellow church members.

Noel had grown up in this town and she still loved living here. It wasn't as hip as Seattle or as rich as Bainbridge Island, but it was comfortable. Whispering Pines almost had it all—family, friends, food and lattes. And now with the nearby mall, there was the added joy of department stores. (Macy's, Kohl's and Penney's!)

As far as Noel was concerned the only thing lacking was a bookstore. The Book Nook had closed two years ago, and it had been a sad day when that happened. She'd worked there since high school and Suzanne Selfors, the owner, had hosted a book-signing party for her when her first Marvella book was published. Suzanne was now living in New York with no plans to return, but Noel still nursed the hope that someone would take that empty space and turn it into a book-lovers' heaven again. Meanwhile, though, there was still the Whispering Pines Library, where her mother worked part-time, and when she wanted to purchase a book, she could at least do it online.

So life here was good. This was where she wanted to stay, where she wanted to get married, raise a family, live happily-ever-after. And the only house where she could envision living happily-ever-after was the one she was in now.

As she waited at one of the three traffic signals

in town she checked her makeup. Lookin' fine. She
practiced a smile. Was it flirty enough? She wasn't
very skilled at flirty smiles. She tried again and
cocked her head. Gave her hair a shake, letting the
long red locks shimmy. Okay, that was pretty good.
She'd have to make sure she did that.

The signal changed and she drove down Pine
toward Ben Fordham's office. There was Riley's
grandma, Mrs. MacDonald, coming out of Tease,
her white locks freshly coiffed. Noel tooted her car
horn and waved, and Mrs. M smiled and waved
back.

She drove past Wellness Drugs, where her sister Aimi worked as a cashier, past the bank, past
Doggie Style Pet Grooming. Every parking space
along the street was taken and on the sidewalks people rushed from shop to shop, trying to finish their
holiday errands.

She wouldn't be doing much shopping now.
Thanks to the latest development with the house
she was pinching her pennies even tighter. Most of
her presents this year would be homemade. She sure
hoped her mom and sister would like the scarves
she'd started knitting for them. (Yarn had been fifty
percent off at The Yarn Barn.) She knew Dad and
Uncle Bill would love the blackberry liqueur she
had stewing in the pantry in her big glass jar. Made
from berries she'd picked in August and then frozen. She'd gotten plenty of scratches picking them,
but now she was glad she'd let Mom talk her into a
neighborhood berrying expedition. She'd probably

never master the art of baking pies but she could manage mixing crushed berries and vodka.

She turned onto the street where Ben Fordham's office was—and saw him leaving. Crud. He was on his way somewhere. He wouldn't be able to talk to her now. She slumped down behind the wheel.

What are you doing? Marvella demanded.

He's going somewhere. He doesn't have time to talk.

You're chickening out, Marvella sneered. *Do you have a brave cell anywhere in your body? How'd you ever think of me, anyway?*

Good question.

He's getting away. Are you just gonna sit here or are you gonna do something?

Do something. She'd follow him. Maybe he was going into town to run some errands. She could bump into him. That would be better than coming to his office, anyway. More natural. He started his big truck and it varoomed to life. Then he made a U-turn and drove down the street right past her. She slumped so low she nearly got stuck.

You're pathetic, Marvella said in disgust.

She was not pathetic. She was, well, she wasn't sure what she was. She whipped a U-turn herself and followed him.

He pulled up in front of Java Josie's and parked. Ah, a perfect place for a chance encounter. *See?* she told Mavella. *I know what I'm doing.*

Marvella grunted and then went away.

Noel walked into the coffee shop and was enveloped in warmth, probably body heat considering how many people were in there. Obviously she wasn't the only one who thought a midmorning coffee break was a good idea. The aroma of coffee beans danced around her nose, and the chatter of voices and hiss of steam wands greeted her.

She gave her hair a practice toss and walked over to where Ben Fordham stood at the end of the order line. Okay, she was here. Now, what to say? "Hi." Wow, that was brilliant.

He turned and smiled. "Noel. I don't think I've seen you in here before."

That was because when she was there, she tended to be invisible, hunched over her computer, doling out adventures to imaginary characters, missing out on them herself.

"You come here often?"

"I do." She used to, anyway. She hadn't been in much since she and Donny broke up. "They make the best lattes in town," she added. Well, that was dumb. They also made the only lattes in town.

"What's your favorite?"

Get flirty, Marvella commanded.

Get lost, Noel told her. She could do this. She wasn't completely hopeless. She tossed her hair again. "I was going to ask you that. I'd love to buy you something to make up for dinner." There. Well done. Jo would be proud.

"There's nothing to make up for," he assured her.

"Noel, I was going to call you."

Noel turned to see Donny, the disaster ex-boyfriend,

behind her. Great. Just what she didn't need. "Donny, how are you?"

He shrugged. "I'm okay. I miss you."

Which was why he hadn't called her in six months. "Still writing?" *Still using people?*

"Actually, I'm working on a children's book."

That explained why he was planning to call her. She could see where this was heading and decided to detour. "Where are my manners? Ben Fordham, this is Donny Lockhart, my, uh…" User ex-boyfriend? No, that was a little too honest. "One of my writing friends." They weren't really friends but Donny was hard to label.

He looked at Ben suspiciously, as if Ben was some sort of threat. Which he could hardly be, since Noel and Donny weren't dating anymore. "Are you a writer?"

"Nope. I remodel houses."

"Oh." Donny was underwhelmed. The line inched forward. "So, Noel, how about lunch tomorrow? I want to tell you about my new book idea," he continued, oblivious to the fact that she'd been talking to Ben.

Who was standing right there with a curious smile on his face.

"Gee, Donny, I'm pretty busy these days."

Donny frowned. "With him?"

Noel could feel her cheeks flaming. "With life. Aren't you seeing someone?"

"I was. She left me for a hack mystery writer."

They were at the order counter now. "Hi, Ben,"

said Ginger the barista. "Noel, we haven't seen you in a while."

Yep, come here all the time. Noel's cheeks kept on burning. "I've been a little busy lately. Can you give me an eggnog latte? And put whatever he wants on my bill, too," she said, nodding at Ben.

"While you're at it I'll have a large Americano," Donny put in, and Noel frowned at him.

"They're all on me." Ben said and took his wallet out of his jeans back pocket.

"Hey, thanks," said Donny.

"You didn't have to do that," Noel told Ben. "I wanted to pay."

"Never say no when people want to do nice things for you," Donny advised her as they moved toward the pick-up counter. "So, how about lunch tomorrow?"

"Donny, I really am busy."

"You can't be that busy. Everyone knows you have no life," Donny said with a scowl.

The flame spread from her face clear up into the roots of her hair. Any minute now someone was going to take a fire extinguisher to her. What had she ever seen in him?

"She's busy with me," Ben said and slung an arm around Noel's shoulders, stirring up all kinds of excitement in long-dormant body parts.

Donny looked completely perplexed. And irritated. "You're with him?"

"People move on, dude," Ben said and handed Donny his drink. "Good luck with the book." Then, to Noel, "I see a table over there." Before she could say anything he'd put her drink in her hand and was steering her to a small table by the window. "Nice meeting you, Donny," he called over his shoulder.

"Yeah. You, too," Donny called after him. He didn't sound as though he meant it.

"Thanks," she said to Ben as they sat down at the table.

"Glad to help. So you and that guy were…"

"We went out for a while." It had made sense at the time.

"Why? Wait, don't tell me, let me guess. He had potential. That's usually why women go out with guys like that."

"Everyone has potential," Noel said in both Donny's defense and her own.

Ben nodded slowly. "So, you're one of those women who believes the best of everyone?"

"I try to."

He regarded her over the rim of his mug. "Even house-flippers?"

"Most of all, house-flippers. They understand potential. They also understand how a person can fall in love with a house." That was subtle. Not.

He set down his mug. "Yes, they do. Noel, I'm sorry you didn't have the money to buy the house. I really am."

This sounded like the beginning of a speech she didn't want to hear. "I know. And I appreciate the fact that you're open to listening to my suggestions for how to keep its character. Can I buy you dinner tonight so we can talk about them? It's Peppermint Blizzard season at Dairy Queen."

"Are you trying to bribe me again?" he teased.

She cocked her head and tried a flirty smile. "Maybe." *Yes, of course.*

"I can't."

Her flirty smile faltered. "Oh."

"I have to go over to my mom's." Just when she was feeling that all was lost he said, "How about tomorrow night?"

She was so happy with this turn of events that she forgot to cock her head or toss her hair. "That would be great," she said and gave him a plain, old Noel smile.

"You have a great smile."

"I do?" She'd always thought her smile was rather average.

"Come on. I'm sure guys tell you that all the time."

"Not really. I guess not everyone sees my potential."

He shook his head. "Cute and funny." Then he sobered. "I wish we'd met under different circumstances."

That statement didn't bode well. It pretty much said, "I like you, but I'm still going to sell your house out from under you for an obscene profit." She tried to think of something clever to say in response but her brain was taking a nap. Even Marvella was strangely silent. Noel attempted to bring back the flirty smile; it refused to make an appearance and her normal one wasn't up to the task.

He felt the awkwardness, too. He cleared his throat. "I'd better get going. I have to check on a house I bought over in Bremerton."

She nodded. All was lost. Why bother with burgers?

There's a winning attitude. Marvella was back. *Don't give up. It's not over till it's over.*

True. She had nothing to lose. "I enjoyed visiting with you," she said. No lie. She had until the subject of the house came up. If only they'd met under different circumstances. If only he didn't have that one character flaw of buying houses someone else was in love with, she could so fall for him.

"Same here," he said and downed the last of his drink.

"I'll see you tomorrow at Dairy Queen," she said, working hard to inject fresh enthusiasm into her voice.

He nodded. "Six o'clock." Then he left.

She watched him go, feeling let down and miserable. Ben Fordham liked her—just not enough to lose money for her.

There were some women men would do anything for, including lose money. What was their secret?

"Are you seeing him?"

She broke out of her reverie to find Donny sliding into the seat Ben had vacated. And what was it about other women that they attracted men like…Donny?

"Oh, Donny, go away," she said in disgust.

"What?" he demanded, clueless.

On second thought, she'd go away. She took her latte and left the coffee shop.

She needed to talk to someone. Riley was teaching, so she couldn't call her. Anyway, Riley wasn't doing any better at managing men than she was. What she needed was an expert.

Jo. Jo had always had boys trailing after her in high school and beyond. Cool attitude, hot looks— she had it all together. Noel parked in the Pineland Supermarket lot and put in a call, hoping Jo might have a minute.

"Mikey's about to wake up. You'll have to talk fast," Jo said.

"I need help."

"The clothes aren't working?"

"It's not the clothes. They're great. It's me."

"What's wrong with you?"

"That's what I want to know. I saw Ben Fordham again. I don't think he's going to budge on making it affordable for me to get my house."

"What a turd," Jo muttered.

"He's not really," Noel said. And when, exactly had she changed her opinion about the man? "He's just a businessman."

"Who's ruining your life? Noel, are you falling for this guy?"

Maybe. "No. Look, I need to find a way to make him want to help me more than he wants to make money."

"Good luck with that."

"What is it about some women that makes men willing to do anything for them?"

Jo laughed. "That's only in books."

"Yeah? What about you? Guys have always tripped all over themselves to do what you wanted."

"Tell that to my husband," Jo said irritably.

"Come on, I'm serious. What have you got that I haven't?" Besides blond hair, style, a husband and a baby.

"Are you asking me what I think you're lacking?"

"As a matter of fact, I am."

"Confidence," Jo said. "You need to practice walking into a room like you own it. When you want something tell yourself, 'I deserve it,' because, Noel, you do. You're pretty and sweet and kind-hearted and you need to appreciate yourself a little more. If you don't, who will? Don't let people turn you into a carpet. Decide what you want and then go about making it happen. That's all there is to it."

"You make it sound so easy," Noel said wistfully.

"It may not be easy for you, but it's what you need to do. Oh, the baby's crying. That's the end of the shrink session for today."

"Thanks," Noel said.

"I'm only telling you what's true. You're special, Noel, you really are. Now start acting like it."

Special. Was she really? She pulled down the car visor and studied herself in the mirror. She wasn't bad-looking. Why on earth didn't she have more confidence?

Oh, yeah, high school. She could still remember

how her tummy churned when she'd tried to talk to boys she was crushing on, could still feel the terrible sting of rejection when the boy of her dreams turned her down after she asked him to the spring dance. She remembered how nervous she'd get when a date wanted to kiss her, sure she'd mess the whole thing up. She invariably did. She'd only had a couple of serious boyfriends, and Donny Lockhart had been one of them.

But she could change. She was going to be more confident. She got out of her car and made her way into the grocery store. Confidently.

At the row of grocery carts at the entrance, she was just reaching for one when a fifty-something woman she'd seen in the store before snagged it and wheeled it off. How rude! She scowled at the woman's retreating backside, commandeered the next cart and followed her inside. Designer jeans, boots, an expensive jacket and cashmere scarf. Diamonds in her ears. Perfectly highlighted, straightened, chin-length hair. Well-off and entitled. She was probably the kind of woman men would do anything for.

Noel thought of her own sweet mom, a little pudgy with streaks of gray in faint auburn hair. Mom never wore designer jeans. Her daughters were grown-up now but she still wouldn't spend that much money on herself. She especially wouldn't now that Dad was laid off. Was Mom the kind of woman men would do anything for? Maybe not, but Dad would, and that was all she needed. "It's what's in your heart that counts," she liked to say. So how to balance a good heart and confidence? Jo managed to do it.

Still mulling over what Jo had told her, she wheeled her own cart to the produce department. She was selecting some apples when she realized the rude, cart-stealing woman was standing only a few feet away, inspecting oranges and talking on her cell.

"Yes, that girl would love to get her acrylic nails into him." Pause and a frown. "Of course I'm aware he's a grown man, but he's still my son and you know he has a real blind spot when it comes to women. Thank God they only went out a couple of times. He's done. I told him what a disaster she'd be."

Yikes! Noel couldn't help wondering what was wrong with the mystery woman who wanted to get her nails into this woman's son. She was probably breathing.

"I've got another call coming in. Talk to you later," the woman said. Her voice turned to syrup as she answered the new call. "Ben, dear. Are you staying for dinner tonight after you pick up Timmy?"

Ben? Noel blinked. No, couldn't be. The Ben she was dealing with wouldn't have this lizard for a mother.

"Good, because I need you to fix that leak under the sink."

There had to be more than one Ben in a town of almost ten thousand who knew how to fix leaks.

"And bring your tool belt. I need you to put up a shelf for me in the laundry room."

And there had to be more than one Ben in a town of almost ten thousand who owned a tool belt.

If there wasn't, and if he really was as hard-hearted as his mother… Okay, Noel was so not going to think about that right now.

Chapter Eleven

Noel was loading her groceries into the car when her sister called. "I'm going over to Mom and Dad's for dinner and to talk about wedding stuff. I thought you'd want to be there since you're my maid of honor."

Always a bridesmaid, never a bride. Was that going to be her? She hoped not. "Sure," she said. She did want to be there. Even though her own love life was nothing to write about, she was still happy for her sister.

She got to her parents' place to find Mom putting the finishing touches on a beef stew. "It smells great," she said, kissing her mother's cheek.

"Just leftover pot roast and some veggies and gravy," Mom said.

Which would, of course, be perfectly seasoned and served with homemade, fluffy herbed biscuits. Mom could have been a chef.

And Noel could have been...the person who enjoyed the chef's creations. Cooking wasn't her forte. She'd confirmed that yet again when she'd tried to make dinner for Ben Fordham. Mom had tried to pass on her culinary gift, but finally gave up when it became apparent that her daughter would rather have her nose in a book than over a simmering pot.

Aimi had been the star of the kitchen, and tonight she was bringing a salad, which Noel knew would be full of yummy extras like pomegranate seeds and bacon bits.

She put her offering (two bottles of sparkling cider) in the fridge. "Where's Daddy?"

"In the den, checking out help-wanted ads."

"I hope something shows up for him soon."

"It will," Mom said, sounding completely unruffled.

She loved her mother's positive attitude. If only more of it had worn off on her.

A moment later her father wandered into the kitchen. "I thought I heard our girl," he said, giving Noel a hug. "How's Marvella doing?"

"Oh, she's busy," Noel said and left it at that. Best not to share that Marvella was spending more time in her head these days, counseling her, than she was on the computer screen. People who weren't writers tended to get concerned when you talked about hearing voices in your head.

Daddy beamed. "Don't we have the most talented daughter?" he said to Mom.

"I think you might be a little prejudiced," Noel told him.

He shook his head. "I don't think so. One of these

days your name will be a household word, just like Dr. Seuss."

If only it already was. Then she'd have been able to buy her house. She kept that to herself, too. Her parents had enough to worry about. They didn't need to hear how her dream house had gotten away from her.

"Isn't it exciting about Aimi and Dan?" Mom said, probably for the twentieth time since Aimi had gotten engaged.

"Yes, it is," Noel agreed.

"I'm glad they want a church wedding," Mom continued.

"I was hoping we could pay them to elope," Dad joked. He opened the fridge. "Looks like elves came and left us some fancy drinks." He held up one of the bottles of cider. "Would you like some, princess?"

Princess. She loved that nickname, loved that her father thought she was special. "Sure."

He poured all three of them a glass. "Here's to Marvella making you a fortune in the New Year so you can buy that house."

Now that it was about to be fixed and flipped, she'd probably need a fortune. She tried to smile, gave up and took a quick sip of her cider.

Another few minutes, and her sister arrived on the scene. She had the same red hair as Noel and a perfect face. Perfect figure. Perfect outfit, too, Noel observed, taking in the red coat, black leggings and boots. Like Jo, Aimi had flair.

Yeah? Well, you've got me, Marvella told her.

Yes, she did, and when it came right down to it, she was fine with that. She liked making up stories, enjoyed the creative process. She was happy being who she was.

Most of the time. Still, was it wrong to want more than a career she loved, to want a good man and a child of her own to read her stories to?

Aimi set down a wooden bowl full of greens and yes, there were the pomegranate seeds and the bacon bits, along with avocado, tomatoes, finely chopped red onions and fresh dill. "Hey, everyone!" she caroled and doled out hugs and kisses. The party always started when Aimi entered the room.

"Hey, Squirt," Dad said and gave her a big kiss. "How was work?"

Aimi shrugged. "Boring."

"At least it's a job," Mom pointed out.

"Yes, but I'm going to need more money now that I'm getting married."

"We told you not to worry about wedding expenses," Mom reminded her. "We're going to pay."

And of course she'd let them, Noel thought with a frown, even though their parents were on a tight budget until Dad found a job. Ever the baby of the family.

"You guys are the best," Aimi said, smiling at Mom.

"How are the wedding plans coming?" Mom asked.

"Slowly. There's so much to do. I think we need a wedding planner."

"How much does that cost?" Noel asked. Could Mom and Dad afford that?

"I don't know, but it'll be worth every penny," Aimi said. "A wedding planner can help keep you on track."

"I can help keep you on track," Noel said but Aimi ignored her.

"The biscuits are done," Mom announced. "We're ready to eat."

"Remember, Mom and Dad don't have a lot of money right now," she whispered as Mom took their biscuits out of the oven and Dad flipped on the radio to his favorite eighties station.

Aimi whispered back, "I know."

Noel wanted to say more, but here was Mom back at the table with the bowl full of biscuits. She settled for giving her little sister a stern look.

Dinner would've been more delicious if it hadn't been seasoned with Aimi's selfishness. She rattled on about everything from flowers to her gown, and the dollar signs danced around the table.

"We need to come up with a budget," Mom said at last.

Thank heaven.

"Budget?" Aimi said suspiciously.

"Darling, we want to give you a nice wedding but we're not a bottomless well," Mom said.

"And Daddy's out of work," Noel added. Her father's smile fell and she instantly regretted bringing that nasty specter to the table.

"We'll come up with the money somehow," he said.

It was the same thing he'd said when she'd first talked about needing money for her house. Then he was laid off and she'd been careful not to bring up the subject again.

"It's not like I'm planning to spend a lot," Aimi insisted, "but weddings do cost money." Her voice was now tinged with the beginnings of panic.

"I'm sure we can find some ways to cut corners," Mom said calmly.

"Where? How?"

"You can start by bagging the wedding planner," Noel said and Aimi scowled at her.

"We'll figure it out," Mom assured her. "Now, show us some of the gowns you were looking at."

This put Aimi in a happier frame of mind. She took out her phone and pulled up the latest website she'd found, then began scrolling through pictures of women in gorgeous gowns.

Each wedding dress was beautiful. Aimi would look fabulous in any one of them. Yes, Noel was happy for her sister. And yes, she was also the tiniest bit jealous.

"They're lovely," said Mom. "Have you gone to Old and New yet? I saw a dress similar to that last one you showed us in their window the other day when I was driving past."

"A secondhand store?"

"A boutique that sells wedding gowns at a very reasonable price," Mom corrected her. "We should at least check it out. You might find the perfect gown there."

Aimi's expression was dubious but she promised to stop in.

"I can go with you," Noel offered.

"I'll let you know," Aimi said, which made Noel wonder if she was going to keep her promise. As the youngest she was a little spoiled, but ever since she'd gotten engaged she'd become completely self-absorbed.

"Are you going to check out Old and New?" Noel asked later as they went down the front walk to their cars.

Aimi made a face. "I don't think so."

"It would save a ton," Noel pointed out.

"I know, but you only get married once."

Noel didn't bother mentioning people who got married twice. Or three times. Or not at all. Riley's aborted wedding and then her own nonexistent prospects sprang to mind.

"It's a good thing because Mom and Dad can hardly afford the one you're planning."

"Jeez, Noel. Can you, like, not ruin my night? We're just in the early stages. I'm not going to break the bank. Okay?"

"You'd better not," Noel said, channeling Marvella.

"Stop being so mean," Aimi said. "Just because you're not getting married doesn't mean you have to make me feel bad that I am."

Good Lord, was that what she was doing? She went home and watched *27 Dresses*.

That night she dreamed she was getting married. On the way to the church she stopped at Old and New and picked up a gown. It had stains on the bodice but the saleswoman gave her a fifty percent discount so she changed into it right there. Then she got on her bicycle (why was she riding a bicycle?) and pedaled off to church. She barely made it in time, hopping off her bike and running up the steps, a reverse Cinderella hurrying to her prince. Aimi served as the world's oldest flower girl, scattering rose petals everywhere, and Marvella was Noel's maid of honor, her blue tail sticking out from under her purple bridesmaid's dress.

Noel followed them. (Walking herself down the aisle—what was that about?) She got to the front of the church, only to discover there was no groom.

But there was Santa, together with Mrs. Claus, sitting in the front row next to Mom and Dad. "Don't worry," he called. "Your groom will show up."

She awakened with one word on her tongue. *When?*

Who knew? One thing she did know. She had work to do and a date tonight. All good.

She spent the morning on her laptop and she and Marvella turned Little Jenny into a confident child who not only boldly raised her hand in class but also won the school jump rope contest and took a shy newcomer under her wing. All in a day's work.

And now she had the afternoon free. Time to decorate for the holidays. She fetched her artificial tree and the ornaments from the garage, as well as the lights she always strung around the front windows—

fat, old-fashioned, multicolored ones that made her small house look like a jewel box.

She did her outside decorating first, replacing the burned-out bulbs on her strings of lights and framing her windows with them. The sky was gray and the air smelled like snow. She hoped it would snow. In the temperate Pacific Northwest they didn't get much of the white stuff, but when they did she made sure to get outside and really enjoy herself, taking long walks and making snowmen with the neighbor children. Her neighbors all lined their houses with lights and hung icicles from the roof, and a couple of inches of snow turned everything magical. She hummed as she worked. *It's beginning to look a lot like Christmas*. Yes, it was. And her house was always adorable all dressed up for the holidays.

This could be her last Christmas in it.

She pushed away the depressing thought and went inside and put up her tree. There. Very festive. A couple of scented candles on the mantel (Bath & Body Works Twisted Peppermint and Fresh Balsam), along with the little porcelain church that had once been Mom's and the vintage choirboy candles from the fifties that she'd found in an antiques mall. Then, with her stocking hung by the chimney with care, she was ready. The brick fireplace was perfect for those old holiday decorations. They wouldn't look the same with some sleek, new design. She'd point that out to Ben.

Ben. Dairy Queen. She checked the time and

realized her afternoon had evaporated. She had to shower and get changed!

She hurried through her shower, threw on some of her loaner clothes then applied mascara and lip gloss and rushed out the door. She should've taken more time with her hair. It wasn't fully dry and she could already feel it curling in all directions. Too late now. She didn't want to keep Ben waiting.

But he was already waiting there when she arrived, parked at a table near the door. He smiled at the sight of her and rose.

"Sorry I'm a little late," she said. "I was decorating. It takes a while."

"I bet it looks great."

"It does. Maybe you'd like to come and see it after we eat."

"Maybe I would," he agreed.

Smoothly done, she congratulated herself. When he saw how beautifully she had everything fixed up, he'd have to admit that she and the house were a perfect match. Just like he and she could be…if only he hadn't bought the place; if only he didn't have the mother from hell. No, that woman in the store couldn't—could *not*—be his mother.

Never mind his mother. Make conversation, Marvella commanded.

Oh, yeah. That. "Do you decorate for Christmas?"

"I put up a tree, but that's it. Not much point bothering when you're in an apartment."

She could feel her eyebrows shooting up. "You live in an apartment?"

"I buy houses to resell, not to live in."

That seemed so…cold. "Wouldn't you rather live in a house?"

"Yeah. Someday. Right now where I am works fine."

Of course, a single man didn't need a big old house, not when he was busy going out with beautiful women. Who had acrylic nails. Ben Fordham and other women wasn't something she wanted to think about. She asked him what he'd like to eat.

"Tell me what you want first," he said, pulling out his wallet.

"No. I'm paying," she insisted and laid a hand on his arm. His hard, solid arm. Her tummy fluttered.

She drew back her hand.

"Okay," he said. "How about a cheeseburger and a Coke?"

"How about a cheeseburger, onion rings and a peppermint Blizzard?" she countered.

"Sure. Why not?"

They settled at a table with their burgers and Blizzards and while he dug into his, Noel tried to think of some witty banter. Nothing came to mind and Marvella was irritatingly silent.

"It might snow tonight," she finally said. Wow, that was a sparkling bit of conversation.

"I hope so. I like the snow."

"Do you? Me, too."

"What do you like about it? Do you ski?"

She shook her head. Skiing was not a cheap sport. Her dad was never the high-powered variety of businessman, and her parents hadn't really had the money to afford ski lessons and the ski bus for two kids. "I'd like to learn someday." The idea of being up there in the mountains, whooshing down a hill with the wind in her face sounded so romantic.

"Nothing like it," he said and took a slurp of his Blizzard.

She could see him filling out a ski parka with that massive chest, those powerful legs working as he zigzagged down a craggy mountain. The image left her spellbound. And speechless. Okay, she needed to say something. She gulped down some of her drink and willed the peppermint to bring her brain to life.

Finally she asked, "Did you buy any houses today?"

"Not today. I probably won't be buying any more now until I sell one. Unless I find a great place at auction."

"How many houses do you have?"

"Well, that one in Bremerton. And yours."

Maybe he'd sell the Bremerton house first. "Does the Bremerton one need a lot of work?"

"Not really. Mostly cosmetic stuff—some paint inside and a new hardwood floor in the living room, updated appliances in the kitchen."

"If you sold that, then you wouldn't need to sell my, er, the other house right away." And she'd have more time to come up with the money. Her agent was negotiating a new contract with her publisher.

If they gave her a contract for two more Marvella books, surely she could pull together enough money for a down payment. Of course, December was nap time for the publishing business. Even if a deal was struck, she wouldn't get her contract until well into the New Year. And then, after that was signed, she'd have to wait several more weeks for her advance money. If she could just stall Ben... "I'll have money in the New Year," she added, thinking positive.

"Oh?" He looked interested and almost...hopeful?

"I should be able to come up with enough for you to make a profit if you didn't do a lot of remodeling in my, er, your house. It doesn't actually need that much work."

"If I flip it, it does."

Flip. There was that four-letter word.

"Could you show me again what you'd do?" she asked. With luck, she could talk him out of it."

He didn't look happy at the prospect of doing that, but he popped the last of his onion rings into his mouth then crumpled the bag. "Let's go."

They drove to Noel's house, with him following her in his truck. It was snowing now and settling on the lawns and roofs, showing off the lights decorating the houses, making them sparkle like jewels. Her house wasn't as elaborately done as many of her neighbors', but it was still festive with its lights and the tree standing in the window.

"Did you do all that yourself?" he asked.

"I did. I'd love to hang icicles from the roof, too, but I don't like going up on ladders."

"They can be dangerous," he said.

Good, send him up on one, said Marvella.

She told Marvella to shut up, let him inside and took his coat then watched as he checked out her decorations.

"Nice job."

"The old-fashioned fireplace is perfect for vintage Christmas decorations."

"I know," he said. "You don't want it modernized. You already told me that."

"You have to admit, it looks really sweet."

He nodded. "It does."

He smiled at her—a killer smile. His coat smelled of the outdoors and some spicy cologne. She suddenly thought of the guy in the Old Spice commercials. Ben Fordham would make a great Old Spice man. An image of him in a towel appeared in her mind, and she told herself to quit fantasizing about impossible things. She turned abruptly and hung his coat in the closet.

"So, what else would you not change about the house?" he asked. "I know you want to keep that built-in china cabinet."

"Of course. It's unique. And charming."

"The kitchen floor. At least tell me you'd get rid of that scabby old vinyl," he said, starting for the kitchen.

She followed him. He turned on the light and yes, the floor was pretty pathetic. "Okay, yes, that," she agreed.

"And the counters. They should be updated."

"Granite," she said in disgust. Why did people like granite so much? "That ugly orange spotty stuff—my friend Riley has it in her kitchen. So does her sister."

"It's not all ugly. A soft gray would look really nice in here. Or you could put in a maple butcher-block counter."

"What would all that cost?"

"Not too much," he said vaguely.

She could see the price on her house rising steadily, like a river about to flood. She bit her lip.

"Come on, let's look around."

They did, wandering through the upstairs rooms. "This bathroom will have to be redone," he said. "There's no getting around it."

"It's not that bad," Noel said. She tried to see it from his viewpoint. Yes, the floor had old, chipped tile that even her bathroom area rugs couldn't dress up. But the claw-foot tub was charming. "That tub is great for bubble baths."

"There's no walk-in shower anywhere in this house. Most people want a shower."

"I guess I'm not most people," she said.

He smiled at that. "I guess not. You know, there's probably room in here for a tub and a shower."

"How much would all *that* cost?" Of course he'd tack that amount on to the price when he resold the house.

"Not that much," came the stock answer.

"If you sell it to me as is, you won't have to do anything," she said.

He said nothing to that, just moved on to her bedroom. His standing next to her bed made it hard for her to concentrate. She kept getting distracted by visions of two bodies in that bed, one of them a big, strong man with big, clever hands.

"Probably don't need to do much in here," he said.

She could think of plenty. *Stop it*, she scolded herself. *What is wrong with you?*

Back downstairs they examined the small bathroom. "I wanted to put a pedestal sink in here someday," she said wistfully. "Maybe a small, vintage dresser for towels."

"That'd look good," he said.

Yes, he'd take her idea and run with it. And the price would continue to soar.

"I suppose you'll bring in someone to stage it," she said. So he could get top dollar. Ugh.

"That's what I usually do. I have an excellent stager," he added with a grin.

Oh, who cares? muttered Marvella.

The one in the office across from him, obviously, but she still asked, "Who?"

"My mother, actually."

I need you to fix that leak under the sink. The conversation she'd overheard in the grocery store came back to her. Oh, no. The lizard from the store was his mom *and* his stager? Surely this couldn't be. Coincidence. It had to be coincidence.

"Your m-mother," Noel stammered.

"What can I say? We believe in nepotism in my family. Mom's office is right across from mine. My cousin's in the same building, too. He's a real estate broker and he writes up all my deals." Then Ben brought them back to the subject at hand. "This house could be a real gem."

With him ripping out walls right and left, and his mother displaying slick, high-priced furniture and decorations in every room. They'd sell it for an obscene profit and cackle all the way to the bank.

"I'll never be able to afford it by the time you're done with it, will I?" She could feel the prickle of tears. Embarrassed, she focused on the old vanity with its chipped wood and wiped the corner of her eye.

Then she felt his fingers, calloused and rough, on her chin, urging her to look at him. "Noel." His voice was soft.

She did and she saw pity on his face. She tried not to let the tears spill.

"I'm not out to ruin your life. Really."

"I know," she whispered.

Now he was gazing at her lips. She might not have been the world's greatest femme fatale but even she knew what that meant.

Go for it, Marvella whispered.

She lifted her chin slightly and that was all the encouragement he needed. He bent and kissed her—a light, sweet kiss, filled with tenderness.

Just as she was about to get into it, he pulled away. "Sorry. I shouldn't have done that."

She blinked.

He clawed a hand through his hair. "This is not

a good road to start down—not until we get things settled about the house."

"Then let's get things settled," she urged.

"Noel, I can't simply give you this place. I have to make a profit. This is my business and I have obligations."

"How much of a profit do you want to make?" Why was she asking? She'd seen plenty of those house-flipping shows.

Sure enough. The amount he told her made her want to stick her head in the toilet and drown herself. "I don't know if I can qualify for a loan for that much."

He paced down the hall. "This was supposed to be an easy deal, quick profit. Get in and get out." He stood there in the hallway, shaking his head.

She hurried over to him. "You can still make a profit. Just don't make all those changes. I don't care about them. I love the house the way it is. Add another ten thousand to the price and call it good." What was she saying? She couldn't afford another ten thousand. She couldn't even afford another five. And neither of those numbers was close to what he wanted to clear. "Carry my contract and let me make monthly payments." She'd have the place paid off by the time she was…sixty. Not exactly turning a quick profit, but… "That would bring in some income every month for you."

He looked torn. She laid a hand on his arm. "Can't you at least think about it?"

At last he said, "Let me crunch the numbers. Okay?"

She wanted to throw her arms around him and kiss him. Promise to buy him Blizzards for life. Instead she smiled gratefully. "Thank you."

"I'm not making any promises," he reminded her.

She nodded. "I understand."

"I don't know if I can make this work," he continued, dousing the fire of hope that had been building inside her.

Baloney, scoffed Marvella. He's caving. *Keep pumping him full of Blizzards and lattes, and this place will be ours.*

Yes! Blizzards and lattes…and kisses.

What obligations did he have, anyway?

Chapter Twelve

There was no better way to spend a Saturday morning than helping your sister give your infant nephew a bath. The help consisted mainly of standing by holding the towel, but it gave her something to think about besides the looming non-wedding date.

One week from today she would've been getting married. She sighed.

Her sister the psychic shot her a sideways glance. "What are you going to do next Saturday?"

"Bake cookies."

Jo frowned. "You know what I mean."

She wished she didn't. The dreaded day was now coming at her like an avalanche.

"I think you should celebrate your lucky escape," Jo said.

Yep, celebrate. Just like she'd done the Saturday before, consuming cookies and streaming old episodes of *Downton Abbey*.

"Let's have a party."

"I'm not sure I'm going to be in a party mood," Riley said.

"Well, let me see if I can help you get in one. Sean is a skunk. You almost married a skunk. And how much do you want to bet there'll be more women after Emily? Your life with him would've sucked. We should declare next Saturday your Independence Day and set off fireworks. Okay, we're ready for our towel."

Riley frowned as she handed over the towel. "I should be relieved I found out what a cheater he is. Why don't I feel more glad?"

"Because the two-legged turd broke your heart. Baby oil."

Riley took the top off the baby oil and handed that over, too, but not before she kept some to rub into one of the baby's little feet. Those tiny toes— so cute!

"Still, you're going to reach a point when you thank God all you had to worry about was canceling your venue. You have canceled it, right?"

She still hadn't been able to bring herself to call the golf club. Canceling the venue felt like buying a coffin for her love life. She bit her lip and shook her head.

"Uh, Riles, you probably need to do that."

Riley could feel tears welling in her eyes. She kept her focus on the baby. Suddenly it felt as if she was looking at little Mikey from under water. "I know."

Jo diapered the baby, and Riley passed her the red-and-white-striped coverall Grammy had bought him, joining the family stampede to buy some baby-boy outfits. "Aren't you adorable, my lovely son," she cooed. Then she returned her attention to Riley. "You probably can't get back any of your deposits at this point, but it's worth a try. How about the photographer? Have you talked to him?"

Riley shook her head again.

"The florist?"

"Uh-uh."

"Cake?"

"No."

"DJ? *Anything*?"

"Nooo." She was always so organized, so on top of things. Now she was on top of nothing, confronted by a pile of ugly to-dos, and all she wanted was to bury her head in the sand like an ostrich. Actually, she'd read somewhere that ostriches didn't really do that. Well, what did they know, anyway? They were ostriches. This head-burying thing was working fine for her.

Sort of.

Riley's cell phone rang. It was Mom. "Hi, honey, just wanted to see how you're doing. Have you canceled your venue yet?"

Were Mom and Jo communicating telepathically? "Jo and I were talking about that a few minutes ago."

"I don't think you can get your deposit back. What does your contract say?"

She hadn't even looked at her contract. She hadn't done anything except swing back and forth between happiness for her sister and misery over her ruined future. "I don't know. I'll have to check."

"I ran into Bett from Floral Bliss at the grocery store, and she said she hadn't heard from you."

"I was getting ready to call her." Someday.

"Well, I talked with her and she says she'll refund your deposit."

Good old Mom. "Thanks," Riley said.

"And Annette at The Cake Box says she will, too."

It was only a hundred dollars, but on her salary that was nothing to sneeze at and Riley was grateful. "That's really nice of her. And of Bett." Bett's refund would help plump up her piggy bank, as well. Small consolation, but it was something.

"You owe them thank-you notes."

Yes, she could use the stationery she'd ordered to write thank-yous for her wedding gifts. Sigh.

"Are you sure you don't want me to call The Pines for you?" Mom offered.

"No. I'm a big ostrich, er, girl. I can do it." She'd take care of it after school on Monday.

"Okay," Mom said dubiously. "I hate to see you going through all this. But," she hurried on, "wedding cancellation misery is better than divorce misery any day."

Mom and Jo were both right, of course. At the moment it was hard to see it like that. She needed to correct her vision.

"What are you doing for fun today? The streets are clear so Grammy and I are going over to the senior center later to check out the holiday bazaar."

A thrilling way to spend a Saturday, looking at

embroidered dish towels and homemade jams. She could hear Grammy in the background. "Tell her she needs to get out."

"Your grandma says you need to get out."

"I am out. I'm at Jo's."

"If Mom's taking you shopping don't let me stop you," Jo said. "Mikey and I are having naps this afternoon."

So, that was the choice—take a nap with Jo and the baby or go to the senior center.

"Come on," Mom urged. "It'll be fun."

It probably would. She enjoyed being with her mother and grandmother. And, if she played her cards right, she'd get invited to Mom and Dad's for dinner.

Her wayward thoughts strayed to what her Saturday nights used to look like—dinners out with Sean, cuddling on the couch with a roaring fake fire in the electric fireplace, hot kisses...

"So, what do you say?" Mom asked.

Anything was better than sitting at home thinking about her old life. "I'll come pick you guys up in half an hour," she replied.

"If anybody's selling fudge, buy me some," Jo said.

There was bound to be fudge for sale. *If Riley buys fudge for her sister instead of herself, how many ounces does she prevent from gluing themselves to her hips? Not enough to counteract the other goodies she'll consume.* But who cared! She deserved a treat.

In fact, she deserved a life, darn it all. On her way to her mom's, she put her Bluetooth to work and called Noel. "Are you doing anything tonight?" she asked.

"No." Noel sounded downright grumpy. This was hardly surprising since she was worried about being able to afford her house.

"Then let's do something." Even though both their lives were in the toilet, they could console themselves by swimming around in there together.

"You want to come over? We can order pizza."

Spending a Saturday night in, eating pizza— when you did that with your boyfriend, it was cozy and fun. When you did that with a girlfriend, it was because you had no place to go. She was *not* going to let Sean reduce her to a life of evenings in.

"Why don't we put on our new dresses and go to The Tree House instead?" she suggested.

"I don't know," Noel said doubtfully.

"Come on. We can't sit home, not on a Saturday night."

"I can."

"Try the heels one more time, okay? I'll pick you up at eight."

Noel said a reluctant "Okay," and Riley ended the call with a smile. Good. The afternoon with her mom and grandma, dinner (hopefully) with her parents and a night out. That took care of this Saturday. As for next Saturday…as Noel would say, she wasn't going to think about that right now.

Mom and Grammy were ready and waiting when

she got to her parents', Mom wearing jeans and a cream-colored sweater accented with a gold necklace, simple black flats on her feet. It was plain to see where Jo got her style sense. She certainly didn't get it from Grammy, who was resplendent in tennis shoes and jeans topped by an ugly Christmas sweater decorated with penguins in Santa hats. She'd accented her ensemble with a Santa hat pulled over her short, spiky gray hair and a necklace of Christmas ornaments that blinked on and off. The green ornament earrings dangling from her ears were blinking, too, but to an entirely different beat.

"Let's go party," she said, leading the way. Watching her blink down the hall, Riley couldn't help thinking of the song about Rudolph and his red nose. If Rudolph wanted Christmas Eve off to play reindeer games, Grammy could easily fill in for him.

"She really wants to go out looking like that?" Riley whispered to her mother.

Mom shrugged. "What can I say? She has her own, uh, unique style. Just pretend you don't know her when we get there."

But of course, that wasn't happening. Grammy wanted to introduce her lovely granddaughter to anyone and everyone. Riley already knew some of the seniors peddling their wares, like Mrs. Wooster, Grammy's BFF, who was selling crocheted mug cozies and sock monkeys.

"Your grandma told me about that awful man who jilted you," Mrs. Wooster boomed. (Mrs. Wooster was hard of hearing and assumed everyone else was, too.) "That piece in the paper was simply awful, but I'd have rammed the vixen, too."

"I didn't do it on purpose," Riley said. She could feel her cheeks flaming. She was aware of the sweet, gray-haired lady sitting at the table next to Mrs. Wooster, eavesdropping shamelessly. In a hurry to change the subject, she picked up a red mug cozy. "Did you make these yourself?"

"Did I what?" boomed Mrs. Wooster.

The woman selling brownies at the next table spoke up. "You know, my daughter is a witch. She could cast a spell."

"Thanks, but I think I'll let him get what's coming to him all on his own." Then to Mrs. Wooster, a little more loudly, "Did you make these?"

"I did."

"Well, then I'll take two."

Mrs. Wooster nodded. "Yes, they're new."

Riley held up two fingers. "Two."

"Buy two, get two free," said Mrs. Wooster.

Goody. Riley fished in her purse. She could use them...hmm. She could give them to...hmm. She'd think of someone.

Meanwhile, the little old lady at the next table was selling more than brownies. "Just a little spell?"

"Uh, no, that's okay," Riley said. "But I will take one of your brownies."

The woman beamed a beatific smile. "You'll want more than one. They're laced with pot."

"I'll take two," said Grammy.

"Mother!" Mom scolded.

"What? It's legal here in Washington," Grammy retorted and Mom made a face.

So far, this wasn't exactly what Riley had envisioned when she'd agreed to come to the seniors' holiday bazaar. At least it wasn't boring.

They moved on to more tables and Riley wound up purchasing a jar of peppermint face scrub and something called Snowmommy's Soup, which was cocoa mix with miniature marshmallows and crushed peppermint candies.

She also bought a handmade birdhouse from a fit-looking older man with a few wisps of white hair fringing an otherwise bald pate. "This'll be nice on your patio," he told her.

"I don't have a patio yet, but I will someday." And if not she'd give the birdhouse to Noel for her place…once she'd gotten it back from the house-flipper. "This is really charming," she added.

"Thanks."

"You sure have a lot of them." There weren't that many people milling around the senior center. She hoped for his sake as well as the others all looking eagerly at the people strolling past their tables that they'd have a late-afternoon rush.

"I like to putter." He grabbed some newspaper and wrapped up her purchase with gnarled hands. "The kids want me to move to one of those assisted living places, but I told 'em that's for old people. I'm not in my grave yet."

"You have a long ways to go before that happens, Felix," Grammy assured him.

"You got that right. Kids these days, they figure just because a man gets old he's useless. I keep telling 'em that even if there's snow on the rooftop, it don't mean there's no fire in the chimney," he said with a wink that made Grammy blush.

"He's cute," Riley said as they moved away. She nudged Grammy. "I think he's got the hots for you."

"Oh, he flirts with all the ladies. When you get to be our age, a man can have his pick of women. He's a good man with lots of life left in him." She shook her head. "His kids want to stick him somewhere and forget him."

"I'm sure that's not true," Riley protested.

"It's true for many people after a certain age. Funny how the longer you live, the smaller your world becomes. Your children get busy with their lives and their own children. You wind up hard of hearing and sitting on the sidelines at family gatherings, watching the fun instead of being part of it."

Riley looked over at where Mrs. Wooster sat. Was Grammy talking about her?

"Pretty soon it's just you and Friday-night bingo. Of course, that's not the case with me," Grammy added. "But it is with a number of my friends. This is the highlight of the year for many of them."

Riley took in the large room decorated with tinsel and red bows, filled with tables and senior citizens smiling at potential customers. Did the ornaments on the tree in the corner look a little worn and tired? Did the smiles on some of those faces look just a little desperate?

As she stopped to chat with the seniors, she heard tales of neglectful children, tight budgets and lonely holidays looming. And she thought *she* had problems. The more she heard, the more she bought. By the time they left, she was loaded down with everything from tea towels to fudge for Jo.

"You're a good kid," Grammy said as they all walked back to the car, Riley with her armload of purchases, Grammy with her pot-laced brownies.

"I'm a sucker," Riley said. "I don't know what I'm going to do with half of this."

"You can give me the mug cozies for Christmas," Grammy said. "I'll use them for my tea mugs. And in return I'll share my brownies," she added with a grin.

Riley wasn't into pot even if it was legal. "No, thanks, Grammy."

"Honestly, Mother," Mom said, clearly annoyed.

"An old woman deserves some pleasure," Grammy insisted.

"You are not deprived," Mom informed her.

Grammy's teasing smile disappeared. "You're right, I'm blessed. I wish all those people in there had a family like mine and something nice to look forward to other than a Christmas dinner in the church basement."

"They've got you for a friend and I'd say that makes them pretty blessed," Riley said.

"Okay, you're back in the will," Grammy joked.

Once they got home Mom issued the hoped-for dinner invitation, and Riley hung around and played hearts with Dad and Grammy before getting treated to her mother's Swedish meatballs. Grammy offered her brownies for dessert but nobody took her up on it.

"I'm driving," Riley said.

"You can stick around," Mom told her. "Spend the night."

"I'm actually going out."

"With a man?" Grammy wanted to know. "Way to go, darling."

"No, with Noel. But we're going to The Tree House."

"Don't let anyone buy drinks for you," Grammy cautioned then lowered her voice and added, "They'll slip you that rape drug."

"I won't," Riley promised.

"And don't leave your drink unwatched. Or your purse."

"Mother, she knows all that," said Mom.

"You can't be too careful," Dad said, siding with Grammy.

"Don't worry, guys, I'll be careful." After hugging everyone, Riley went home and got ready for her big night out. She'd been saving her new dress for New Year's Eve, but what the heck. Why wait? She slipped into it, put on some black peep-toe heels and the silver necklace with the small ruby (her birthstone) that her parents had given her for her twenty-first birthday, and she was ready to go.

She picked up Noel and saw she was wearing her

new dress, too. "Good. You wore your dress," she said as Noel grabbed her coat.

"I figured I may as well get my money's worth." Noel locked the front door and tottered to the car. "I just don't know about these shoes."

"They look great," Riley told her. "*You* look great." Indeed she did, with her red hair falling in soft waves to her shoulders. Noel was so pretty. Too bad she never saw herself that way. But tonight she was bound to attract a lot of men. Who knew? Maybe one of them would turn out to be a wonderful guy with a super-good job. Maybe he'd fall in love with both her and her house. They'd be able to buy the place and fill it with kids who would brag about their talented mom to all their friends.

"Aww, thanks," Noel said as if Riley was just saying that to make her feel better.

"No, really, you do. You're going to have men fighting over you."

"I've never had men fight over me."

"You've never worn clothes like that," Riley pointed out.

"I have to admit, I do feel kind of sexy in this dress," Noel said. "I wonder if Ben Fordham ever goes dancing," she mused.

Hmm. "Are you falling for this guy?"

"Me? No, no. He sure is gorgeous, though," Noel said wistfully.

"Just remember that he bought your house out from under you," Riley cautioned. "No sleeping with the enemy."

"No sleeping with the enemy," Noel repeated.

"And keep your antennae up. You never know who you might meet."

As for Riley, all she wanted tonight was to have some fun, flirt a little, shore up her sagging confidence. Whispering Pines wasn't exactly the big city, but there had to be some decent man kicking around, someone she hadn't met. Like a certain good-looking cop. Did Officer Knight have a girlfriend? If not, what sort of girlfriend would he be interested in? Did he like blondes?

The Tree House was located downtown at the end of Pine Street. Back in the sixties, the place had been a bowling alley. Then it was a fitness gym. Now it was a club, complete with pool tables and a huge dance floor. It offered pizza by the slice, nachos, microbrews and all manner of cocktails. The parking lot was always packed and you could hear the music half a block away. Two dwarf pines sat in pots on either side of the front entrance, decorated for Christmas. Inside, the walls were painted with murals of various trees—fir, alder, maple and pine, along with various blooming varieties. Tables and chairs were rustic and the music was frenzied, rather like the mob out on the dance floor. Everybody was in a holiday mood, many of the revelers sporting Santa hats. Yes, this was going to be fun.

Riley and Noel managed to snag a table and order a couple of drinks. Noel got daring and ordered something called Angel's Delight that included triple sec and grenadine, which would satisfy her sweet tooth, and Riley opted for a Grinch, a green cocktail with melon-flavored Midori and lemon juice.

Their cocktails hadn't even arrived before someone was at the table asking Noel to dance. "Go for it," Riley encouraged her and she tottered off on her red stilettos. Noel was right. Fabulous as they were, those shoes were not a fit.

Riley sat back and watched the scene. Everyone was so happy, smiling, laughing, drinking. What was she doing here? Oh, yes. Having fun. The waitress brought their drinks and Riley paid up and took a guzzle. Yummy. Too bad she was driving. She'd have ordered another…three or four or six. Seven. Seven was the number of perfection.

Okay, she couldn't sit around and get gooshed. She needed to dance. She scanned the dance floor. Maybe she'd just go out and throw herself into the crowd, boogie on over right next to a good-looking man like…

Aack! What was Sean doing here? And Emily. There they were, out in the middle of the floor, having a wonderful time, gazing at each other as if they were the only two people in the room.

It felt suddenly very hot in this big, old place. And stuffy and close. Riley needed some fresh air. She darted from the table, trying to skirt the crowd. Did her ex see her running away, looking pathetic? She cast a quick glance over her shoulder and immediately ran into something solid, spilling her drink in the process. On the something solid…

Who was almost six feet tall, dirty-blond with green eyes and…a frown. "What the—?"

"Oh, my gosh, I'm sorry."

The something solid frowned and brushed at his red sweater. "You might want to take it easy with those," he said, nodding at her glass. "They pack a wallop."

"This is my first one. Uh, was my first one," Riley corrected herself. This man looked vaguely familiar. Where had she seen him before? The grocery store? Had he been at the gym when she'd stopped by to visit Sean? In a clothing catalog, modeling men's suits? He was certainly attractive enough for that. "I'm sorry about your sweater," she said.

The music was ending now. People were coming off the floor to rehydrate. And, oh, no! Here came Sean and Emily. She should scram. But that was the coward's way out. Sean had to see that she was doing fine without him. Just fine.

Crap. Here they were and the only thing she was proving so far was that she was dangerous. "Could you do me a favor?" she asked.

He looked at her warily. "Maybe."

"Good," she said and grabbed his sopping sweater and yanked him up against her.

"Whoa," he said just before she glued her lips to his. But then he got into his part. The guy sure could kiss.

"Riley?"

Riley took her time letting go of the stranger and turned to stare at Sean in faux surprise. "Sean, what are you doing here?" *Having fun with the woman you left me for? How nice.*

"Just out, uh… How are you?"

"I'm fine. I'm moving on."

He frowned. "I can see." He stuck out a hand. "Sean Little."

The something solid took it. "Jack Logan."

Sean leaned over to Riley. "You didn't wait long, did you?"

"At least I waited." She glared at Emily. Bad enough that she had to see the woman at school. She wasn't going to stand around The Tree House and talk with her. Riley gave her fake love interest's arm a tug and hauled him out on the floor for a slow dance.

"Thank you," she said. "That was…awkward."

He didn't return her smile. "So, old boyfriend with new girlfriend. Make him see what he lost? I don't like doing favors like that."

"Well, that wasn't what this was."

"Yeah?" The expression on his face dared her to spill her guts.

She supposed she could clarify that this was more a case of convincing the fiancé who'd dumped her that she wasn't home cutting herself. But it was all too humiliating to spill to a stranger. Anyway, this stranger had already judged her and declared her petty and vindictive. If there'd been anything left in her glass she would have dumped it over his head.

"Thanks for the kiss," she snapped.

"Thanks for the drink," he retorted, holding out his soaked sweater.

She marched back to her table, hoping that Sean wasn't watching. A new song had started, the beat fast and pumping, and people were going crazy out on the dance floor. She hopped into the throng and went crazy, too. *Take that, Sean. Take that, Jack Logan. Take that, every man here.* Who needed a man to have fun, anyway?

The dance ended and she returned to her table and sat down, feeling hollowed out in spite of her empowering self-talk. This should have been fun, darn it all!

Noel came right after her, stilettos dangling from her hand. "My feet are killing me," she said, falling onto her chair.

"Do you want to go?"

Noel took a gulp of her drink. "You're not having fun?"

"Sean and Emily are here."

"Oh, no." Noel cast a longing look at the dance floor then gave a determined nod. "Yes, let's go home."

"You can stay if you want," Riley said. "I'll leave you money for a cab."

"Not in these shoes. Let's go back to my house, watch a Christmas movie and drink eggnog," she suggested, slipping the stilettos back on.

"Good idea," Riley said, grabbing her purse and coat. So much for her exciting night out. But trying to keep pretending there was life after Sean was simply too stressful. Hopefully, he wouldn't notice her leaving with Noel.

But what if Sean saw Jack Logan by himself later on or dancing with another woman? Maybe she should try to find him, explain more of what happened, offer to pay him to leave with her. Offer to pay to have his sweater cleaned.

She scanned the crowd on the dance floor as they skirted it, hoping to catch a glimpse of him, but all she saw was Sean and Emily glued together for a slow dance. Never mind worrying that he'd see her alone. Sean was in his own little world—Emily World.

"Are you okay?" Noel asked as they picked their way across the slushy parking lot.

"I'm fine," Riley said. Yes, she was. Absolutely. So what if Sean was out with Emily practically having sex on the dance floor? She was going to her friend's house to drink eggnog.

Sean was probably going back to Emily's house later and they'd drink eggnog, too. But Riley was willing to bet that they wouldn't watch a movie. How cozy. Just the two of them, Sean the Cheater and Emily the Man-Stealer.

Riley ground her teeth as they got into the car. She revved it and backed out of the parking spot. She didn't back too far before she banged into yet another something solid. What the heck?

"Oh, my gosh, we hit someone's car!" cried Noel, stating the obvious.

Riley let down her window and craned her head. "Oh, no," she groaned. "Not another accident."

"We'll have to take up a collection to pay for your car insurance," Noel predicted. "Do we need to call the police?"

For a fender bender? She and the poor injured party probably only needed to exchange insurance information. Except if the police came... A vision of handsome Officer Knight popped into her head. On second thought, it was always good to call the police when there'd been an accident, wasn't it?

"Call 911," she said to Noel then got out of the car.

She practically ran into him, which would've made the second time that night.

"You," he said in disgust.

Oh, no! "I'm so sorry. I didn't see you back there."

"It's a Hummer. What are you, blind?"

This man was the biggest jerk on the planet. "I said I was sorry," Riley said stiffly.

Jack Logan let out a long-suffering sigh. "Never mind. Just tell me you have insurance."

"Of course I have insurance."

"Okay, let's exchange information."

"We have to wait for the police."

"You called the cops? Seriously?"

Riley raised her chin. "There's been an accident."

"More damage to your car than mine and you were at fault. This seems pretty straightforward to me."

Now Noel had joined them. "They're on their way."

Jack Logan frowned and shook his head. "I can't believe you called the cops for this."

"It shouldn't take long," Riley said to him. "And you're not with anyone, so you can't be in that big a hurry to get home."

"I'm not with anyone because someone spilled her drink all over me and I need to go home and change," he growled.

"I said I was sorry."

"For the drink. No apology for using me to trick your ex."

"Well, I'm sorry for that, too. I'm sure if your fiancée had dumped you for one of your groomsmen three weeks before the wedding, you'd have been much more noble."

"What?"

Darn it all, she hadn't intended to share that. He'd gotten her so mad she'd lost all control of her mouth. "Never mind," she said, pointing to the approaching patrol car.

"Never mind? You might have told me that before you lip-locked me and got me all excited for nothing."

Riley was aware of her friend gaping at her. It was pretty frosty out here in the parking lot but there was a roaring fire on her cheeks.

"There wasn't time," she said. "And what do you mean, got you all excited?"

"Well, I thought you were coming on to me."

"I'd never seen you before."

He shrugged. "Thought you'd had too much to drink," he said as the patrol car rolled up.

"And you were going to take advantage of that?"

"No," he protested. "What do you think, I was planning to haul you off to a dark corner and rape you? You kissed me right in the middle of a crowded club."

"Is there a problem here?"

Riley turned, expecting to see Officer Knight in Shining Armor. Instead she saw mall cop Kevin James to the third power. "Where's Officer Knight?"

The cop frowned. "He's off tonight. This better not be a frivolous call."

"It's not," said Jack Logan. "The ladies assumed calling the police was the thing to do. But really, we can handle this by exchanging information and reporting it to our insurance companies."

"Well, I'm here now," the cop said, sounding grumpy. "May as well fill out an accident report."

"Bored," muttered Jack Logan as the officer went to his patrol car to fetch his accident report forms.

Riley and Noel looked at each other. Obviously, this had been a bad idea.

Ten minutes later Riley had a citation for reckless driving and a headache, and even though this latest mess was entirely her fault, she had an unreasonable desire to kick the irritating Jack Logan in the shins.

"I'm sorry I caused you so much trouble tonight," she said to him. "Don't worry about any damage to your vehicle. I have very good insurance." And now it was also going to be very expensive insurance.

She just hoped that after her back-to-back fender benders the company wouldn't drop her.

"Your car got the worst of it."

"And if you need a new sweater..."

"I'm fine. About what I said earlier..."

A total stranger now knew that she was a love loser. Well, what the heck, they'd already kissed. Heaven help her, what Christmas elf had put it in her head that it would be fun to go out tonight?

She nodded, feeling that flame spreading across her face again. Then, before he could finish his sentence, she got into her car, Noel taking up her position riding shotgun, and waited for Jack Logan to drive away. Far away, where she'd never see him again.

Chapter Thirteen

It was Monday and Riley had run out of excuses for canceling her venue. Of course she should have done it right after Sean and Emily wedding-bombed her, but even though she hadn't wanted to admit it, she'd kept hoping Sean would realize what a mistake he'd made and beg her to take him back.

Watching them dancing at The Tree House had killed that dream, and she knew there'd be no resurrecting it after she saw him picking Emily up after school and kissing her. There'd be no begging. No wedding.

She tried not to think about that kiss as she drove to the golf club, but it had lodged in her brain like a burr. The image of Emily giving him a sweet, quick, we're-a-couple kiss, kept playing over and over. And over. And...over.

Emily the Man-Stealer had probably already moved in with him. They were sharing breakfasts and toothpaste and the same bed and...

What was this? A patrol car right behind her, and he had his party lights on. Nooo.

She pulled over to the side of the road and began to cry. She was going to have her insurance canceled for sure. Sobbing and sniffling, she looked in her rearview mirror and saw Officer Knight approaching. Where was he on Saturday when she'd looked cute and wasn't having a nervous breakdown accompanied by a runny nose?

She lowered her window and greeted him with, "Please don't give me a ticket. I've been having a terrible December."

"You were speeding," he pointed out gently. "And the snow has made the streets slick."

"I had another accident since you stopped me and now I'm on my way to cancel the venue for my… my…my wedding," she finished on a wail. "Who breaks up with you three weeks before your wedding? And on Thanksgiving Day no less!"

Officer Knight was regarding her with a sympathetic expression. "I'm sorry. I know how that feels."

"You do?" Had someone broken his heart, too? Maybe they could help each other heal. Maybe… well, Santa had said she'd meet her Mr. Right in a memorable way. The way they'd met had certainly been memorable.

He nodded. "Oh, yeah. My ex-girlfriend dumped me for a sailor."

"I'm sorry." Maybe he needed consolation.

"Then I met my new girlfriend and everything's good."

Everything's good. So much for that stupid shopping mall Santa.

"I'm going to give you another warning," said Officer Knight, back to business. "but you have to promise to be more careful."

"I will," she managed, her voice shaky.

"I mean it," he said sternly. "Next time I'll cite you."

She bit her lip and nodded.

"And don't worry," he said. "Someone better will come along."

After Sean anyone would be better. She thanked Officer Knight in Shining Armor for the warning and continued slooowly on to the golf club.

She shouldn't be torturing herself like this, she thought as she drove up the long drive lined with evergreens, the golf course peeping out between. She should simply have called in her cancellation. That was what phones were for, to save jilted brides from self-flagellation. But maybe, if she showed up in person and looked pitiful enough, Sharla Green, the events coordinator, would give her back a small part of her deposit. It was Christmas, after all.

And she was delusional.

Only weeks ago, she'd envisioned herself going down this same drive in a limo with her groom. Wearing her beautiful wedding gown, drinking champagne. Life was so unfair sometimes.

No, not life. Just Sean.

She walked into the clubhouse lobby, and again it was hard not to imagine how beautiful this was all going to be…before it wasn't. The lobby was richly decorated with a grouping of leather chairs and a love seat around a glass-topped table, potted plants artistically placed. Beyond it was the ever-popular Olympic Room, where so many people held their big events, with its sweeping views of the Olympics and Case Inlet, its baby grand piano, linen-draped tables, generous dance floor. Ugh. She should've called.

But she was here now, so she made her way to the office where Sharla worked her magic. Sharla was in her midthirties, happily married with two kids, a big believer in happily-ever-after. She loved planning events, especially weddings. She'd left three messages on Riley's phone last week.

"Riley," Sharla greeted her. "Did you get my messages? I just wanted to make sure you didn't have any last-minute questions. You all ready for the big day?"

This was quintessential *awful*. "There isn't going to be a big day," Riley said, trying to keep her lower lip from wobbling. "The wedding's been called off."

Sharla's perky smile turned into an empathetic frown. "I'm sorry."

"Don't be. He was a weasel."

"Well, you sure don't want to marry the wrong man. So maybe this was a lucky escape."

That was what everyone kept telling her. Riley wished she felt more relieved.

Now that condolences had been bestowed, Sharla got down to business. "I'm afraid we can't give you back your deposit at this late date."

Of course, canceling a week before the wedding was beyond too late. Ridiculous, even.

So much for her special wedding supper—marinated chicken breast and truffle-scented crab salad, rosemary cracker-crusted cod. Then there was the cake. That would've been *so* gorgeous—white fondant trimmed with gold ribbon and red poinsettias, with votive candles all around it. She'd planned everything with such love and attention to detail. All that money and effort for nothing. Riley felt ill.

"Can't be helped," she said, resigned to her miserable fate.

"I'm really sorry," Sharla said. "I hope next time it all works out."

At the rate she was going, maybe there'd never be a next time. She could feel the tide of tears rising, so she said a quick goodbye and hurried out of the office, down the hall and back to the lobby. She didn't see the man coming out of the pro shop until she bumped into him.

"Sorry," she said as he steadied her.

"No prob— You? Please don't tell me you're taking up golf. I'll have to resign before you run me over with a golf cart."

Oh, no. Not Jack Logan again. "No, I'm canceling my wedding reception," she said stiffly and took a swipe at the rivulet of tears rolling down her right cheek.

His expression softened. "Well, shit."

"It's okay. It's only money." She wiped her left cheek. More tears came, along with a sob. She was pathetic.

"Here," he said, taking her arm and steering her

toward the café. "You can't go running around all upset. Not the way you drive."

"Very funny," she muttered and started sobbing in earnest.

He sat her down at a table and went to order a coffee then returned and put the mug in front of her. There was a small container of sugar packets on the table and he pushed it toward her. "I'm guessing you like sugar in your coffee."

Still crying, she nodded and dumped in two packets. *When Riley is upset how many packets of sugar does she need in her coffee? One more.* She took another.

"Can you say adult-onset diabetes?"

She glared at him and grabbed another packet.

"Okay, sorry. I get that you're upset."

"I'm not. I'm well rid of him. I just hate that I spent all that time planning our wedding and all this money on the reception, and it was all for nothing. He wasted two years of my life and most of my savings and a bunch of my parents' money, too." She'd pay her folks back what they'd given her, every penny, darn it all. She ripped open another packet. Sugar spilled everywhere and she threw the packet on the table.

"He was a shit," Jack said.

"Yes, he was." She grabbed a napkin and blew her nose.

"But at least he backed out now before you got married."

She scowled at him. "You men all stick together."

She took a sip of her coffee. Okay, maybe she'd gone a little overboard with the sugar. She shoved it away.

"Hey, don't lump me in the same category as your dude."

"Former dude," she corrected him.

"I wouldn't do that."

"Well, I never thought Sean would, either."

"Sean? Sean Little?"

"You know him?" They were friends? Okay, this conversation was officially over.

Before she could leave, he said, "The guy recently joined the club. He wants to take golf lessons. His girlfriend is a...oh."

"Golfer?" Why not add that to the list of Emily's many sporty talents? And now she and Sean were joining the club. A fresh flood of tears began.

"Hey, now," Jack said, stretching his hand across the table and laying it on her arm. "Don't start again. You really don't want to be with a guy like that, do you?"

"I did," she sobbed, reaching for another napkin, "before I knew he was a guy like that."

"Well, now that you know he is, you ought to be thanking your lucky stars you escaped. You ought to be celebrating."

Riley plucked another napkin from the dispenser. "That's what my sister said."

"Your sister sounds pretty smart." He smiled. "You should go dancing."

That pulled a reluctant smile from her. "I tried that."

He leaned back in his chair and regarded her. "You're cute when you smile." Then, before she could feel too flattered, he added, "You could give Rudoloph a run for his money with that red nose of yours."

She took a sugar packet out of the holder and threw it at him and he chuckled. And she chuckled. "Thanks," she said. "Somehow I feel better." She sighed. "Except I wish I wasn't out a small fortune."

"That's crappy," he agreed. "I hope you're gonna do something besides sit home and mope."

She shrugged. "I thought maybe I'd bake about two dozen cookies and eat them."

"That's one way to teach the bastard a lesson, eat cookies and get fat."

Riley scowled. "Great. Another fitness freak."

"Not me. But I'm thinking you could do better than sitting around and self-medicating with cookies. Do something epic. You know what they say. Living well is the best revenge."

"Living well was the reception we were going to have," Riley said bitterly.

Jo's words came back to her. *Let's have a party.* Hmm. She'd already paid for the venue. She had her gown. Why let all that go to waste? Did she really want to sit around and mope on what would have been her big day?

She slapped the table. "I *am* going to live well, darn it all."

He nodded approvingly. "Way to rock it."

"I'm going to un-cancel my cancellation. So what

if I don't have a groom? I've got a dress and a venue. And I'm going to celebrate!" She jumped up and hurried back to Sharla's office.

"Go for it," he called after her.

Sharla was at her desk, working on her computer. She looked up in surprise. "Riley?"

"Never mind about canceling," Riley said. "We're having a party to celebrate my lucky escape."

Sharla grinned. "Well, way to go."

Riley grinned back. Suddenly she didn't feel so bad. Yes, she almost felt—was it possible?—happy.

"We'll make sure it's wonderful," Sharla promised.

Riley nodded and started out of the office. Then she remembered Jack. "I met a Jack Logan. He must be a member here."

"He's our golf pro. Nice guy."

Riley would never have labeled him a nice guy in light of their first two encounters, but after this last one she was revising her opinion.

"And he's single. Not that you're looking. I mean, it's probably too soon."

"It is." Not. It was far from too soon for revenge. If she was going to do that living-well thing, she should have a date for her non-wedding reception.

She went back down the hall and entered the pro shop, hoping she'd find him there.

Sure enough. He was handing over a bucket of practice golf balls to an old guy in golf attire and a cap and winter jacket.

"Damn snow," the man muttered. "I hear we're supposed to get more of it later today."

"Spring'll be here soon, Andy," Jack said to him.

"Yeah. Meanwhile, I'll have to content myself with the driving range. Glad we put in those heated stalls. At least I can take a few swings to keep the old shoulder limber. Now, what was that tip you mentioned the other day?"

"If the ball goes off to the left, your shoulders are getting ahead of your hips and if it goes off to the right, your hips are getting ahead of your shoulders. Try to keep that swing even."

"Got it," said the old man. He took his bucket of balls, turned to leave and caught sight of Riley. "Well, hello there. Are you new here?"

"I'm not a member."

Old Andy gave a knowing nod. "Here to see our boy, huh?" He winked at Riley. "He sure can pick 'em."

Riley felt herself blushing.

"I should be so lucky," said Jack.

"Well, then, if you're not taken and you like older men with lots of money, I'll be around," Andy told her.

She smiled at him. "I'll remember that."

"You never want to underestimate us older guys. The outside might look like a jalopy, but inside it's a Ferrari." He chuckled at his own wit and left for the driving range.

Jack shook his head. "I think he really believes that."

"He's sweet," Riley said, watching him go.

"He's lonely. Wife died two years ago. He's here every day, rain or shine. If you decide to bake those cookies, Andy'll be happy to help you eat them."

"I'll do better than that. I'll invite him to come here Saturday night and eat non-wedding cake. How about you? Want to see what a non-wedding reception looks like?" Now that she'd issued the invitation she felt ridiculously self-conscious. She hardly knew this man.

He nodded. "Yeah, as a matter of fact, I do. Can I kiss the non-bride? You owe me a favor, after all."

Her cheeks were sizzling but she smiled and said, "Maybe."

He grinned.

She grinned, too. Jack Logan was turning out to be a pretty cool guy.

Of course, she'd thought the same about Sean when she first met him. They'd both been at a fundraiser for autism research. She'd been there because she liked to support any children's cause. He'd been there because he had a cousin who suffered from it and he wanted to help raise awareness. He'd said he loved kids. And he admired teachers. She'd thought Sean was perfect. Boy, had she been deceived.

Well, she already knew Jack wasn't. So maybe she *would* let him kiss the non-bride.

She bade him farewell and left the club, still feeling—was it truly possible?—happy. A few light snowflakes were starting to drift onto her windshield and she decided to stop by the grocery store to stock up on soup and instant hot chocolate. At even a hint of snow everyone panicked and cleared the shelves. If she didn't go now there'd be nothing left.

She was picking up some more flour in case the urge to bake overcame her when she ran into Mrs. Wooster, whose tall, skinny frame was wrapped in a long, black parka. "Hello, dear, stocking up for the storm? I hear we're supposed to get three inches. I'm not poking my nose out the door until it's all gone."

Mrs. Wooster made it sound as if they were in for a blizzard. "I think it's supposed to turn to rain by Thursday," Riley said.

"Rain by Tuesday?"

Riley raised her voice. "By Thursday."

"Good. The sooner, the better. The snow's pretty but I hate going out in the stuff. At my age it only takes one fall and then you're in trouble. I have no intention of getting a broken hip for Christmas." She pointed to Riley's cart. "Are you going to bake cookies?"

"I thought I might."

"Tonight you say?"

"I might!"

Mrs. Wooster looked almost wistful. "I don't bake much anymore. Not much point when there's just me. Sometimes I wish my children lived closer."

Poor Mrs. Wooster. It had to get lonely living all by herself.

Riley remembered the old man she'd met at the country club and a new idea popped into her mind. "Mrs. Wooster, what are you doing this Saturday?"

"Saturday? I don't know. Maybe I'll see if your grandma wants to come over and play Scrabble."

"How'd you like to come to a party?"

The old woman's eyes lit up. "Are you having a party, dear?"

"As a matter of fact, I am. I'm celebrating a lucky escape and having a reception at the golf club," Riley said. "Dinner, dancing, cake."

"What are you going to make?"

"Cake!" Riley shouted.

"Cake?" Mrs. Wooster repeated eagerly.

"I'd love to have you come," Riley said, speaking loudly enough for Mrs. Wooster's hearing aid to pick up. "In fact, tell your friends. This is going to be the party of the year."

"Well, I guess," Mrs. Wooster said. "Thank you for inviting me. I sure am going to be praying that snow goes away."

"We'll get you there no matter what," Riley promised.

Mrs. Wooster's eyes actually teared up. "It's very generous of you, my dear, to think of an old woman."

Riley was thinking of all the older people she'd had contact with lately. They'd lived a lot and many of them had lost a lot. Just because they were old, it didn't mean their lives were over. They deserved to have a good time. They'd be the perfect guests to invite to her non-reception.

She patted Mrs. Wooster's arm. "I'll be delighted to have you." She'd be delighted to have anyone whose life wasn't quite going according to plan.

She said goodbye to Mrs. Wooster and hurried to the checkout. She had loads to do when she got home. She needed to design invitations to take to the senior center and the nursing home, needed to send out e-vites, call her family and have them spread the word, get everyone on board.

Once she was home she called Mom.

"How are you doing, sweetie? How was school?" Mom asked.

"I'm doing great. Mom, can you do me a favor and call Bett at Floral Bliss?"

"Honey, I already did. Remember?"

"I know. But now could you call her and tell her I still want flowers? I need those table arrangements, too, and ask her if she can put a hundred single red carnations in a bucket to give away. Also, please tell Annette I still want the cake."

"I don't understand."

"I can't get a refund on the club, so I'm having the reception, anyway."

There was silence on the other end.

"I know, it seems crazy, but I'm going to have a non-wedding reception. I'm inviting every senior in town and all our friends and family who can make it. And I'm going to wear my wedding gown!"

"Are you sure?" Mom asked. She sounded worried. *My daughter has lost her mind.*

"Yes, I am. The money's already been spent, so why not get what I paid for? Anyway, if I just sit at home and feel sorry for myself, that gives Sean and

Emily power over me, and I refuse to let them have it. I'm going on with my life, starting this Saturday."

"I'll make the calls."

"Thanks, Mom. And tell Grammy to invite all her friends. I want to fill the Olympic Room to over-flowing."

"All right!" Mom said, catching the vision.

Oh, yes. This was going to be fun. Riley called Noel. "Do you have plans for Saturday?"

"I wish," Noel said.

"Well, now you do. Dig out your bridesmaid dress. I'm still having my reception at the country club."

"But you're not getting married," Noel pointed out.

"That doesn't mean I can't have a party. The venue's already paid for and I'm going to use it. Oh, and tell your parents. And invite a date if you want."

"I don't know who I'd invite."

"You could bring the house-flipper," Riley suggested. "You are still trying to butter him up, aren't you?"

"No. Yes. It's complicated."

"Well, if you want to, you can," Riley said and left it at that. Then she called Jo.

"Good for you!" her sister cheered. "I'm proud of you."

Riley smiled. Yes, good for her. She could hardly wait for Saturday.

Chapter Fourteen

Wow! Riley was so inspiring. How had she managed to turn around such an awful disappointment? Noel wished she knew.

She also wished she knew how Ben was doing with his number-crunching. She hadn't heard back from him and she was leery of calling him for fear of becoming an irritating pest. At least that was what she told herself. Deep down she was afraid to call for fear of hearing that the numbers had refused to crunch and she was out of luck.

She set her cell phone back on the desk and returned to working on her new project, plan B.

Trevor Truman had never seen such a beautiful woman. From her obsidian eyes to her ruby-red mouth, she was everything he'd ever dreamed of.

Pathetic, scoffed Marvella.

Actually, it was.

You need to come up with a better plan B or we're going to wind up homeless.

A better plan B. Like what? Robbing a bank? Selling her body? (Would she get any takers?) She heaved a sigh. If she couldn't find a way to make a deal with Ben, what kind of house could she get that would be comparable to this one?

Probably nothing. She'd have to rent an apartment. At a higher rate than she was paying now.

Like you can afford that, Marvella jeered. Marvella was not being very helpful today.

"So then I'll move back in with my parents until I can figure something out," Noel muttered.

She sat back and stared at her pathetic start to a romance novel. This was not going to work. Even if she could come up with a brilliant idea and get it written in the next three weeks, it would take time to market it. Maybe an ebook?

No. She needed immediate money. She went online to the *Whispering Pines Chronicle* site and checked out the classifieds. Harrison Hospital in nearby Belfair was looking for nurses, Got Gutters wanted someone with gutter experiences and...what was this? The Rusty Saw was now hiring for their morning shift.

She could handle taking orders and delivering pancakes and coffees. She donned Jo's skinny jeans, the classic white blouse and her boots, put on some makeup and braved the snowy streets to go to the restaurant, with visions of dollars dancing in her head. Why hadn't she thought of moonlighting some place like this a year ago? She'd have had a lot more money in savings.

Oh, yeah. A year ago she'd thought she was going to be a household name by now. A year ago she'd been very naive. Having three children's books published did not a Dr. Seuss make. At least not in her case.

The Rusty Saw was once an IHOP but that chain had hopped on long ago and the place had been taken over by a former truck driver named Randy (nickname Rusty) Sawyer. The decor was stuck in the seventies but that didn't bother Rusty's customers. They came for the oversize waffles with blackberry syrup, the biscuits and sausage gravy, and the chicken-fried steak. The place always did a good business. And good business surely meant good tips.

Rusty himself was seated at a booth in the back, reading the paper. He was a big hulk of a man who dressed in flannel and jeans. His hair still held hints of the red that had probably earned him his nickname.

He smiled at Noel. "Now, who have we got here?"

"Have you hired a server yet?" she asked, twisting the strap of her purse.

Stop that! Marvella commanded. *You're acting desperate.*

I am desperate.

"Not yet." He set aside his paper and looked her up and down.

At that moment Mrs. Sawyer made her appearance, carrying a coffee mug. Her body was as wide as her husband's. Her smile...not so much.

"Are you applying for the job?" she asked, sitting down across from him.

"Yes, I am."

The woman looked her up and down, too. "Got any experience?"

"No, but I'm a fast learner."

"When can you start?" Rusty asked, grinning at her.

His wife frowned at him. "Not so fast. You need to fill out a job application. And we need references. Where have you worked before this?"

"Well, I used to work at The Book Nook." If the bookstore hadn't closed two years ago, she could've gone back there to supplement her writer's income. Suzanne would have rehired her in a heartbeat.

"Where have you worked since then?" asked Mrs. Sawyer.

"At home. I'm self-employed."

Now Mrs. Sawyer was looking suspicious.

"I write children's books," Noel explained.

Mrs. Sawyer suddenly looked friendlier. "Would we have heard of you?"

"I don't know. I write books featuring a monster who helps children."

"Marvella?" the woman asked eagerly.

This had to be a good sign. Noel nodded.

"Our granddaughter loves your books," gushed Mrs. Sawyer. Then she looked suspicious again. "But you're a writer. Why do you need this job?"

Because I'm a writer. "I'm trying to earn extra money so I can buy the house I'm renting."

Rusty smiled encouragingly at Noel while his missus sat contemplating.

At last the true decision-maker spoke. "Okay,"

said Mrs. Sawyer. "We'll have you fill out the application and a W-2 form. Come in tomorrow and we'll give you a try. You'll work a five-hour shift starting at six."

Noel nodded. "And what's the salary?"

"Minimum wage," Rusty said. "You make up for it in tips," he assured her.

They were probably right about the tips. Everyone knew that was how restaurant servers made their real living. Which was why, when she could afford to go out, Noel always tipped generously.

"Thank you," she breathed. Surely that extra paycheck and the tips would plump up her bank account. She'd go by Ben Fordham's office later and tell him she was well on her way to pulling together the money he needed if he could give her a little more time. Hopefully, he wouldn't ask her to be specific about how *much* time she needed.

She duly filled out the forms and then was given two yellow polo shirts printed with *Rusty Saw* and the diner's logo, a plate of pancakes sitting on a tree stump, to be worn over black slacks.

"We'll take the cost out of your first paycheck," Mrs. Sawyer explained.

Between that and taxes her first paycheck would be pitiful. But there'd be tips. This was going to work. Yes, it was.

Back home she called her mother and told her the good news. Mom was working her shift at the library, but she always answered her cell phone when her daughters called.

"Guess what! I got a job," Noel crowed.

"That's very nice, but why were you out looking for a job? Oh, no. Didn't your publisher offer you a new contract?"

"They're going to, but I need some extra money."

"The house," Mom guessed. "You should have told us. We'll help you."

"This isn't a good time for you guys, especially with Aimi getting married now."

"We have some money in savings."

Which Aimi would probably burn through. "You need that money yourselves," Noel reminded her.

"We want to be able to help our children. Is Mrs. Bing going to sell the house to you?"

Maybe she shouldn't have called her mom. "Um, no."

"I thought she wanted to sell it."

"She did. She sold it already."

"Oh, Noel, I'm so sorry."

"I might still have a chance to buy it. She sold it to a house-flipper."

"Oh." Yes, Mom watched those house-flipping shows, too, and she knew what that meant.

"I'm hoping to work out a deal with him."

"Sweetheart, there'll be other houses," Mom said gently.

Not like hers. "I have to at least try."

"Well, then, tell me about this new job of yours. I hope it won't interfere with your writing."

"No. I'll be able to work my writing around it just fine."

"What's the job?"

"I'll be waiting tables at The Rusty Saw."

"Waitressing is hard work," Mom said. "I did it when I was in college."

"Yes, but the tips are good, right?"

"Depends on where you're working. If you're at a high-end restaurant, yes."

The Rusty Saw wasn't exactly a high-end restaurant.

"Are you working nights?"

"No, I'll be doing the morning shift. Which will be great because then I can come home and write."

"I'm not sure you'll make that much in tips serving breakfast," Mom said. "The big tippers are the dinner crowd."

This was disheartening. Still, what else could she do? She didn't have any valuable art to sell, nothing to put on eBay. And the classifieds hadn't exactly been brimming with job opportunities.

"When do you start?"

"Tomorrow morning. They hired me on the spot. It turns out their granddaughter likes my books."

"Everyone likes your books," Mom said.

"Not enough everyones."

"Oh, honey, your time will come. I feel bad that you're having to do this, though."

"You always say there's nothing wrong with good, honest work," Noel told her.

"That's absolutely true, but you're already working hard on your writing career."

"I can handle it."

"I do admire your ambition," her mother said. "Oh, and speaking of work, send up a little prayer. Daddy has a job interview tomorrow—managing the office for a nuclear pharmacy in Silverdale. It'll be a bit of a commute but the salary is good."

Her father was itching to get back to work. It had been so wrong when his company laid him off. Downsizing and hiring younger men for less money. So unfair. Daddy was fifty-seven now, not an easy age for a man to find employment.

"I will," she promised. "I sure hope he gets this."

"It would be a real boost. And then," Mom added, "we'd be in more of a position to help you, to help both our daughters."

"Don't worry about me. I'll be fine," Noel said.

"I know you will. Now I'd better get back to work. I'm in the middle of cataloging."

And Noel had some new pages to write. But first she wanted to share her news with Jo and Riley.

Jo was her usual succinct and to-the-point self. "You're nuts. Just sleep with the house-flipper," she said, echoing Marvella.

Riley wasn't much more encouraging. "It's an awful lot of work for not much money."

"I can't think of anything else to do," Noel said. "I have to prove to Ben that I mean business."

"Well, I hope it works out, and I hope you won't be too pooped to have fun at my non-wedding party."

"I won't. I'm so glad you're doing this. If I were

you, I'd be curled up in a ball, sucking on chocolate. You're my hero."

"It beats sitting home feeling sorry for myself."

Yes, that was a waste of time. Noel needed to follow in her friend's footsteps. No matter what happened, she was going to make the best of things. But meanwhile she'd work hard to ensure that she got her house. She'd keep trying to make this work until Ben told her straight out to forget it. *Quitters never win and winners never quit.*

Oh, stop already and get to work, said Marvella.

Right.

She got a lot written and rewarded herself with a frozen pizza for dinner. She ate it cuddled under a blanket on the sofa watching *Jeopardy* and *Wheel of Fortune*. Then she pulled out her favorite Georgette Heyer Regency romance and took it to bed. She set her alarm for 5:00 a.m. and then read herself to sleep. She was just dreaming about eloping to Gretna Green in a carriage with Ben Fordham, who was all dressed up in a powdered wig and breeches, when the alarm yanked her out of his arms and back into cold reality. The job.

This would be fun. She'd have a chance to meet people, make them happy serving them pancakes and bacon and eggs. Yes, this had been a good idea.

Oh, but why did the good idea have to start so early in the morning?

A shower woke her up and some coffee got her going. She toasted a slice of bread, smeared peanut butter on it then ate it while putting on her makeup.

Then she pulled her hair back in a ponytail, donned her uniform and headed off to work.

Mrs. Sawyer let her in. A chunky college-age girl was stuffing sugar packets into their holders. She waved and called a cheery hello; Noel smiled and nodded at her.

"Get back to work, Summer," said Mrs. Sawyer. "This is a training day for you so you won't get paid," she told Noel.

Noel blinked. What kind of deal was this? "Is that legal?" Oh, dear. Maybe she shouldn't have said that out loud.

Now Mrs. Sawyer blinked. "Well, I guess we can pay you something."

Don't let her walk all over you, Marvella urged.

Noel was sweating now and her heart was pumping. "I'd like it if you'd pay me what we agreed on." For someone who'd just walked in the door, she was being awfully assertive. This was it. She was going to get fired for sure. Fired before she even started.

Mrs. Sawyer heaved a long-suffering sigh, her massive chest rising like a swell on the ocean. "Very well. Come on. I'll show you around."

There wasn't that much to show. The open kitchen was a long, stainless-steel counter and grill behind the lunch counter. A skinny guy in his thirties with tattoos on both arms and his neck was busy getting organized for the morning breakfast. He wore the typical white chef's apron and toque.

"This is Bradley, our head grill operator," Mrs. Sawyer said.

Bradley grunted, which Noel translated as hello.

"Hang your dupes here," Mrs. Sawyer said, pointing to the apparatus Noel had seen in any number of restaurants with order slips hanging from them.

"Dupes?"

"Your orders."

"Oh." Noel could feel her cheeks warming. She nodded.

They moved on to the break room, which was down the hall at the end of the world. Tiny and slightly dingy. Then to the drinks station and the computer, where she'd input orders and print out the checks. Mrs. Sawyer escorted her to the back of the restaurant and motioned to several tables and three booths. "This will be your station."

"All these tables?" It sure seemed like a lot. What if a whole bunch of people came in at once?

"A good waitress can handle that without a problem," Mrs. Sawyer said.

"Of course," she murmured, her cheeks going from warm to sizzling. Old Bradley could probably fry pancakes on them right now.

Another waitress was nearby, busy filling salt and pepper shakers. She was somewhere in her forties and she looked tired. "This is Misty. She'll help you out if you get into trouble," Mrs. Sawyer said.

"I can't help you out too much," Misty warned.

Noel wished the cheerful Summer was working back here with her.

"Your shift extends into the beginning of lunch. You'll set up tables as customers leave," Mrs. Sawyer said. "Morning shift always fills the salt and pepper shakers and makes sure there's plenty of sugar and sugar substitute packets in their holders. Our son Grady does the busing. He gets ten percent of your tips. We have a pretty big breakfast crowd so don't stand around visiting with the customers. Your job is to get their food to them and keep their coffee coming. Got it?"

Noel nodded, attempting to look both eager and capable.

"Good. You can go ahead and help Misty set up. We open at seven."

Noel got to work.

"You done this before?" Misty asked.

"No."

Misty shook her head. "You'll run your butt off. It's a killer on the feet, too. I don't know what you were thinking wearing those shoes," she added, pointing to Noel's flats.

Of course, she should've thought of that. Tomorrow she'd wear tennis shoes.

The doors opened promptly at seven and the customers started wandering in—a few men in business suits, a couple of guys in coveralls and a smattering of retirees. Mrs. Sawyer morphed into a happy woman, giving everyone a friendly greeting and showing them to their tables.

Noel stood by one of hers, a ready-to-please smile on her face. The smile faded as Mrs. Sawyer scattered the customers around in the other two waitresses' stations. Okay, the woman had to give her some customers at some point.

Meanwhile, as the customers were seated, a burly guy with red hair and freckles started carrying glasses of water to the various tables. Grady, son of the Sawyers and heir apparent to The Rusty Saw. He looked a lot like his dad but judging from the lack of a smile, he'd inherited his mother's disposition. Friendly work environment.

Finally Mrs. Sawyer sat two older men at one of her booths. "It's her first day so be nice," she told them playfully.

One of them, a grizzled little guy with a stoop, smiled at Noel. "We'll help you out, honey."

She fetched menus to hand them but the skinny one waved them away. "We want the same thing we have every morning. Jesse here will have eggs over easy with bacon and coffee and orange juice, and I want The Rusty Saw special, same as always."

"The Rusty Saw special," she repeated, and wrote that on her order slip.

"What the hell is this?" growled Bradley from the grill.

"It's what my customer ordered," she said.

"How the hell am I supposed to know what that is?" He threw the ticket back at her.

"You're the cook. I thought you'd know," she said. Her first order and she'd already messed up.

"I don't have time to stop and figure out what the special is," he snarled as he flipped pancakes.

Noel fled back to her section and looked up the

special in one of the menus. Two eggs, three slices
of bacon and one pancake. Judging by the picture,
it could double as an area rug. She wrote that down
and turned in her order again.

"How'm I supposed to know how they want their
eggs?" Bradley snapped.

Crud. She took her order and hurried back to
the table. "I'm sorry," she said. "How do you want
your eggs?"

"Sunny side up. And we'll take that coffee anytime."

Oh, yes, coffee. She brought back the order, praying that this time it would get the Bradley stamp
of approval, then hurried to the table with her coffeepot.

"You're doing fine, honey," said the little man
with the stooped shoulders. "First day of any job is
always hard."

"Thank you for being so patient," she said.

As she finished pouring coffee, Mrs. Sawyer
came her way with a family in tow. Not just any
family. There was Ben Fordham, a little boy of about
four or five holding his hand and skipping along beside him. And with them was a woman. Not just any
woman, but the horrible one from the supermarket.
Noel swallowed hard.

Ben stopped at the sight of her. "Noel?"

"Hi," she stammered.

He looked as self-conscious as she felt. "What
are you doing here?"

"Working," she said lightly.

"Look, I haven't forgotten what we talked about. My accountant's been out of town."

"No problem." *No pressure. Keep the smile going.*

"My name's Timmy," the little boy piped up.

Are you staying for dinner tonight after you pick up Timmy? The woman's one-way conversation that Noel had heard in the grocery store came roaring back into her mind. So this little boy with the same brown eyes, dark hair and irresistible smile was related to Ben. And the lizard.

"It's my birthday," the child announced.

Noel bent down. "How old are you today, Timmy?"

He held up one hand. "Five!"

"You're a big boy. I'll bet that next year you get to go to kindergarten."

He nodded eagerly. "I go to preschool now. After school today, I get to have a party at Nana's house."

At Nana's house, not Mommy's. Where was Timmy's mother?

Nana was smiling fondly at the child but when Noel looked at her the smile vanished. Maybe she was related to Mrs. Sawyer.

"Do you mind if we sit down?" the woman asked.

"Sorry," Noel said and got out of the way.

"We're on a tight schedule," Ben explained as his mother the lizard slid into the booth.

"Of course." Noel handed out the menus. "May I start you off with some coffee?"

"I want apple juice," Timmy said, squirming happily in his seat.

"One apple juice coming up," Noel said, smiling at him. He was so cute. Where *was* his mommy?

"We'll take coffee," Ben added.

Noel fetched a glass of juice and the coffeepot.

"She's renting the house I bought," Ben was saying to his mother when Noel returned.

So the third degree about her had already begun. Soon this woman would be back on her cell phone telling her friend, "There's no way I'll let that cheap little waitress with her unmanicured nails anywhere near my son."

She set down Timmy's apple juice and poured the coffee, then, cheeks burning, said, "I'll be right back to take your orders."

"Hey, darling," called one of her little old men as she passed, "we'll take some more of that coffee."

Oh, yes, of course. She needed to work more efficiently.

And here came Mrs. Sawyer, bringing her more people. Riley's grandma and her friend Mrs. Wooster. She sat them at a table near the two men, who ogled them as they walked past. Riley's grandma reached out a hand and caught Noel's arm. "We heard about your new job. Wanted to come support you."

"That was so sweet of you," Noel said. "Thank you."

"Not really. It gives us an excuse to get out."

"You don't have time to visit," Mrs. Sawyer whispered nastily in Noel's ear then hurried back to the front of the restaurant, greeting more customers.

"I'll get you some menus," Noel said. "Would you like some coffee?"

"Is that coffee you're holding?" asked Mrs. Wooster. "Pour me some, dear. I need something to settle my nerves. Terrible weather to be out in."

"Oh, nonsense," said Riley's grandma. "The snowplows have cleared the streets."

"They haven't cleared the sidewalks," Mrs. Wooster retorted. "We'll be lucky if we don't fall and break every bone in our bodies."

"Waitress!"

Noel gave a start and turned to see Ben Fordham's mother scowling at her.

"If you're not too busy we'd like to order," the woman said irritably.

"Yes, right away." Noel rushed to ditch her now-empty coffeepot and returned to Ben's table, order pad in hand. "What would you like?"

"I want pancakes," Timmy chirped.

"Pancakes and eggs," corrected his grandmother. "You need protein so you can grow up big and strong like Daddy."

Timmy didn't look all that excited about the prospect of eggs.

"Make the eggs well-done. He won't eat them if they're runny," Mrs. Fordham continued. "I'll have the egg white omelet. Rye toast."

"Rye toast," Noel repeated, scribbling frantically. She was aware of more people being seated at the table behind her. *Don't panic. You can do this.*

"I'll have the special, eggs over easy," Ben said.

She nodded and was about to dash to the kitchen to place the order when he asked, "Why are you here, Noel?"

"Just earning a little extra money."

He frowned. "Does this have anything to do with the house?"

"Actually, yes."

"We need water over here," said one of the new arrivals.

"We're in a hurry," Mrs. Fordham reminded her.

We're in over our heads, Marvella said.

Boy, were they ever. Noel speed-walked to the kitchen counter and turned in the Fordhams' order then rushed some glasses of water to the new table, where three harried businessmen sat. In her haste she managed to tip the first water glass, making Mr. Businessman scoot his chair back...right into Mrs. Wooster, who was on her way to the restroom.

Mrs. Wooster teetered sideways and, in a panic, Noel grabbed her just before she fell, dropping the other two glasses in the process. Broken glass everywhere and Mrs. Wooster's legs were now wet.

"I'm sorry," Noel said to both her and the businessman.

"My pants are soaked," he growled.

"I'm so sorry," she said again. "It's my first day. Are you okay?" she asked Mrs. Wooster.

"Yes, no thanks to this man," Mrs. Wooster said, glaring at the angry businessman. "You almost knocked me head over teakettle," she scolded him. "I have osteoporosis and I could have broken my hip."

"Don't blame me," the man said stiffly. "Blame your waitress here. I'll catch up with you later," he said to his friends. "I'm going to grab a croissant and coffee at Java Josie's. Should've done that in the first place," he finished.

"I'm really sorry," she said to his back as he stalked away.

Mrs. Wooster continued to the restroom and here was Grady with a broom and dustpan to clean up her mess. "This stuff happens," he told her and she wanted to hug him for that scrap of kindness.

"Just bring us pancakes," said one of the other businessmen. "And coffee."

She nodded and went off to place their order.

The Fordham family's orders were up and she took two of the plates. Oh, dear. There was the third. She'd seen waitresses do that balance-the-plate routine. She wasn't sure she could manage it.

"I'll come back for this last one."

"The hell you will," snarled Bradley. "Get that plate outta here. I need room to put up more orders."

Misty was picking up one of hers. "You gotta do it sometime. Keep your arm steady. You'll be fine."

Noel took a deep breath, maneuvered the plates around and hoped she'd get back to her table without dropping one. That plate on her arm was pretty hot. She tried to walk quickly while balancing it. *Don't spill, don't spill, don't...*

She made it to the Fordhams' table before the

plate tipped off her arm. There went the over-easy eggs, easily over onto Mrs. Fordham, who let out a horrified shriek.

"I'm so very sorry," Noel said, setting the other two plates down. Ben calmly delivered his son's breakfast to him.

"It's okay," he said.

"It certainly is not," snapped his mother.

"Nana, you look funny," Timmy said with a laugh.

Nana, however, was not laughing.

Noel grabbed a napkin from a nearby table and tried to wipe the egg off the woman's sweater. Cashmere, ugh. First cheesecake on Ben, now eggs on his mother. This was not the way to make a good impression. And why was she trying to clean the woman off? People did that in the movies and it never worked.

It didn't work now. The woman pulled away and yanked the napkin from Noel. "This is ruined."

"I'll get you another plate right away," Noel promised Ben.

"You'll also get the bill for a new sweater," Mrs. Fordham warned.

Mrs. Sawyer arrived on the scene. "Is everything all right?"

Of course, nothing was all right.

"This server of yours is a disaster," Mrs. Fordham informed her.

"Yes," said Mrs. Sawyer, frowning at Noel. "I see that. Noel, go get a fresh plate."

Noel hurried off, Mrs. Fordham's words chasing her. "That girl has ruined my sweater. What are you going to do about it?"

Noel was pretty sure she knew.

Mrs. Fordham cleaned off enough of the egg to stay for Timmy's birthday breakfast, but when Noel returned with the new plate she leaned as far away as possible.

"It could happen to anyone," Riley's grandma consoled her when she delivered their orders. "You can't let little things like that upset you."

Dumping eggs on the mother of the man she'd been trying to butter up didn't count as a *little thing*, but Noel simply thanked her.

Mrs. Sawyer didn't seat any more people in Noel's station, even though there were people waiting by the door. That didn't bode well.

The two older men both left her a five-dollar tip, and as they passed, Jesse said, "You can come clean house for me if she fires you." Then he gave her a pat on the bottom and shuffled off.

In his dreams, said Marvella.

Riley's grandma and Mrs. Wooster each left her two dollars.

Ben asked for the check, and she told him she'd cover the bill.

"And so she should," Mrs. Fordham muttered, sliding out of the booth. "Do not leave that girl a tip."

Ben stood up, sent Timmy off after his mother then pulled out two fifties and laid them on the table.

"Oh, no," she began.

"Oh, yes," he said. "I'm sorry about...all this."

She sighed as she watched him go. So was she.

Once she'd cleaned off her tables and reset them, Mrs. Sawyer made her appearance. "Noel, this is not going to work out. I think you know that."

"I'll get the hang of it."

"I'm already out the cost of that ruined breakfast and a sweater. I can't afford to give you a second chance."

Noel handed over her tips. "This should help."

Mrs. Sawyer's eyes were as big as eggs. "You got that much in tips?"

"I think everyone felt sorry for me."

Mrs. Sawyer shook her head. "They should've felt sorry for me." Then she did something surprising. She gave Noel's arm a comforting pat. "You're not cut out for this, but that's okay. You were meant for greater things. Do us all a favor and go home and write another book."

Mrs. Sawyer's unexpected kind words, coupled with her disastrous morning, brought Noel to tears. She nodded, did her best to blink them back and went to collect her coat and purse.

Misty was too busy laying down plates of pancakes to say anything, but as Noel passed, Summer managed to say, "Sorry it didn't work out."

That made two of them.

Chapter Fifteen

T he branches of the phone tree had been shaking with calls going out to all the wives. Shelley Stilton had called Jo the night before and shared the good news, cryptic but perfectly understandable to a navy wife. "The family event will take place tomorrow at 2:00 p.m. at the bowling alley."

Tomorrow. The very word had started Jo's heart fluttering. It had been a long three months, but now Mike was coming home.

For all of three months. The baby wouldn't even be crawling by the time he left again. The fluttering had stopped in a hurry.

But that was yesterday. Today she was excited to see her man.

Early in her marriage, she and the other newbie wives had gone to the pier to meet the sub. It had been late coming in to the Bangor Naval Base, and they'd spent two hours waiting and almost froze to death. Of course, it hadn't helped that they'd all dressed sexily. Big mistake. The waterfront piers where the boats tied up had cranes and various cables and other obstacles waiting to trip an unsuspecting woman wearing heels. One of her friends had tripped and sprained her ankle. The cold wind coming off the water had raced up their skirts and left them all shivering.

They got smart after that and became more practical in their choice of clothing. They also took to waiting at the bowling alley where it was warm and they could order pizza and let their excited offspring run wild. When the time came, buses hauled them to the pier.

Jo still was going to dress cute, but it was winter so maternity leggings and a long sweater would have to do. After she'd fed Mikey and put him down for his nap, she got into her welcome home outfit. Her legs still looked great and the sweater helped hide some of the baby fat she needed to lose. Concealer took care of the dark circles under her eyes that proclaimed her a new, sleep-deprived mother. Mascara, eyeliner and lipstick brought her face to life. She inspected herself in the mirror and gave herself a passing grade.

Her mom showed up for baby patrol a little before one. "You look lovely," she said, hugging Jo.

"I feel like a whale."

"Everyone does after having a baby. You'll lose it in no time. Now, where's my adorable grandson?"

"Napping. I've pumped some milk for him in case he wakes up. It's in the fridge. I tried him on a bottle last night and he took it fine so that should hold him until we get back. If he spits up I've laid out another outfit on the changing table. And if there's any problem, call me. I don't know how long I'll be. If the boat is late coming in…"

"Don't worry, dear. I've done this a few times before," Mom assured her.

Still… "I can come back if necessary and Mike can catch a ride to town." That probably wouldn't make him happy but now they had someone in their lives to consider besides themselves.

"We'll be fine. Go," Mom said.

Yes, she needed to get out the door.

She made the drive to the naval base outside Poulsbo in record time. In fact, she arrived at the base bowling alley a little early. Most of the other wives were already there. Pizzas had been ordered. Someone had hired a face-painter and she was busy painting stars and lightning bolts and rainbows on the younger children. Many of the kids were bowling. Some of the older ones were playing arcade games. The toddlers were mostly fussy, wanting their afternoon naps.

Jo found her pal Arlene Mendoza seated at one of the lanes, holding a sleeping six-month-old on her lap while her two older children were bowling. Both had their faces painted. Her four-year-old daughter, Amanda, sported a rainbow on her cheek and her six-year-old, Anthony, wore lightning bolts.

Arlene greeted her with a disappointed expression. "You didn't bring the baby." Then, multitasking, she called to her son, "Anthony, it's your sister's turn to bowl. Let her have her turn."

Jo sat down next to her. "My mom's watching him. It's his nap time."

Arlene gave a knowing smile. "And you don't want him around all these germs."

"Well, yeah." That had been the main reason. The little guy wasn't quite two weeks old. No sense taking him out and exposing him to heaven only knew what.

"I was the same way with my first. With Maxie here I haven't bothered. And you know, he hasn't been sick a single day."

"So far." Who could tell what horrible snotty cold poor Maxie would pick up around all these people?

"He'll be fine," Arlene said.

Well, it was her kid.

Amanda dropped her ball instead of throwing it, and the ball crawled down the gutter, bouncing off the alley bumpers as it went. Pleased with her efforts, she jumped up and down, clapping.

Meanwhile, her brother, impatient for his turn, ran over to the alley and launched his, too, even as Arlene said, "No, not yet, Anthony!"

Anthony's ball bounced into his sister's and she sent up a howl of outrage. Arlene got up, gave her son a stern talking-to and pointed out to her daughter that her brother's ball was helping hers on its way. All was well once more.

Three kids. How did she keep from going bonkers when her husband was gone?

"I don't know how you do it," Jo said when she

returned to her seat. "Dealing with them all by your-self, I mean."

"You get used to it," Arlene said.

"I don't know if I want to."

"Girlfriend, you don't have a choice. You may not know it, but you're in the service, too."

That made Jo scowl.

Arlene nudged her shoulder playfully. "Hey, it's not so bad. Come on, look at all the fun we have when the guys are gone." Her son took his sister's ball and hurled it down the alley for her and the little girl broke into angry wails. Arlene was up again. "Now, why did you take your sister's ball?"

"I was helping her," Anthony protested.

"Now you can just help yourself to a time-out," Arlene said, pointing to a plastic chair.

He obeyed, crying all the way.

"Yeah, you're sure having fun," Jo said as Arlene walked back to her own seat.

"You think this stuff wouldn't happen when your husband was home? You're delirious."

"Well, at least I'd have someone to share the misery," Jo muttered.

"There are benefits to being on your own. I like it when Tony's gone. I'm in charge of everything and it all runs smoothly. No one to fight with over money or what I buy for the house or the kids. When Tony's home, Anthony plays us against each other, the little stinker."

"What do you mean?"

"You'll find out. Of course it's not all bad when

Tony comes home. Honeymoon sex all over again. Oh, yeah. Today it's out for hot fudge sundaes with Daddy, then the kids are staying at Grandma and Grandpa's overnight and we're off to the Alderbrook Inn for a romantic dinner and a night of wild monkey sex. Of course, by the time he's been home for three months, I'll be done with this normal life stuff and ready for him to ship out again," she added with a grin.

What a crazy, emotional, seesaw way to live. Arlene was right. The men weren't the only ones who were in the service.

Their conversation came to an end, since the buses had arrived. It was time to go meet the sub. Jo put in a quick call to her mom to make sure the baby was doing okay.

"He's fine. Don't worry. Go greet your husband."

The noise level had risen to high tide with excited chatter and children yelling and jumping up and down like crazed kangaroos as the families made their way out of the bowling alley and onto the buses.

Everyone buzzed with excitement as the bus lumbered down to the pier. Jo felt as if she was on caffeine overload. The air was cold and unwelcoming when she got off the overheated bus, but she barely noticed because there, among the other uniformed seamen walking down the pier, was a tall, handsome sailor. Her sailor. She joined the throng of wives rushing to greet their men.

He smelled awful, the scent of submarine and

men living in close quarters for too long was woven into the very cloth of his uniform but she didn't care. She wrapped her arms around him and kissed him for all she was worth.

"Oh, baby, I missed you," he said once they finally came up for air.

"I missed you, too." He couldn't keep doing this to her, darn it all.

He kissed her one more time, practically devouring her right there on the blustery pier. It was an epic kiss, equal to the one in that famous World War II photograph you saw everywhere. Of course, there were a lot of epic kisses taking place on that pier. And then, hurrying off the pier, couples anxious to get home and celebrate.

"Where's our son?" Mike asked as they followed the crowd.

"With Grandma. I didn't want to bring him out so soon."

"I can hardly wait to see him," Mike said. He hugged her close to him as they walked. "It's good to be home."

"It's good to have you home." *Where you belong.*

"Man, I can hardly wait to get out of these clothes," Mike said once they were on the road. "I stink."

"Yes, you do," Jo agreed and he chuckled. They both knew about that peculiar odor that seeps into clothes and possessions after three months in confined quarters. Mike's boat things would be stored in the garage.

Little Mikey was awake when they got to the

house and had just had his bottle. He was changed and contented, and to look at him you'd think he didn't even know how to cry. Looks were deceptive.

"I imagine you'd like to hold your son," Mom said. She got up from the couch and put the baby in Mike's arms.

He beamed down at the baby. "Hey, there, buddy. Sorry I wasn't here to greet you."

So was Jo. That was such an incredible moment. It would've been great if they could have shared it.

"They had quite the adventure," Mom said. "Did Jo tell you they got stopped by the police on their way to the hospital?"

He looked at Jo in surprise. "Really? What was that about?"

"Riley was speeding." A detail she hadn't planned on sharing. Mike didn't have a very high opinion of her sister's driving abilities.

Mike shook his head. "And whose idea was it for your sister to drive you to the hospital?"

"Not mine, that's for sure. But we were at the mall when my water broke. Anyway, you weren't here to take me."

Mom, ever the peacemaker, sensed a potential bump in the happy homecoming road and quickly added, "He gave them a police escort."

Mike smiled down at the baby. "A police escort. Already an important man."

"Just like his daddy," Mom said and Jo felt a little guilty. She should've been the one to come up

with that supportive remark. Once upon a time she
would have.

Mom left and Jo got the baby out of his now con-
taminated outfit and put him in his bassinet while
Mike deposited his smelly clothes and gear in the
garage. He came into the house naked and looking
like Michelangelo's David.

"You're a tease," Jo said as he came through the
kitchen, where she was making him some coffee.

"No teasing here." He lifted her hair and kissed
her neck. "Come take a shower with me."

"Babe, I just gave birth," she said sadly. "It's too
soon." Not only that, but what was he going to think
when he saw her post-baby bod? Oh, but it had been
soooo long.

"We can get creative," he said softly, nibbling
on her ear.

A few more kisses, along with sweet whispers of
love and, well, what the heck. She wouldn't mind another shower. And, after three sex-deprived months
on a sub, he probably wouldn't mind that she had
some extra weight around her middle.

He led her off to the bathroom and quickly reminded her of one of the many things she loved
about him. Darn it all, if only he'd stay put.

Dried off and comfy in sweats, they went to the
family room for coffee. Jo also put out Mike's favorite cheese and salami along with some of the cookies her mom had brought over.

"Man, I love Christmas," he said.

"I'm glad you're going to be home for the holidays." At least they had that.

The baby monitor on the kitchen counter announced that Mikey was stirring. She could hear the little snuffling noises he made when he was warming up for a good cry.

"I think somebody's hungry again," she said.

"Does he need to be changed?"

"Probably."

"I can do that," Mike offered, so they both went to the bedroom where she had the bassinet.

En route they passed the nursery. Pink Land. The walls were pink, and so were all the accents from the curtains to the changing table and the crib blankets. The only blue thing in the room was the stuffed bear Noel had bought for the baby, which was sitting on the (pink) dresser.

"We're going to have to change that," Mike said.

"We were expecting a girl," Jo reminded him.

"Are you disappointed you didn't get your girl?" he asked as they approached the bassinet.

She smiled down at her son. "No. This little man is perfect."

Mike stood next to her and put an arm around her. "We'll have a girl next time."

Another child to be upset every time Daddy left. There was a depressing thought.

The baby was starting to cry in earnest now. "We'd better get this guy changed. He's ready for some chow," Mike said.

"Are you sure you can handle this?" Jo asked.

Mike made a face. "I'm not an idiot."

"Okay," she said and handed him the baby, but she followed him to the nursery and stood next to him at the changing table, supervising the procedure.

Meanwhile, Mikey's cries became ever more lusty.

"Okay, time for Mom to take over," Mike said, handing him back.

Jo settled in the rocking chair and gave her baby the breast. The whole nursing thing was getting easier, thank God.

Mike watched with rapt interest and she suddenly felt a little shy. "What?" she said defensively.

"My baby feeding our baby. That's the most beautiful sight I've ever seen." He whipped out his cell phone and snapped a picture.

"If you post that on Facebook I'll kill you."

"Facebook, hell. This is just for me." He came over and knelt beside her, putting an arm around her. "I love you, Jo. Thank you for our son."

She smiled down at her boy and stroked his downy head. "He is beautiful, isn't he?"

"Yes, he is."

She almost asked, "And do you really want to leave him in three months?" But she held her peace. It was Mike's first day home and there was no sense in spoiling it with a fight. Because she was sure that was exactly what would happen.

While she finished feeding the baby, Mike went to fetch Chinese takeout and stop by his parents' for a quick hi. While he was gone, she tried to imagine what her life would be like if they continued this pattern. She couldn't picture herself coping like her pal Arlene. All she could envision was Mike missing important milestones like the baby's first steps, his first words, kindergarten graduation, important sports events.

When he came back, she tried to push the images out of her mind but they didn't want to leave. In bed that night, she lay awake stewing over how things were going to work out between her and Mike. Between that and getting up with the baby, it was a wakeful night.

She was just settling into a decent sleep when Mike brought her breakfast in bed—orange juice, a fried egg and toast. She groaned and dragged herself awake, shoving her hair out of her eyes. She'd have taken sleep over breakfast but it was a nice gesture and a reminder of what a good man she had.

"Wow. Do I have to tip you?" she joked, sitting up.

"Maybe." He laid the tray on her lap and sat on a corner of the bed. "You look gorgeous."

With dark circles and bed head. "You need glasses. Where's your breakfast?"

"I ate. Still used to getting up at 0-dark-hundred."

That brought the old elephant lumbering into the room. Mike's reenlistment plans. She hated to bring up the subject when he was being so sweet. But the elephant was on the bed with them now and couldn't be ignored.

"I don't want you to leave again."

His easy smile fell away. "Do we have to talk about this right now?"

"Yeah, we do. We need to settle this, Mike."

"And how are we going to do that? You don't want me to re-up. I think I should."

"Do you really want to miss out on your son's life for months at a time?" She'd seen how he'd looked at the baby. He was already crazy in love with his child. "What kind of relationship can you have with him when you're gone so much?"

"You and I manage okay," he pointed out.

"I'm not a child." Although he probably thought she was acting like one about this.

"Jo, I've been in the navy for eight years. It doesn't make sense to pack it in now."

"It does to me."

"Yeah? And what am I going to do when I get out?"

"Plenty. You're smart. You can do anything."

"Yeah, I can. But I won't find a job here doing what I do. You like being near your family. How far away are you willing to move? And what about Mikey? Do we want him to be able to go to college? We could fund an education account for him with my signing bonus and never have to worry about money."

"We don't have to worry about money now. We have plenty saved."

Jo felt overwhelmed. It had to be the darned hormones. Or the fact that she was tired. Whatever the cause, she started to cry.

Mike moved the tray from her lap and sat next to her, slipping an arm around her. "I'm sorry, babe. I'm not trying to upset you. I'm just trying to be practical."

"I don't want to be practical. I want to be happy!" Oh, yes, that was mature. Now she was really crying. Where were those chocolates Georgia had given her?

"I hate to see you like this," he said softly. "What can I do?"

"You can go away. I need a nap!"

That was when the baby started to snuffle and stir in his bassinet. "Oh, never mind," Jo said, dashing away the tears and throwing off the covers.

Mike sat on the bed and watched as she picked up their son and settled back in bed with him. She pretended to ignore him, but she was aware of him looking at her sadly. She didn't say anything. The old silent treatment, just what a man wanted when he came home from sea.

Finally he heaved a sigh and left the room, leaving behind her unfinished breakfast.

Great, Jo, fight with your husband on his first full day home. Obviously, there was more than one baby in this bed.

Chapter Sixteen

Everyone at school now knew why Riley and Emily were no longer friends and why Riley was no longer engaged, and Emily's approval rating had dropped to nil. No one confronted her, but no one included her in lunch break conversation, either. And although everyone was talking to Riley, nobody came right out and brought up the awkward subject of her lost groom.

Except Marge. "I think it's disgusting that he had the nerve to show up at the winter concert," she said as she visited with Riley in her room after school. "The man should be ashamed. They both should."

"You know what? I'm so over him," Riley said and shoved her desk drawer shut. "I'm so over both of them. I'm moving on."

"Good for you," Marge approved.

"In fact…" She held up the paper with the invitation she'd printed out. "I'm having a non-wedding reception on Saturday. I hope you haven't made plans."

"I have to admit I'd crossed you off my calendar," Marge said. "But I'll be happy to put you back on."

"Good. I'm going to hang this in the teachers' break room. I hope everyone will come."

"I'm sure they will. We all love you, Riley."

Riley found her throat suddenly tight. It was good to be loved, even if not by the man she'd thought she was going to marry. Well, onward and upward as Mom would say.

She hugged Marge then went to the break room and pinned her invitation to the bulletin board. That took care of the teachers. Next stop, the senior center.

The center was quiet when Riley walked in. Senior yoga and line dancing classes were over for the day, and the only person in the large room where many of those activities took place was Grammy's buddy Felix, who was setting up for the evening's bingo.

Riley ducked into the office where Henrietta Black sat at her desk, buried under paperwork as always. She smiled at Riley, showing the deep lines around her eyes and mouth. "Winnie's granddaughter, right?"

Riley nodded.

"Are you looking for your grandma?" Henrietta asked, obviously confused as to why a thirty-one-year-old would be hanging around the senior center.

"No, I was looking for you. I have an invitation for your members."

Now Henrietta really seemed confused. "We have over two hundred members."

Riley gulped. Yes, she'd lost all the groom's family and friends from her guest list, but Sean hadn't had two hundred people coming. She couldn't make room for that many extra.

"Of course, they're not all active," Henrietta said. "A lot of our members join simply so they can take trips or be on the seniors' softball team or attend classes for free."

"How many active members do you have?"

"About eighty."

That was manageable. "I'd like to ask your active members to a party."

"A party?"

"Actually, it's a reception."

"Oh? A reception for whom?"

"Me."

Yes, there was that confused expression again.

Riley explained about the canceled wedding. "So, I'm going to have a party this Saturday. I'm wondering if some of your members might enjoy coming to a fancy dinner."

"I think they would," Henrietta said eagerly. "I sure would. I've been at sixes and sevens since my husband died last summer and I'm always looking for ways to fill the weekend." Her expression turned wistful.

"It would make me very happy if you'd come," Riley told her. And she meant it. The more people like Henrietta who came, the more she'd like it. Her non-wedding reception was no longer so much about her as it was about giving a holiday lift to people who could really use it. "Here's the invitation," she said, sliding the sheet of paper onto the desk.

Henrietta picked it up and read, "'Come one and all to The Pines this Saturday at 7:00 p.m. to help Riley Erickson celebrate the holidays. (And her lucky escape from marrying the wrong man!) Dinner, dancing and non-wedding cake provided. No gifts. Your presence will be the best gift of all.' That's sweet. Your grandma's always saying what a class act you are."

Riley didn't know if what she was doing counted as classy but she hoped it would be fun. Anyway, it beat sitting home feeling sorry for herself.

"Don't be surprised if you get a ton of RSVPs," Henrietta said.

"That's what I want," Riley told her. She said a cheerful goodbye to Henrietta and left, her next destination the nursing home.

The Watermark served as both a retirement and nursing home. One corner of the property was occupied by a three-story building made up of retiree-friendly two-bedroom condos. It came complete with a workout room and a party room that residents could reserve for entertaining large groups, as well as some short, scenic trails for walking. Most of the rooms had a lovely water and mountain view. And, snugged in by trees as the place was, none had a view of their future—the nursing home, which was the next, close-by step for residents who couldn't take care of themselves anymore.

According to Grammy this was the last stop before the Grim Reaper escorted you off the party bus. "Don't even think about putting me there," she'd say. "If I reach that point, just hit me over the head with a hammer and put us all out of our misery."

But Riley knew that many of the nursing home residents were only there temporarily, recovering from various surgeries and going through PT. Some of them might have a family member who could bring them to her party.

The walls of the nursing home were painted a calming blue, and the windows had curtains that looked like they'd been stolen from an old farmhouse. Other than at the main entrance, the walls were devoid of pictures. In spite of the cleaning personnel who were diligently mopping the floors, a faint odor of urine hung in the air. Riley could see why her grandmother didn't want to end up here. The place needed an interior decorator, not to mention stronger cleaning solution.

An old lady was walking down the hall. When Riley came within reach, she leaned on her walker and stretched out a frail hand. "Hello," she said. "Welcome to The Watermark. My name is Margaret."

Riley took her hand. It was thin and fragile, down to skin over bone. "I'm Riley."

"You're very pretty," said Margaret. "Are you visiting someone here?"

"No, I'm here to drop something off."

"The desk is right over there." The woman nodded but didn't release Riley's hand, and Riley couldn't help wondering how many visitors she got. "I'll come with you," Margaret offered.

"I'd appreciate that," Riley said.

The old woman let go of her hand to turn her walker around. "Don't leave."

"I won't."

Once pointed in the right direction, Margaret started toward the reception desk and Riley slowed her pace to match her new friend's.

"Speaking of dropping things off..." Margaret began. "People have been showing up with Christmas cookies. Carolers came last week and brought those frosted ones to give out." She frowned. "We're not allowed to eat them, though. Liability issues, don't you know."

If the nursing home didn't allow people to distribute cookies, would they allow her to invite the residents to her party?

"I'm ready to leave this place, let me tell you," Margaret continued. "I hope to be back in my house by Christmas."

Their progress down the hall was slow. If they'd been racing a slug, the slug would have won. Still, Riley enjoyed visiting with the woman as they walked.

"I was once a Rockette," Margaret said. "I was quite a high kicker back then."

"I'll bet you were great."

"Oh, I had a wonderful time. I love to dance. When my husband was alive we used to go to the Elks every week for the tea dance. I was still dancing clear up until October when I fell and broke my hip."

"I'm sorry," Riley said.

"Oh, I'm so much better now. I'd sure like to dance again."

Maybe she could. "Do you have family around here, Margaret?" Riley asked.

"My daughter and her husband are snowbirds but they're around all summer. They're planning to come back for Christmas, so I'll see them soon. My granddaughter moved to Alaska. Can you imagine? The very thought of living up in that cold wilderness makes my old bones ache."

"So there's no one here for you now?"

"Oh, there is. My handsome grandson comes to visit me every week. In fact, this is his day. I was watching for him when you arrived." The look Margaret shot Riley was positively cagey. "He's single."

And probably living in his parents' basement while they did their snowbird thing.

"What did you say your name was, dear?"

"It's Riley."

"And are you single?"

"Yes, but I'm not looking right now," Riley said. She was waiting for Santa to drop the perfect man down her chimney. That could be a little hard to do, considering the fact that she had an electric fireplace.

They arrived at the reception desk and the receptionist, who was about Riley's age, asked, "May I help you?"

"Yes, thanks, I have an invitation I want to drop off."

The receptionist smiled. "Nice. Who's it for?"

"For anyone who wants it."

The receptionist's brows knit. "I don't understand."

"I broke up with my fiancé," Riley explained.

This brought a sympathetic frown. "That's too bad."

"Yes, it is. But we're having the reception, anyway, and I thought you might have some residents here who'd like to come."

"I'd like to come," Margaret said. "Will there be dancing?"

"We'll have a DJ," Riley said.

"And cake?" Margaret asked eagerly.

Riley smiled. She couldn't believe she was actually smiling about this. "Of course."

"Wow," said the receptionist, staring at Riley as if she'd announced that she'd completed the Boston Marathon and ended world hunger...while running the Boston Marathon. "That's sweet of you. I'll pass it on to my boss," she said as Riley handed it over.

"It's this Saturday, so if you could pass it on right away that would be great," Riley said.

"I'll be there," said Margaret.

"Now, Margaret, we have to check," said the receptionist.

The old woman scowled at her. "Last time I looked this wasn't a prison."

"But we'll need your doctor's permission."

"He'll give it or I'll find myself a new doctor."

"Gram, are you causing trouble?" came a male voice from behind them.

That voice sounded familiar. Riley turned to see…Jack Logan.

Margaret lit up like a kid on Christmas morning. "This is my handsome grandson."

Jack blushed. He covered his embarrassment by rolling his eyes. "That's my gram, biased and blind."

Riley didn't think her new friend was either. Jack Logan was good-looking, no doubt about it. And obviously he was a devoted grandson.

"Are you visiting someone here?" he asked Riley.

"No, I'm just dropping off an invitation."

He grinned. "To your non-wedding reception?"

"You guessed it."

"I'm going," his grandmother announced.

"You want to go, Gram? You can be my date."

"We'll need her doctor's permission," put in the receptionist.

"I'll take care of it," Jack said. Then he returned his attention to his grandmother. "What's for dinner tonight?"

"Chicken and mashed potatoes, same as last week."

"Good thing I like chicken and mashed potatoes," Jack said. Then to Riley, "Want to join us?"

"Oh, please do," said Margaret.

"Well…" She didn't really have anything else to do at the moment. "Sure."

Jack smiled. What a smile. "You're in luck— there should be chocolate pudding for dessert. Right, Gram?"

"Oh, yes," Margaret said happily.

At the lunchroom Jack insisted on paying for Riley's meal then scoped out three places for them at a table already occupied by two women who looked as frail as Margaret.

"You're lucky to have such a fine grandson," one of the women said once they'd all settled at the table. "And is this his girlfriend?"

Riley's cheeks felt warm. She sneaked a glance in Jack's direction and he was smiling. Again.

"We're new friends," he said.

"That's so sweet," cooed the woman.

A waitress came to take their orders. Big choices— did they want peas or carrots with their chicken? And did they want decaf coffee or tea?

"What do you think of my grandma?" he asked Riley as the women told the waitress their preferences.

"She's charming," Riley said.

"She's a firecracker. If the doc doesn't give permission for her to come to your party, she'll probably beat him up with her walker. Guess we've got a chaperone."

"I guess so," Riley agreed. She lowered her voice. "I don't know what had her more excited, the dancing or the cake."

"Might be a toss-up. Mostly I think she's excited to get out. This place is making her buggy. It would me, too," he added under his breath.

"It's kind of you to bring her," Riley said.

"I have many good qualities."

"I'm beginning to suspect that."

"Wait until Saturday night. I'll be happy to confirm your suspicions," he said.

Dinner conversation was an interesting combination of reports on aches and pains and the disappointing behavior of family. Not everyone at the table had a grandson who offered weekly visits.

Margaret did her best to cheer up her table companions, though, assuring them they'd be feeling better soon and predicting visitors for them. "Meanwhile, I'll share my grandson and my new friend," she said, beaming at Riley and Jack.

"You young people are so fortunate," one of the women told them. "You've got your whole lives ahead of you."

"We still have some time left to us," Margaret informed her. "And then eternity with the Lord. Now, that's something to look forward to." The other woman frowned at her plate, and Margaret leaned across the table and said to Riley, "I'm a glass-half-full kind of girl. How about you?"

Three weeks ago Riley had been more of a glass completely empty kind of girl. Thank heaven she didn't feel like that anymore. "Definitely half-full," she replied with a nod.

Jack winked at her and she decided maybe her

glass was a little more than half-full. Possibly up to two-thirds.

Dinner ended, and they escorted Margaret to her room, which she shared with another woman. "Betty's been a very nice roommate," she said, "but I'll be glad to go home and have my bedroom all to myself again. She snores."

"It won't be long," Jack reassured her as she lowered herself onto her bed. "You're getting around better all the time."

"I'm certainly getting around well enough to go out for an evening," she said. "Don't forget to order me a pass, darling."

"I won't."

"And now, you two young people probably have things to do, so I think I'll just read for a while and then rest my eyes."

"Last time I came in and found you 'resting your eyes' you were snoring yourself," Jack teased her.

"That must've been Betty," she said, waving away his teasing. "Give me a kiss, you rascal."

He obediently bent and kissed the top of her head and she smiled. "Come give me a kiss, too," she said to Riley, who was happy to oblige.

"And now I'm going to read about murder and mayhem," Margaret announced, holding up a paperback mystery with a very gory cover. "Next time you visit, I'll have a full report on who done it."

"Can hardly wait," Jack said as he and Riley slipped out of the room.

"What a lovely woman," Riley said.

"It runs in the family. My mom is, too."

"And what about your sister?"

"She suckered me into dressing like a girl for Halloween when I was eight," he said, making a face, and Riley chuckled. He checked his phone. "Six o'clock. Cocktail hour. Wanna get a drink?"

"I might spill it on you."

"I'll take my chances."

They wound up back at The Tree House, sitting in the bar area, and this time Riley managed to keep the Grinch in her glass.

"So what do you do when you're not making passes at strangers and hanging out with little old ladies?" he asked.

"I'm a teacher."

"Ah." He nodded. "Loves kids, wants five of her own."

"Loves kids and only wants two. I've seen first-hand how much school supplies cost, and that's just the tip of the iceberg. Kids are an expensive hobby."

"I wouldn't mind having a couple of 'em, though," he said. "Down the road. I'm in no hurry."

She almost asked him if he was in a hurry to find the right woman and get married. Almost.

Instead she took another sip of her drink. "I suppose you're busy entering golf tournaments."

"I've done a few," he said and drank some of his beer. "You ever played golf?"

She shook her head. "I'm not athletic at all."

"Then what do you do for fun?"

She shrugged. "Watch movies, read, go out with

my girlfriends, go dancing." She used to go out with Sean. Oh, no! No thinking about Sean allowed. She quickly moved on. "I like to play cards with my family." Did she sound boring?

"Yeah? I like to play cards. Poker," he added.

A sudden image of playing strip poker with Jack Logan came to mind. *Don't go there*, she scolded herself. *You barely know this man.*

"I like movies, too," he said.

"Action ones, right?" she guessed.

"Is there any other kind?"

"Romantic comedies. Movies based on Jane Austen books?"

"Who?" She looked at him, shocked, and he laughed. "Just kidding. I know who she is. But I gotta say, those movies bore me to tears. All that... talking."

"That's what we're doing now."

"Yeah, but this is different. We're talking about us."

Of course he meant *us* as in each of them individually, but she for a moment couldn't help imagining them as a couple. They might have gotten off to a bumpy start but those bumps were smoothing out nicely. Oh, how she'd like to be an *us* again with someone. The right someone this time.

"What else do I need to know about you?" he asked. "Are you, by any chance, a nymphomaniac?" Her face flamed and he grinned. "A closet nympho, I bet. But moving on, tell me some more about yourself."

"I love Christmas."

"That explains the Christmas wedding," he murmured.

She shrugged.

"You have poor taste in men."

"I'm having a drink with you," she pointed out.

"Your tastes are improving," he said, saluting her with his beer bottle. "What else?"

"I'd like to travel." Sean had promised to take her somewhere glamorous for their honeymoon.

"Yeah? Where?"

"Someplace with very blue water and warm beaches. I've never been to Hawaii."

"That's definitely an oversight."

"I suppose you have," she said.

"Yeah. Maui is the best. Waterfalls, great scenery, good hiking. Oh, except you're not athletic."

"I can hike. And I love beautiful scenery and waterfalls." Maybe someday she'd get to Hawaii. She was already having a non-wedding reception. Why not a non-honeymoon?

"Lots of hiking around here," he said. "Done any of the trails in the Olympics?"

She shook her head. She'd only said she *could* hike. She hadn't said she actually had.

"Something to think about this summer," he said and took a drink.

Something to think about right now. She could see herself hiking in the mountains with this man. She could see herself doing plenty of things with him.

Remember, you're not in a hurry. She didn't need

to host a second non-wedding reception. So after finishing her drink, she said she had to go.

"Well, then, I'll see you Saturday."

Yes, Saturday. And now, even though she was determined not to rush into anything, she was excited all over again. She was having the party to end all parties and Jack Logan was coming. Life was good.

She called Noel when she got home to report in.

"He sounds great," Noel said after Riley had described her afternoon with Jack.

"I think he probably is," Riley said. "Of course, it may not turn into anything."

"Sounds like he wants it to if he's asking you out for drinks."

"Maybe," Riley said, not wanting to get her hopes up.

"So funny that you two are hitting it off after the way you met. Just like Santa said," Noel added. "Isn't that weird?"

"Coincidence." Riley was done trying to explain their strange Santa encounter. "How about you? How's the job going?"

There was a moment's silence, followed by, "It's not."

"You quit?"

"No, I got fired."

"Fired!"

"On my first day," Noel said, her voice tinged with misery.

"Oh, no. I'm sorry. What happened?"

"I had a slight accident."

Shades of Noel's disastrous dinner with the evil house-flipper. "What kind of accident?"

"I spilled eggs on Ben Fordham's mother."

"What was he doing at The Rusty Saw?" Talk about bad timing.

"Birthday breakfast with his son."

"He's got a son?" If he had a son, that meant he had a woman somewhere. No wonder Noel was having so much trouble persuading him to let her have her house back.

"I don't know what the deal is with that, but I do know Ben's mother guards him like a dragon. She made me so nervous," Noel said and went on to describe the whole grisly scene.

"That's terrible," Riley said.

"Maybe I should go and apologize to his mom, bring her chocolates or something."

"She doesn't deserve chocolates. She sounds like a real be-atch."

"I think she is," Noel said.

"It wasn't like you did it on purpose."

"I know. But still. Or maybe I should forget about the house, let the whole thing go."

"Don't do that. Did you invite him to my party?"

"There wasn't exactly time at the Saw."

"You should invite him."

"I don't know," Noel said miserably. "I think someone else is going to wind up in my house. I'll have to move back home with my parents like a big failure."

"You're not a failure," Riley said. "Don't even go there. And you can always move in with me."

"Thanks. You're such a good friend." Another sigh. "I love this house."

Riley could've told her that there'd be other houses, but that would have cheered Noel about as much as it had cheered Riley every time someone told her how lucky she was to be rid of Sean.

Of course, now she could see that there *were* other men out there. A girl could move on.

Still, she hoped Noel wouldn't have to. If she got the house-flipper to the party, if he saw Noel in her fancy green bridesmaid dress...well, who knew? It was Christmas, after all, the most wonderful time of the year. Anything could happen.

She thought of Jack Logan. Oh, yes, indeed, anything could happen.

Chapter Seventeen

Noel and Marvella were busy helping a little boy master sleeping without a night-light when Noel's cell phone rang. She didn't recognize the number.

Don't answer it, advised Marvella. *We have work to do and it's probably someone wanting to sell you a vacation time-share.*

Probably. Noel let the call go to voice mail.

But she had a hard time concentrating on little Edgar's troubles. Who was that mystery caller? She finally picked up her cell phone and listened to the message.

"This is Ben Fordham," said a deep voice.

Ben Fordham! She'd missed a call from Ben Fordham. She knew she shouldn't have listened to Marvella.

"I, uh, got your number from Mrs. Bing. You might not want to talk to me after what happened at the Saw. I wanted to call and see if you still had your job. Uh, actually, well, I, uh, feel bad that you felt you had to take the job in the first place. I hope we can work out something about the house."

Joy! Elation!

Ha! The old sympathy ploy worked. Looks like you've finally got the poor slob where you want him. Bet he'll let you have it for next to nothing now.

Marvella's words threw cold water on the fire of enthusiasm. Yes, Noel had wanted to butter him up so he'd make a deal, but she wasn't out to use him. She only wanted him to cooperate with her. She certainly didn't need his pity.

Pity, shmitty. Who cares as long as you get what you want?

Sometimes Marvella wasn't very noble. "It's a good thing I don't let your ugly side come out in books," Noel muttered.

Never mind my ugly side. Call the man back.

She started to call him then decided she'd rather go to his office. Maybe he'd even ask her to lunch.

She changed out of her fuzzy pajama bottoms, ratty old sweater and Hello Kitty slippers and put on more of her borrowed classy lady clothes. On her way to his office she decided to stop and buy a peace offering for his mother. Chocolates. And, while a box of candies wasn't the same as a new sweater, it was the thought that counted. Right? Anyway, Mrs. Sawyer had taken enough money from her to pay for a new one.

Cashmere? Who was she kidding? She decided to buy a really big box of chocolates.

At Northwest Gifts she chose a large box of chocolate truffles tied with a red velvet bow. She hoped her offering would win some points with Ben's mother. While she was at it, she got a small box for her father by way of congratulations. He'd gotten the job and they were all going out to Pepe's for Mexican that night to celebrate.

"This is our biggest seller," the clerk informed her as she rang up Noel's purchases. "They're made by a chocolate company in Icicle Falls and people love them."

She hoped Ben's mother counted as people. "She'll love them," Noel assured herself as she parked in front of Ben Fordham's office. Still, she found her feet getting colder with each step toward the building, and it had nothing to do with the slush on the ground. Did she really want to face Mrs. Fordham?

You bought 'em. You may as well deliver 'em, said Marvella.

Maybe she'd deliver them to Ben and he could give them to his mother. Yes, that was a much better plan. She'd give him chocolates to pass on and they could settle things about the house, hopefully in a way that would make them both happy.

She had just gotten to the Fordham Enterprises door and was about to walk in when the door of the office across from it opened. "May I help you?" said a female voice in a tone as close to a snarl as one could get and still be civil.

Startled, Noel dropped the box of chocolates. What was it with this family that every time she was around them, she dropped something? She scrambled to pick it up and hugged it to her.

Will you stop looking so pathetic? Marvella said. *And you're holding that box of chocolates like it's a shield. Try to show some confidence.*

Confidence. Noel lowered the box, keeping a firm grip on it. Okay, her grip was firm but her knees felt weak. "Yes, actually. Mrs. Fordham, it's nice to see you again." What a lie.

The woman didn't bother with small talk. There she stood, fashionably dressed as usual in gray slacks, black heels and a white blouse, which she'd accented with a red scarf and a frown. "What do you want?"

"I wanted to give you these." Noel managed a smile and held out the chocolates. "As an apology for ruining your sweater."

Mrs. Fordham made no move to take them nor did she smile back. "I'm afraid I don't eat chocolate."

Which would explain why she was as thin as a snake. "Oh. Well, I just wanted you to know that I felt bad. I hope Mrs. Sawyer gave you my money for a replacement one."

"My son was in there yesterday and she gave it to him. Is there anything else?"

Noel's eyes sneaked a glance at Ben's office door.

This didn't go unnoticed by the lizard. "I understand Ben has purchased the house you've been renting."

"Uh, yes. I'm hoping to buy it back from him." A perfectly penciled eyebrow shot up and Noel could feel a guilty heat zooming from her neck to the roots of her hair.

"I'm sure his Realtor will be happy to talk to you when the time comes," Mrs. Fordham said.

She didn't have to add, "Now, scram." That was implied and Noel got the message loud and clear. But darn it all, she didn't want to scram. She wanted to see Ben. She reached to open his office door.

"I hope you don't have designs on my son, young woman."

Noel's hand dropped from the door handle and she took a step back. "Designs?"

Mrs. Fordham pointed a finger at her. "Don't play innocent with me. I know what you're up to."

The heat on Noel's face got hotter. "I don't understand what you're talking about," she lied.

"You're not the first woman to try to take advantage of his soft heart, but I can tell you right now he listens to me and I'm going to have a few things to say about you when we have our meeting today."

"Mrs. Fordham, you don't even know me," Noel protested.

"Oh, yes, I do. I've met your type before."

Shy writers?

Noel was trying to form an answer when the door to the Fordham Enterprises office opened. Maybe it was Ben. Maybe she could ask to see him privately, put in a good word for herself before his mother got to him. What that good word was going to be she had no idea, since Mrs. Fordham was absolutely right. She *was* hoping to take advantage of his soft heart—now that she knew he had one.

Sadly, it wasn't Ben who came out. It was his

secretary. She hesitated uncertainly, glancing from Noel to Mrs. Fordham.

"Janelle, what are you doing out here?" Mrs. Fordham demanded.

Janelle looked almost as cowed as Noel felt. "I'm on my way to lunch?"

Lunch hour already. How time flew when you were being intimidated.

"Well, go on, then. No one's stopping you."

"Yes, Mrs. Fordham," the secretary said and began speed-walking toward the stairs.

"Now, if you'll excuse me," Mrs. Fordham said, opening the door Janelle had just come out of. She slipped inside and shut it firmly behind her.

Noel started speed-walking for the stairs herself, anxious to get away from the scene of her humiliation. She'd almost reached Janelle when she realized she was about to step into another unpleasant conversation, this time with her rival. She stopped with the speed-walking.

But Janelle had heard her coming and paused on the stairs, waiting for Noel to catch up with her. Great.

Surprisingly, the expression on the secretary's face was far from adversarial. She looked almost sympathetic. "Don't feel bad. She doesn't like me, either."

"Did she call you a user?"

"No, she called me a complication, something her son doesn't have time for. He's raising his kid all alone. It's upsetting for Timmy to have women parading through his life. Blah, blah."

"Why is he raising Timmy alone?" Noel asked.

"I don't know the details, but I wouldn't be surprised if his mother drove his ex away. That woman is a dragon. Nobody gets past her." Janelle pointed to Noel's chocolates. "Bribery doesn't work, either. Believe me, I tried. If the dragon had her way, she'd replace me with someone who's fifty and fat. But I'm not going anywhere." Janelle smiled, but with her eyes narrowed it changed to something far from sweet. Mrs. Fordham had better not be anywhere near the stairs when Janelle was. She could wind up having a sad accident.

Janelle's evil twin vanished and she added some syrup to her expression. "If you want I can give the chocolates to Ben. He loves chocolate."

That was unexpectedly nice, especially considering that before this, Janelle hadn't been much warmer to her than Mrs. Fordham. "Thanks," she said, handing them over. "Someone may as well enjoy them."

"Don't worry. Someone will," Janelle said as she took the box.

Hmm. Had she just been duped? Would Ben even see those chocolates? Noel sighed inwardly and continued, and Janelle went back up the stairs with the candy. Well, she'd tried. And that was all she could do. She returned to her car feeling depressed.

A text from her sister didn't lift her spirits.

Just got bling from Dan. He couldn't wait to give it to me.

Cool, Noel texted back. Nice that life was falling into place for somebody.

Can't wait to show you. See you tonite.

Yes, tonight. What was Ben Fordham doing tonight? She'd never get a chance to find out, not with his mom on patrol. Might as well return Jo's clothes. She texted Jo and suggested she drop them off.

You can't be done with them already, Jo replied.

Not much point anymore.

Are you having a crisis?

Did giving up count as a crisis?

No. Just thought you'd like them back.

Can't fit into them yet. Keep them a little longer. Next month we'll go sale shopping and get you some big-girl clothes of your own.

In other words, fashion model stuff like Jo wore. Noel wasn't sure she saw the point, but she thanked Jo. Then she asked about the baby and how things were going with Mike home.

Readjusting, Jo texted.

Noel hoped she meant that in a good way. She said bye and then drove home where she changed back into fleecy bottoms, her ratty sweater and her slippers. She made herself a cup of tea, sat down at her desk and got very aggressive with the monster who was picking on little Edgar. Well, Marvella got aggressive. Noel simply took dictation.

The chapter finished, she sat back, read what she'd written and pronounced it good. If only she could influence the outcome of real-life events the way she could fictional ones. Her phone pinged, announcing a new text. This one came from… She almost dropped her cell. Ben Fordham.

Mom says she talked to you.

You could call it that. Yes.

Can I see you tonight?

She couldn't help feeling intrigued. Why did he want to see her? Her heart rate began to pick up. He got the chocolates and he wanted to thank her. He'd told his mother off and decided he needed to sell Noel the house and then move in with her. He'd…

You can't see him. You've got your family dinner. You're busy, Marvella reminded her. *Anyway, you need to make him sweat.*

Him? She was the one with the rapid heartbeat here. She wouldn't be at the restaurant all night. Ben

could come over later for hot chocolate. And conversation. And...ooh, just think of the possibilities.

She texted back:

Can you come at 8?

Don't get excited, she told herself. *You don't even
know why he wants to come over.* After talking to
his mom, he was probably coming to let her down
easy, tell her he'd changed his mind about trying to
work out a deal and that she'd better hurry up and
start packing her stuff.

Too late. She was excited. She couldn't stop herself.

I'll get a pizza.

I'll bring wine.

Yuck.

Scratch that. You don't like wine.

He remembered. That had to mean something.
*It means he's not going to waste money on wine.
Don't get all sloppy sentimental,* Marvella said. *You
need to keep your wits about you.*

How about cola?

Super.

They settled on eight and she immediately ended her workday to clean her house and herself. Maybe she'd even give herself a mani. And a pedi.

She hummed as she cleaned up her place and had a shower, and she was smiling as she changed back into what Jo referred to as big-girl clothes. She was still smiling when she drove to Pepe's and the smile stayed with her clear through dinner. It never even faltered when Aimi showed off the diamond earrings Dan had gotten her. He didn't make a lot and he'd probably saved for months to buy them. Lucky Aimi that he was so willing to sacrifice for her.

That's okay, she told herself, still smiling, *you're going to work things out with Ben Fordham. Life is good.*

After dinner Dad broke open the chocolates she'd brought and shared them. Oh, yes, life was indeed good.

On the way home she picked up a frozen pizza. Once in the house she brushed her teeth, touched up her makeup, put on more perfume and shed her shoes so she could show off her toenail polish—Christmas red with white tips, a lovely job if she did say so herself. And staying barefoot was a much better idea than running around in red stilettos. There would be no tripping or spilling tonight.

She got her pizza in the oven, lit a scented candle and flipped on her Christmas lights. Then she stood in her doorway, taking in the winter scene. The neighbors all had their Christmas lights on and there was just enough snow left to make everything look festive. The kids down the street had built a snowman and he seemed to be waving at Noel with one of his stick arms. She loved nights like this when everything was quiet and pretty.

She loved her neighborhood. She liked chatting about gardening over the back fence, liked giving out candy bars to all the little trick-or-treaters at Halloween. Her next-door neighbors, the Demmings, often brought her fresh crab after they'd been crabbing, and the Nordlies down the street always invited her to their New Year's Day open house. What if she didn't get to stay here?

It was getting cold. She shut the door.

She had just taken the pizza out of the oven when Ben arrived with a large bottle of pop. And well, well. What else did he have? Chocolates? Just like the ones she'd bought for his mother.

"Something smells great," he said, stepping inside.

"The pizza."

"No, it's something else."

"Oh, the scented candle."

"No, that's not it." He leaned over and sniffed her neck and all her nerve endings got giddy. "It's you."

Good thing you put on that perfume like I suggested.

Scram, Noel told Marvella.

You might need me.

Not tonight. She could handle this.

Or not. "Well, um, thanks," she stammered.

He held out the chocolate box. "I thought we

might want dessert. My secretary got this for me, but I can't eat all that by myself."

"Your...secretary." You couldn't trust people.

I could have told you that.

Will you SCRAM?

Fine, Marvella huffed. *Go ahead, do this on your own. You'll be sorry.*

"You do like chocolate, right?" Ben asked as she put the box on the hall table.

"Every woman likes chocolate."

"Not my mom." He removed his coat and she took it.

She knew that now. The very mention of his mom made her face flush hot. She turned her back and busied herself hanging up the coat.

"Look, about Mom," he began.

The last thing she needed when they were trying to come to some agreement about the house was the ghost of his mother hovering over them, scowling. "I'm sure she's a very nice lady," Noel lied. "Our pizza's ready." She hurried to the kitchen and began cutting it. Rather vigorously. It started to slide on the cutting board.

Just as she thought she was going to lose half of it, a large hand reached out and saved the day. "How about I cut it for you?"

"I'm really not accident prone," she said. "But sometimes I get nervous and..." Her words petered off. "Let me pour you some of that pop."

He caught her arm and stopped her from turning away. "Did my mom make you nervous?"

Oh, no, not his mom again.

"You should know a few things about her, about us."

She bites the heads off chickens and you're adopted. Please say you're adopted.

"We're close."

This didn't bode well for working out any kind of deal—except one where Noel disappeared. She grabbed the bottle of soda pop he'd set on the counter and got busy pouring him a glass.

"My dad left when I was three and it's always been just the two of us. She worked hard, put in long hours as a bank teller and did interior decorating on the side. But she always made time for me. Never missed a football game. She was the best," Ben finished and took a long drink of his pop.

"She sounds like a very dedicated mother." So, underneath that cold exterior beat a heart of—well, beat a heart.

"She was. She hardly dated at all when I was growing up. Of course, when I was a kid I liked being the man of the house and I did a pretty good job of chasing away the few guys who tried to come between us."

Kind of like what she's been doing to you, Noel thought. She found she couldn't look at Ben. "So, does that mean there's no room for anyone else?"

"Not necessarily. But I haven't always been smart about relationships." He picked up a piece of pizza from the cutting board, examined it then took a bite.

Noel waited for the story to continue.

It did. "Had a couple of real duds in high school and college. I wasn't much smarter when I got older. I met someone a few years back. She was hot." He smiled ruefully. "Who doesn't want a hot girlfriend, right? Yvonne and I had fun together." He shrugged. "We decided to get married."

"I guess you didn't live happily-ever-after."

"Not even close. Money was tight, she lost her job and we were struggling. Then she got pregnant. She didn't want to keep the baby. I had to beg her, bribe her, actually. She got a new car out of the deal. The day after Timmy was born, she said she wanted a divorce."

"And so that was that?"

"Not at first. I thought it was postpartum depression or something. Mom just thought she was a bitch. Turns out Mom was right. She wanted out and she pretty much made my life miserable until I agreed."

Some women didn't know how good they had it. "Where is she now?"

"Living in Vegas with a high roller. She gets Timmy for two weeks every summer."

"Your poor son."

Ben shrugged. "He's okay. He's got Mom."

Grandma Lizard. Except maybe she wasn't such a lizard, after all. Maybe she simply wanted to shield her son from further heartbreak.

"Anyway, I've picked some real winners and it's usually cost me one way or another. I can't blame my mom for being suspicious. According to her, most people have a hidden agenda. Everybody's out to use you."

Noel had reached for a slice of pizza but now she didn't feel hungry. In fact, she felt sick to her stomach. She put it back on the cutting board.

She couldn't keep trying to manipulate this nice man into giving her what she wanted. "I can't do this."

His brows knit. "Do what?"

"I was out to butter you up. I just wanted to find a way to get my house back."

The indulgent smile closed down. He set his glass on the counter without meeting her eyes. "I knew you wanted the house, but I thought under all that, there was something more going on."

"There is. And that's why I can't keep trying to… manipulate you." How she hated making herself look like his ex-wife. "Don't worry. I'm giving up on the house. I won't bother you anymore. You can tell your accountant to forget about the number-crunching."

He gave a cynical grunt and looked at her with contempt. "What's this? More manipulation?"

She shook her head. "No. If I got this house that way, I couldn't live in it. I guess if it was meant for me, Mrs. Bing would've sold it to me. So go for the granite countertops and the modern fireplace. I know you'll find the perfect buyer for the place. And like I said, I promise I won't bother you anymore or bring you coffee." Except she wanted to see this man again. She'd given up on the house but she hated to give up on him, too. Maybe, after the house sold, they could be friends. Or more. "Not until after you've sold the house," she amended.

He stood there and endured her whole speech, but as soon as she finished, he nodded and left without so much as a word. A moment later she heard the front door shut.

She wished he'd yelled at her, called her names. She wished he'd stayed long enough for her to say she was sorry. She wished she could turn back time and start again. She sat at the kitchen table and indulged in a good cry.

She was still sobbing when a big hand came down on her shoulder.

She let out a screech and nearly fell off her chair. Then she looked up to see Ben Fordham staring at her.

"You left," she said stupidly.

"Now I'm back. What did you mean about bringing me coffee after the house sells?"

She blinked. Her eyes seemed to be the only part of her body working at the moment. Her mouth sure wasn't in good operating order.

Don't just sit there. Say something! Marvella commanded.

"Um."

He took a seat opposite her. "Tell me."

Noel could feel a simmer on her cheeks. It was suddenly hot in the kitchen.

If you can't stand the heat, get out of the kitchen... and go to the bedroom.

Marvella was not helping. And yet—she was

right. Noel wanted the house, but she wanted Ben more. "I just thought, maybe after all is over... I mean, well..." Oh, for heaven's sake. Where were the words she needed?

"Noel, when you use people, you use them and then forget about them. You don't talk about bringing them coffee after you've lost what you wanted. And you sure don't tell them you're using them."

She hung her head. "I wish I hadn't. It's embarrassing to confess. I just kept hoping that if we talked enough, if I proved to you I'm a good risk..."

"I get that you love this house."

"But you bought it fair and square."

He took her hand. "You know I don't keep houses. Once I've renovated them, I move on. Fix, sell and make a profit. That's my business."

She bit her lip and nodded. He had such big hands. Strong.

"But in the end, real estate is about deals, so let's do a deal. I did talk to my accountant, and I think we can make this happen."

She looked up, startled. What was he saying?

"I'll bag the renovations, sell the place to you as is. You give me a down payment and I'll carry the contract."

That was exactly what she'd been hoping for, but it wouldn't work. She'd been struggling to come up with what Mrs. Bing wanted. She'd never be able to buy the place from Ben.

She sighed. "I wish I could. Just flip the house and put us both out of our misery."

"Come on, work with me here."

"Even without renovations, I'm sure I can't afford to pay you enough to make a profit."

"Tell me what you can afford."

She did, her face flaming as she mentioned the pathetically low amount. Then she told him what she had in savings for a down payment. It was laughable.

To her astonishment, he didn't laugh. "I can live with that."

She blinked. Were her ears working? "That's all you want? That's what I offered Mrs. Bing and she wasn't interested."

He shrugged.

"But…there's hardly any profit for you," she said, feeling increasingly guilty. "I can't."

"Yeah, you can."

"You just said you sell houses for a profit."

"I know what I said. But I got a steal of a deal at auction today—a house on Bainbridge Island that will turn a nice profit. I think I can afford to be generous. Anyway, it's not like I'm *giving* you this place."

Considering the profit he'd lose, it certainly felt like it. "Really?"

"Yeah, really," Ben said. "You love this house and the more I think about it, the less I like taking it from you. We'll both feel better if we can work this out so you can stay."

"Charge me the current interest rate," she said, determined to be businesslike.

"Don't worry, I will," he said with a grin.

"I can't believe you're doing this," she said, tears in her eyes. "But are you sure?" she asked, guilt setting in again. "I mean you have a son to take care of. I didn't know that when this all started. I should've let things go the minute I found out."

"We'll be fine. Anyway, it's Christmas and I don't want to be a Scrooge."

"You're not a Scrooge, you're a saint," she said, and threw her arms around him and kissed him.

He kissed her back and wow, happy holidays.

Chapter Eighteen

The following morning Noel stopped at Java Josie's on her way to Ben's office to pick up his favorite latte. She was just leaving when Donny the ex walked into the coffee shop.

"Noel, you're by yourself," he observed with a smug smile. "Want to have coffee together?"

Honestly, what had she ever seen in him? "No, thanks, I've got a date." Going to Ben's office to discuss the house deal—that was sort of a date.

Donny frowned. "That guy. He seems like a real user to me."

"I guess you'd know about that sort of thing."

"Damn straight I would," he said, missing her sarcasm. "He probably just wants to sleep with you."

"One can always hope," she said and pushed open the door.

At Ben's office Janelle looked surprised to see her.

"I'm here to talk to Ben," Noel said, stating the obvious.

"The dragon didn't burn you to a crisp yet?"

If she dated Ben, the dragon would be part of her life, as well. Noel decided it was best not to let this conversation go any further. "So, is Ben in?"

Janelle frowned and picked up her phone. "Someone's here to see you. Should I tell her to wait?"

Oh, we are a little jealous, Marvella whispered.

Janelle's frown remained in place. "Yeah, that's her. Okay, fine." She hung up. "You can go on in," she said reluctantly.

Ben was already at the door when Noel entered the Fordham Enterprises inner sanctum. "Hey, there." He shut the door and took the coffee out of her hands, setting it on his desk, then pulled her to him and kissed her. What a great way to start the day!

"Now, there's a great way to start the day," he said, echoing her own reaction. "I thought about you all night."

"Really?"

"Does that surprise you?"

"Yes, actually, it does," she admitted.

"You know, I'm beginning to suspect you're pretty special."

Was he kidding?

He shook his head at her. "You don't believe that, do you?"

"Well…"

"You're beautiful and talented and kindhearted. I'd say that all adds up to special."

She felt both warmed and embarrassed. "You're pretty special, yourself," she murmured, suddenly shy.

The minute the words were out of her mouth she

remembered what the mall Santa had said about bringing her a good man to go with her house. *Santa, if this is the man, you outdid yourself!*

"Yeah?" Ben grinned and kissed her again.

She could go on doing this forever. She did finally stop, though, and got a check out of her purse. "I had to postdate it," she explained. "I did an online transfer from savings, and the money won't be available until tomorrow." There was now nothing in her savings account but she had no regrets about draining it.

"You are efficient."

Not so much efficient as afraid she'd dreamed everything that had happened the night before. Except if she had, the dream was still continuing, and it was great.

He stuffed the check in his pocket. "Come on, sit down." He led her over to his desk and pulled out a pad of paper.

For the next twenty minutes they went over payment schedules and how long it would take her to pay off the house, which basically added up to forever. "That's a long time for you to wait to get all your money back," she said when they were done.

"Steady income, though," he said as he walked her to the door. "You told me that yourself. And if you become the next J.K. Rowling you can pay it off early, no penalties. My cousin can draw up the papers. If you want, we can sign them later this afternoon."

By afternoon the house would be hers. Sort of. "I

can come back, no problem," she said. "I still can't believe you're doing this. I can't even begin to tell you how grateful I am."

"I'm hoping you might feel something more than gratitude."

She blushed. "Of course I do."

"But no strings," he hurried to add.

"I like strings."

That made him grin, but he said, "I'm doing this because it's the right thing to do. You don't owe me anything."

"Other than eternal gratitude," she said, beaming at him.

"Maybe that. So, how about having dinner with me tomorrow? I think I can get my mom to babysit."

"Actually, I have something tomorrow evening."

His smile fell away but he nodded. "Oh. Sure."

"But I'd like an escort. Would you be interested in going to a dinner with me? It's kind of a dress-up affair," she said then held her breath.

The smile jumped back on his face. "Yeah, I can dig up a suit. What's the occasion?"

She told him and he shook his head. "Now I've heard everything. Yeah, I want to see what a non-wedding reception looks like. Count me in."

As he walked Noel to the door, a new thought occurred to her. "Um, if we were to start seeing each other…"

"We already are as far as I'm concerned," he said with a smile.

"I just want you to know that, no matter what, I'll never welch."

"I never thought you would," he said. "I don't think you've got it in you." With that he kissed her once more before opening the door and sending her happily on her way.

Janelle took one look at her and scowled. "I guess you won the jackpot. How the heck did you manage it?"

Noel shrugged. "I went to see Santa."

The minute she was at her car, Noel texted her good news to both Riley and Jo. Then she called her mother.

"That is wonderful news, indeed! What a nice man." Mom barely paused before adding, "Is he single?"

"As a matter of fact, he is, and he's coming to Riley's party with me."

"Well, well," Mom said.

"It may not work out." Oh, how she hoped she was wrong about that and Santa had come through for her. "But it's going to be fun to have a date." She'd settle for that right now. After all, she had her house. She didn't need to be greedy.

Ha! Too late for that, Miss Piggy, sneered Marvella.

Yeah, it probably was.

Later that afternoon she met Ben at his cousin's office on the first floor and signed the papers that declared their deal done. It was the frosting on the red velvet cake when Ben smiled at her and said, "I'll pick you up tomorrow at quarter to." She practically floated back to her car.

This called for a celebration. Hot chocolate! She swung by Pineland Supermarket to pick up some cocoa mix.

She'd gotten her cocoa and was at the holiday display contemplating a candy cane to go with it when she heard a familiar female voice on the other side. "You'd think after what Yvonne put him through that he'd be more careful, but no, here he is chasing another user."

Noel stiffened. She knew that voice and she knew who the *user* was. Sure enough, she rounded the display and saw Mrs. Fordham talking on her phone, her hand hovering over the cans of Almond Roca.

Doesn't eat chocolate, huh? sneered Marvella.

Crud. Of all the people to run into! Noel started to back away.

You have to face her sometime, Marvella said. *Suck it up and be brave.*

Marvella was right. And wasn't this what she and her alter ego were always telling the children in her books? Be brave and face your fears.

You can do it. You created me.

Yes, she could. She cleared her throat. "Hello, Mrs. Fordham." She almost added that it was nice to see the woman, but that would've been stretching it.

Mrs. Fordham gave a start and nearly dropped her phone. She recovered quickly, putting on a frosty expression. "I'll call you back," she said into her phone. "Noel."

Her name had never sounded like a dirty word before. This was hardly encouraging, but she plunged on. "Are you stocking up for the holidays?"

"My son likes these," the other woman said stiffly.

Noel was tempted to thank her for the tip and grab a can, but there was no point in deliberately provoking her so she resisted, simply nodding.

"It would appear that you and he have come to some sort of agreement."

Noel could tell how much she approved of that. "Yes, we have. He's carrying my contract and I'm paying him the going interest rate."

"Very noble of you, considering you got the house for a song."

"So did he," Noel pointed out.

This didn't endear her to Mrs. Fordham. She looked ready to run Noel over with her grocery cart. "Well, I hope you're happy."

"I am, actually. But I'm not just happy about the house. I like your son." There. She'd said it. "I like him a lot."

Mrs. Fordham stabbed a well-manicured finger at her. "Do not even think that you are going to start something with my son."

Noel's knees were feeling very weak. She gripped the handle of her shopping basket with both hands. "I know about his ex-wife. I'm not like her."

"You could have fooled me."

"I doubt anyone can fool you, Mrs. Fordham. I know what it's like to be used. It's not fun. And yes, I'll admit, when I first met Ben my goal was to convince him to let me have my house. I love it and I want to stay there."

The older woman's expression said, "I knew as much."

"But I came to realize that I had to let go of that dream. And I would have. Your son was really generous and offered to sell the house to me at a price I can afford. And in the end, I took him up on the offer. But I was willing to walk away, and you need to know that."

"You got it anyhow," Mrs. Fordham sneered.

"I did."

"Then you can go on your way," Mrs. Fordham said airily and started to wheel her cart down the aisle.

"I don't want to go anywhere."

Mrs. Fordham stopped, ready to breathe fire on Noel.

"I meant it when I said I like your son. He's a nice man."

"And he deserves a nice woman."

Noel raised her chin. "I am a nice woman." Mrs. Fordham looked extremely doubtful and Noel continued. "I don't want to rip him off. I would never do what his ex did. And I happen to like children. I write books for them for a living."

Mrs. Fordham cocked an eyebrow. "You do? Ben didn't tell me that."

You were probably so busy dissing me, he couldn't get a word in edgewise. "I do. It hasn't made me rich, but it's enough to cover my bills and it'll be enough to pay Ben what I owe him." Mrs. Fordham didn't say anything and Noel went on. "I'm sorry we got off on the wrong foot. I understand your wanting to protect your son from being hurt. I guess I'd feel the same way if I were you. I can only tell you I'm not out to do that. You don't know me very well, but you can believe me when I say that. I'm hoping eventually you will."

Whew, that had been a big speech. Noel found she was suddenly out of words. Mrs. Fordham didn't seem inclined to give her a hug and say, "Let's be friends," so she scurried away to the checkout stand, reminding herself that dragons didn't slay easily. If things didn't work out between her and Ben, it wouldn't matter whether or not Mrs. Fordham liked her, anyway.

If they did work out, she'd have to find Santa next year and ask him to give the woman a new heart. For now, Noel had been brave, and that was all that mattered.

She was waiting in line when Riley called in response to her earlier text. "You got your house! I'm thrilled for you."

"I know. I'm so excited." There was the understatement of the century.

"How'd you finally wear down the evil house-flipper?"

"Actually, I think it was more a case of him wearing me down. I was ready to let it go."

"I'm glad you didn't have to," Riley said.

"Me, too. And I did invite him to your reception. He's coming with."

"You are not wasting any time. When did this all happen?"

"Last night. We had a serious talk. I confessed about trying to butter him up and..."

"That worked?" Riley sounded shocked.

"What can I say? He's got a bigger heart than I ever thought. I still can't believe how everything turned out."

"I'm glad. You deserve it."

"I was wrong about him. He's been so wonderful to me, and he's so handsome and he's just..."

"Perfect?"

"Yeah, I think maybe he is. Perfect for me, anyway. I know it sounds dumb, but I keep thinking about what that Santa said when we went to see him."

"He promised you your house."

"And a good man to go with it. Kind of a strange coincidence, isn't it?"

"Yeah, I have to admit it is."

"Of course, that's all it is. I mean, who believes in Santa at our age?"

Women who talk to their imaginary characters? Marvella suggested.

"Nobody in her right mind," Riley said. "But I still believe in love."

"Considering what Sean did to you, that's saying something."

"Things have a way of working out for the best. I think there's someone better out there for me."

"Like the golf pro you ran into?" Noel couldn't resist teasing. "Are you seeing him tonight?"

"No, not until tomorrow."

"So, nothing to do tonight?"

"Only my nails. Want to hang out?"

"Absolutely."

"Come on over, then."

"Great. I'll bring the cocoa mix." It was still too early to be sure, but Noel strongly suspected they both had a promising future to toast.

Chapter Nineteen

Am I a bitch? Jo texted her sister.

Of course not, came the reply.

I don't want to go tonite. I think that means I'm a bitch.

It means you're tired. You'll have fun once you get there.

Jo hoped so. It was time to hang out with the in-laws. Mike's mom had planned the dinner for this evening so as not to interfere with Riley's big bash on Saturday. Always considerate of others, that was Georgia.

Mike's brother and sister would both be present at dinner and it would be a full-on Michael Wilton Admiration Society meeting. And rightly so. He'd given his little brother, Rich, (who was now six foot four,) countless basketball tips and spent hours on the half court in the family's backyard, helping him become the star of the Whispering Pines Otters and go on to win a basketball scholarship to Seattle U. He'd watched over his sister's love life like a hawk, chasing away the bad guys and bringing around good ones. She'd finally married one of them, his best friend, Charlie. Mike was the perfect son who never gave his parents any trouble and now he was the epitome of noble, serving his country. No one else in the family (besides her) would even dream of asking him to give up his naval career.

Jo, who'd been readily accepted and loved from the day Mike first brought her home to meet the parents, had felt her popularity slipping after she complained about his being gone so much. As a result, she wasn't looking forward to this family gathering. She also hated taking the baby out so soon. The little guy was only two weeks old. What if he caught a cold?

"He'll be fine," Mike kept telling her. What did he know?

She bundled up the baby and, with the diaper bag stocked with diapers and baby wipes, they drove to his parents' house, which was only a few blocks away from her parents' house. "Handy for holidays," Mike had predicted and he'd been right.

The Wilton home was a two-story brick Tudor with a charming arched front door accented with stone, stucco and half-timbering. Someday Jo wanted to upgrade to a house like it, with lots of character and at least three bedrooms so they could have more kids. But…what was the point of a bigger house with more bedrooms and more kids and more chaos if Mike wasn't there to share it with her?

"We are gonna have fun, aren't we?" he asked as they parked in front.

Fun had been rather a sporadic thing since his arrival. She'd swung from delight that he was back to resentment that he was back for such a short time. She'd found interesting job possibilities in the paper—everything from security guard positions to openings at the shipyard in Bremerton, which wouldn't be much more than a forty-minute commute—and printed them out, leaving them on the kitchen table for Mike. Her discoveries hadn't exactly inspired gratitude. They'd squabbled, and then made up, only to squabble some more. The baby was sleeping four hours at a stretch, which was good, but once she was awake to feed him at 2:00 a.m. she had a hard time shutting off her brain, which was bad. She was feeling sleep-deprived, put-upon and cranky—and guilty for being such a crummy navy wife. The guilt made her even crankier.

No crankiness tonight, she told herself and pulled up a smile for her husband. "Of course we are."

He smiled back. Put that smile up on Wikipedia under "relieved." Poor guy. This should be a happy time for him, back home with his family and a new baby, and here she was the human cloud, raining on everything.

He took her hand and kissed it. "I love you, babe."

"I love you, too." The big question was, did she

love him enough to hang in there if he re-upped? And did he love her enough not to? Ugh.

They got out of the car and he carried Mikey up to the house. Mike was always holding that baby, every chance he had. *Oh, Mike, how can you stand the thought of leaving him?*

"Well, look who's here," boomed his dad, throwing the front door open wide. "Come in. Let's see the little bugger."

The scent of a freshly cut tree rushed out to greet them. The folks still believed in putting up a real fir, and inhaling the fragrance, Jo understood why. Still, she'd stick with her fake tree. It was a good one and she didn't have to worry about picking needles out of the carpet.

They were barely inside before Mike's dad had the baby. Darrel Wilton was as wide as he was tall, and in his big arms the baby looked practically microscopic.

Georgia was right behind him. "How sweet. You know, he looks just like Mike when he was a baby. Here, let's get that snowsuit off him before he roasts to death," she said and took the baby into the living room, laying him on the couch and stripping him out of his fleecy outerwear like a pro. After three kids, of course, she was.

Brother Rich and his wife were already there, and so was Mike's sister, Tanya, with her husband and toddler in tow. Everyone was dressed in holiday sweaters and beaming. A huge tree sat in the corner, decked out in colored lights and a lifetime of collected ornaments, a few presents already under it, awaiting the big day. It made Jo think of a movie set with actors ready to spring into action.

Which they did the minute Mike and Jo entered the room. Mike and Rich exchanged bro hugs and Tanya hung on to him as if he'd been gone for years. Her son came up to the couch to check out his cousin and sneezed, and Jo almost had a heart attack.

She practically snatched him away from Georgia.

"Don't worry," said Tanya. "We think it's allergies."

Don't worry? Was she kidding? "I don't want to take any chances," Jo said. "He needs to eat, anyway," she added and slipped away to the guest bedroom to nurse Mikey and compose herself. Oh, man, it was going to be a long night.

It was, indeed. Everyone wanted to hold the baby and Jo fretted with each new pair of germy hands that took him.

When she wasn't worrying about the baby, she was feeling guilty that she hadn't given her husband a better welcome home. His brother had brought Mike's favorite wine; his mom had made pot roast with all the trimmings, his favorite meal. Why hadn't Jo done that? His sister had made fudge and his dad was talking about a guys' night out at the bowling alley. The prince was back.

Well, it was good that someone was fussing over him, since his own wife hadn't done much of anything but complain.

"How long are you home, son?" his dad asked. He asked the same question every time.

The answer was the same. "Three months."

"It always goes so fast," Georgia said, rubbing his arm.

I'm not the only one who hates to lose him, Jo thought. Why, in all these years, had that never occurred to her? Of course, it had to be hard for his mother to let go. She was so upbeat though, never complained. In fact, her mother-in-law was so darned perfect that if she didn't know better Jo would have sworn she was an android.

After dinner, it was time for the Wilton Christmas tradition and out came Georgia's DVD of *It's a Wonderful Life*. Jo had heard of the movie but never seen it before she met Mike. She sure knew it well now, and while it had been okay the first couple of times, after all these years...ugh. But this was Mike's big homecoming dinner and no way was she going to spoil it.

"Before we start the movie, we have a little something for you," Georgia said. She got a small present from under the tree and handed it to Mike. He opened it and pulled out an ornament in the shape of a bear holding a blue blanket. *Mikey's First Christmas* was printed on the blanket.

Mike grinned as if he'd been given a million dollars. "Look, babe. His first Christmas present."

"It's really cute," Jo said. And it had been sweet of Georgia to get it. Jo suspected they'd receive a similar offering from her parents. No one could say this baby wouldn't be loved, with two families to dote on him and a dad who already adored him.

And would be gone in three months. Jo sighed.

"Oh, you're tired," Georgia said.

Yeah, she was. Both physically and emotionally.

"Would you like me to take the baby?"

Georgia was dying to hold her grandson. Jo turned the baby over to her, and sat next to Mike on the couch and prepared to be bored. He placed an arm around her and snuggled her against him and for a moment she forgot to be cranky. She had her husband beside her, they had a new baby and it was Christmas. How could she be cranky at Christmas?

The opening credits began to roll and the chatter died down as everyone settled in to watch Clarence the angel get his wings and George Bailey get a clue. Jo wasn't much for analyzing stories—she came to Arlene's book club but mostly for the wine and appetizers; half the time she didn't get around to reading the book—but tonight she noticed something in the movie's plot that she'd never noticed before. (Besides the fact that dirty rotten Mr. Potter never got caught taking the Baileys' money.) George Bailey had a good life, but he never followed his dream. Even though he kept trying, other people continued to impose on him. And eventually he exploded and started knocking things over and snapping at people and running off looking for a bridge to jump from.

Mike loved the navy. What if she imposed her wants on him and made him quit? How would he deal with that in the long run? Would he feel he'd been cheated out of doing what he really wanted to do? Would he explode one day? Would she ruin his life and would he resent her?

The movie ended with all the townspeople happily caroling and helping George Bailey in his moment of crisis and, like all the other women in the family, Jo found herself wiping her eyes.

"I love that movie," Georgia said with a sigh. Hot news flash. Not. She said that every year.

"Why do you like it so much, Mom?" Rich asked. "I mean, it's pretty sappy. Hardly anybody my age even knows about it."

"That's a shame," Georgia said. "I suppose it is compared to what we see today." She kissed Mikey's head. "But I like the message behind it. Everyone's life counts. Everyone has a purpose."

Jo suddenly felt squirmy.

As she and Mike drove home, thoughts chased each other around her brain like Sugar Plum Fairies on speed. What if a navy career was Mike's purpose? Did she want to cheat him out of it? Was her life all that bad when he was gone? She wasn't incompetent. She could handle Mikey on her own, and surely he'd adjust to Daddy coming and going, like so many other kids whose parents were in the service. The country needed good men like her husband. It was wrong of her to stop him from doing his part to keep her and those they loved safe. She was a selfish bitch.

"You're quiet," he observed.

"Just thinking."

"About what?"

"About us."

His hands tightened on the steering wheel. "Yeah?"

"I'm sorry I've been so awful lately." The words had trouble crawling up her throat.

"You've been through a lot."

That was Mike, always giving her the benefit of the doubt. "It was childbirth, not chemo." Jo shook her head. "I've been selfish. I don't want you to be like George Bailey."

"Huh?" He shot her a puzzled look.

"I don't want to keep you from your dreams. If you need to reenlist, go for it. I'll support you." Oh, Lord, what was she saying?

What she needed to say. This marriage wasn't simply about her and what *she* wanted. And it wasn't just about what *she* thought was best for them. She and Mike were a team, and lately she hadn't been much of a team player.

"Are you sure?"

"Yes." Other wives in her position might've had a different answer, but she knew that for them this was the right one. Although she wasn't happy about it, she'd get there. Or close, anyway. Eventually.

"What changed your mind?"

"I don't want you to be like poor George Bailey, never getting to live your dream."

"It's just a movie, Jo."

"I know. But this is real and I don't want you to

look back years from now and say, 'I could've been so much more if it wasn't for my wife.'"

"I would never say that," he protested.

"Maybe not to me but you would to yourself. That's not how I want us to be."

He nodded and his grip on the steering wheel loosened. They got home and she fed the baby and put him to bed. Then she and Mike went to bed.

He held her in his arms and kissed her hair. "Thanks, babe. That took a lot."

She smiled at him. "What can I tell you? I'm a sucker for a man in uniform."

Chapter Twenty

Maybe it was crazy to be happy on the day she should have been getting married, but Riley was. Response to her invitations had been enthusiastic and she was going to have a full house for her party. Most of her extended family except the farthest-flung were coming, as well as her friends and fellow teachers (except Emily), and the senior center was bringing a busload. Even a few of the more spry residents of the nursing home would be attending. Her non-wedding reception was the talk of the town.

It had especially been the talk of the teachers' lounge. "I bought a new dress for the occasion," Marge had informed her. "And I'm making Leo wear a suit."

"That'll be something to see," her best friend Stella had said. "I still can't believe you're doing this," she'd told Riley just as Emily walked into the room.

"There's no sense wasting a good party," Riley had replied, "and I may as well celebrate my lucky escape," she'd added, which made Emily frown.

"We're happy to help you," Stella had said. "I think we should pin a medal on you for courage under fire. Here you've had to put up with seeing that woman every day but you managed to be civilized. If my friend had betrayed me like that, I'd have pulled her hair out."

Emily's face had turned as red as a Christmas stocking and she'd fled the room.

"Stella, she heard you," Marge had scolded.

The offender had merely shrugged. "The truth hurts. It's about time we stopped tiptoeing around the subject, anyway."

For a moment Riley had felt almost sorry for Emily. Almost. She hoped Sean was worth it for her.

And that was the last thought she gave to Sean and Emily. She had more important things to take care of, like getting ready for her big day.

Jo was worried about taking the baby out again after the family visit the night before, convinced that he was going to come down with a cold any minute. So at five o'clock on Saturday afternoon, Riley went to her place to get fixed up, bearing her wedding gown and all the trimmings.

Mike let her in. He had the baby in one arm and hugged her with the other.

"Welcome home," Riley said, juggling her party duds.

"Thanks. It's good to be home."

Good to be home. That was a positive sign. Maybe he and Jo had worked out their differences regarding his reenlistment. She pointed to the sleeping baby. "Look at you. Daddy of the year."

"I'm workin' on it. Go on back to the bedroom. Jo's got a bunch of makeup and curling irons and shit ready for you. Us guys'll hang out here and watch ESPN," he said and went to the living room.

The living room resembled a magazine layout with everything in place. The bedroom was just as neat. Even the bed was made. "How do you keep this place looking like a model home?" Riley asked as she laid her gown on the bed. "Didn't you give birth two weeks ago?"

"We're not that messy. Well, the kitchen is. Mike's been cooking."

"It must be great to have him home," Riley said. Mike looked happy, her sister looked happy. Another positive sign.

"It is. Come into the bathroom and let's do something with your hair."

"So, everything's okay with you guys?" Riley persisted as she followed her sister into the bathroom.

"Everything's great."

"He's not reenlisting?"

"He is. I told him he could."

Riley practically fell onto the edge of the tub. "Seriously?"

Jo shrugged. "I was being unrealistic. You know, in the end I want him to do what he needs to do. I want him to be happy. He'd want the same for me."

"So you can live with him being gone."

"I've done it for eight years. I'll manage. And it's not like I don't have a support system in place. You guys will all be there for us, and so will Mike's family. I'm sure Mikey will never have a Little League game that doesn't have somebody there rooting for him. And it's not like I'll be lacking in childcare. Heck, if Mom had her way we'd move in with her and Dad, and she'd watch Mikey twenty-four-seven."

Jo did a good job of making it sound like a breeze to let her husband go every three months but Riley knew better. "You're pretty amazing, sis."

Jo shrugged. "Not really, not compared to the wives who've been doing this for a lot longer than me and with more kids to handle. I guess when a man enlists, so does his family. Anyway, that's enough about me. Today it's all about you." She picked up the curling iron. "Come on over here and let's make your hair look fabulous. Up with some soft curls falling on one side of your face, right?"

"That's what I'm thinking."

"Okay, then," Jo said and got to work. "By the way, if you want to talk about amazing, I'd say you've been pretty amazing yourself. You not only bounced back from getting hurt, you also soared, and I'm proud of you. We all are. I hope you know that."

Riley looked at their reflections in the mirror—her stylish sister and her, about to become stylish (for the evening, anyway). They were both smiling. Caption this moment *Happiness*. Life had its downs, its sad times and bad times, but in moments like this they faded into the shadows.

She reached up and squeezed her sister's hand. "Thanks, sis. I love you."

"Right back atcha," Jo said and got back to styling her hair.

Twenty minutes later it was a thing of beauty. They moved on to makeup and in another ten minutes it was time to shed her blouse and jeans and get into her gown. Finally, made up, sprayed, perfumed, gowned and adorned with Grammy's pearls, Riley studied herself in Jo's full-length bedroom mirror. "Wow."

"Wow is right," Jo said. "You look like a princess."

"I feel like a princess," Riley said, grinning at her lace bodice and the sparkly tulle skirt. The faux fur stole was enough to keep her warm on her way to the party.

"You really should wait and let us drive you to the club."

"No. I want to get there early and check everything out," Riley said. And perhaps allow herself a moment of…reflection. Not mourning. She wasn't going to mourn the loss of Sean. She refused. This was going to be a happy night.

"Okay," Jo said dubiously, handing over the bag she'd put Riley's other clothes in. "Be careful with the hair and for heaven's sake lift your skirt when you get out of the car."

"I will," Riley assured her. "Thanks for making me beautiful."

"You already were beautiful. See you in an hour."

Another hug and Riley was ready to roll.

"You look stellar," Mike said when she came back down the hall in her gown. "Sean was a fool."

She murmured her thanks and sailed out the door, Princess Riley going to the ball.

About halfway to the ball, Princess Riley's coach had a flat tire. "Oh, no," she groaned. "Seriously?"

She stepped carefully out of the car and checked the back left tire. Yep. Flat as a pancake. How could that happen? And on her non-wedding day of all days! "Just shoot me now." So much for getting to the golf club early. She'd be lucky if she even made it there on time.

A truck rolled by with a couple of teenage boys in it who lowered the window and hooted at her. "Thanks for helping," she called after them. Sheesh. Where was Prince Charming when you needed him?

Stopping right now. Except the car pulling up behind her didn't contain Prince Charming. It held Prince Poop and his new princess—who wisely stayed in the car while Sean got out. "Riley, are you okay?"

Resentment reared its ugly head but she smacked it away. "Actually, I am now."

He had the grace to look chagrined. "I'm a shit. What can I say?"

"Not much. But you know what, no hard feelings," she added. "I forgive you." She glanced over at Emily, who was hiding. "Both of you."

He nodded, obviously embarrassed. "Looks like you've got a flat."

He didn't say anything about her wearing a wedding dress, the coward. Emily had probably told him all about the party.

"Flip your trunk."

"You don't need to help. I'll call Triple A."

"I'm here and I'm happy to help."

"No, it's okay."

He took a step closer. "Riles, I really am sorry about what happened. Let me at least change your tire so you can get to your party. You look great, by the way."

"Thanks." She hadn't wanted him to see her in her wedding dress until the big moment. Funny. Now there was no big moment, but here he was, seeing her in it. Did he feel the tiniest bit of regret?

Did it matter?

Another car pulled up, a patrol car, which was becoming an all-too-familiar sight. Out stepped Officer Knight. "Is there a problem here?"

"I had a flat tire," Riley explained.

Officer Knight seemed confused. "You're getting married, after all?"

Sean's face reddened and Riley could feel hers heating up, as well. "No," she said, not looking at Sean. "But I'm having a party, anyway. Why waste such a fancy gown?"

Officer Knight grinned. "Good for you. Well, let's get you on your way."

"I've got it, Officer," Sean said. "Riles, pop the trunk."

"Oh, Officer Knight, this is my former fiancé,"

Riley said, taking perverse pleasure in introducing the offending former groom. No resentment—really—but, hey, she was human.

Officer Knight didn't offer a hand to shake. In fact, he looked as if he'd like to cite Sean for having the nerve to stop.

"We, um, it didn't work out," Sean said lamely and darted a glance at Emily, as if hoping for some kind of telepathic moral support. No support there. She was still slumped in the passenger seat of his car, trying to be invisible.

Yet another person joined the party. Here came Lizbeth Parker, girl reporter, smelling a good story. "Hi, there," she said to the three of them. "What's going on?"

"Nothing, Lizbeth," said Officer Knight. "Move along."

"I had a flat tire on the way to my non-wedding reception," Riley told her. Then couldn't resist adding, "My former fiancé stopped to change my tire. Wasn't that sweet of him?" Was it totally evil to put Sean in the hot seat? Would Santa cross her off his list for being naughty?

Lizbeth grinned, a coconspirator in naughtiness. "Do tell."

"I guess if you don't need me, I'll leave," Sean said.

"I don't." And wasn't it a relief to realize that!

He skedaddled and Officer Knight got busy changing Riley's tire while Lizbeth Parker pumped her for more details.

Okay, this probably sounded stupid. Riley shrugged as she finished. "It was too late to cancel the venue."

"This will make such an inspiring story," Lizbeth gushed. "Can I take your picture? I just happen to have my camera in the car."

Why not? Practically everyone in town knew she'd been dumped and was now a non-bride. If her story could inspire someone else who'd gotten her heart broken, why not? "Sure."

Lizbeth hurried to grab her camera. "Stay where you are by the tire," she told Officer Knight. "Let's get you in the picture, too."

He shook his head but cooperated. After all, this kind of thing was good publicity for the police department.

"This is really impressive," Lizbeth said after she'd finished with her shots. "I bet that party's going to be something else."

Hint, hint. "Would you like to come?" Riley asked.

Lizbeth smiled. "Would I? Oh, yeah. You're going to be a local hero by the time I'm done with you," she promised.

That would be a change from Lizbeth's last write-up on her, but Riley didn't care about being a local hero. She just wanted to have a good time tonight and provide a fun evening for a lot of other people, as well. The tire fixed she thanked Officer Knight, promised to throw the non-bridal bouquet in Lizbeth's direction and then got in the car and finished her journey to the club.

The Olympic Room looked elegant and inviting

with candles shimmering on linen-clad tables, crystal winking in the candlelight. There, in one corner of the room, sat her cake with its gold ribbon and red poinsettias, surrounded with more candles. Two buckets dressed up with ribbons and containing red carnations waited by the door, ready to go home with the guests when they left. The whole scene was fit for a fairy tale.

Without Prince Charming. Who needed him, anyway?

Sharla Green was there, checking everything off on her list. At the sight of Riley she hurried over. "You look beautiful."

"Thanks." Riley took a little spin, making her skirt flare out. "I feel beautiful."

"I'm glad you went ahead with this," Sharla said. "I hope you have a wonderful evening."

"I will. I'm glad I didn't cancel the party."

"That's the spirit," Sharla said encouragingly. "Everything's ready in the kitchen. If there's anything you need, I'll be around."

Riley thanked her and then went over to the window to enjoy the view. Here it was, the big day, the day she'd been planning for so long, the day she'd thought was ruined. She did feel a moment of melancholy, but that was all she allowed herself. Things hadn't worked out with Sean, but surely in the end it was for the best. If they'd been meant to be together, he'd never have left.

"Here's our girl!"

She turned to see Mom and Dad and Grammy

entering the room, coats over their wedding finery, all beaming at her. Mr. Right might have been all wrong, but you could survive that when you had such a loving family to fall back on. She hurried across the room and hugged them all.

"You are a vision," Mom said. "Jo did a beautiful job of getting you ready."

"You forgot one thing." Grammy held out a small silver gift bag with spangled tissue paper peeking out of it.

It wasn't hard to guess. "My garter?"

"I made it for you to wear. You may as well break it in tonight."

Riley hugged her again. "You're the best grandma ever."

Grammy smiled. "I know. But we won't tell that to the other grandma."

Who had flown in from Arizona, along with her third husband. "I won't," Riley said.

"Give me your coats," Dad said, "and I'll take them to the coat check."

While he went to get rid of their coats, Riley slipped on her garter.

"Hey, there are some things a brother doesn't want to see," called Harold, walking into the room, his wife beside him and their daughter, Caitlyn, bouncing ahead, adorable in her red velveteen flower girl dress.

Riley smiled and lowered her skirt then held out her arms to her niece, who ran to her gleefully. "Don't you look pretty in your party dress."

"I get to stay up late," Caitlyn informed her.

"She'll be buzzing with cake and mints, anyway, so what the heck," said Harold, who came up and hugged Riley. "You look good, sis."

"Better than good," added his wife, hugging her, too.

"I feel better than good," she said. "This is going to be fun."

New guests arrived, cousins from Seattle, bearing gifts.

"Oh, no. No presents!" Riley exclaimed. "I thought Mom told you."

"She did," said Riley's cousin Melanie, "but we figured you ought to at least get some cool stuff out of this."

More guests came with more presents and the same attitude.

"I feel guilty," Riley told her mother.

"Don't," Mom said. "Think of it as an early Christmas."

Soon the room was full of people, some milling around visiting in groups, others finding their seats at the tables.

"This is quite the party," Mrs. Wooster said, resplendent in a sequined gown resurrected from the early sixties and a purple boa. "I hope you're going to toss the bouquet. I feel lucky."

Jack and his grandma showed up next. "Aren't you lovely!" exclaimed Margaret, taking Riley's hands. "Isn't she lovely, Jack?"

Jack looked her up and down appreciatively. "She sure is."

Margaret leaned over and whispered in Riley's ear, "You know, he's not seeing anyone."

It was rather a loud whisper and judging by the grin on Jack's face, Riley knew he'd heard. She smiled back at him and said, "What a coincidence. I'm not, either."

"Yeah, what a coincidence," he said, and the look he gave her set her nerve endings tingling.

Grammy with her nose for potential romance joined them. "And who is this?"

Riley introduced Jack and his grandma, who was happy to tell Grammy the story of her life.

"A dancer. You'll have to show me some of your moves on the dance floor," Grammy said.

"This could get embarrassing," Jack whispered. "You may be sorry you invited us."

"I don't think so," she said and he smiled again. "I'll just have to distract you by dancing with you."

That sounded like an excellent idea.

Noel entered a moment later, dazzling in her green velvet bridesmaid dress and towing a handsome, supersized man in a black tuxedo. The no-longer-evil house-flipper.

"This is Ben," she told Riley, stating the obvious.

Ben seemed at a loss for words. Hardly surprising since he didn't know her and here she was, a bride without a groom, running around in her wedding dress. He did manage a smile and a "Thanks for having me."

"Thanks for coming. Any friend of Noel's is a friend of mine." If the look he and Noel exchanged was any indication, she wouldn't be surprised if her friend beat her to the altar.

Seniors arrived by the busload. Literally. Riley felt a rush of happiness as she saw the delighted expressions on so many faces.

"This is quite the shindig," Grammy's friend Felix said to her. "I hope I'm going to get a chance to dance with the bride."

"I think that can be arranged," Riley told him.

Soon the tables were filled with celebrants all dressed to the nines, and Riley sat at the head table with her parents and sister and brother and their spouses. Baby Mikey was at home, safe from germs, with Georgia watching over him. Riley suspected Jo wouldn't stay long, but she was grateful to have her here, even if it was just for a little while. The way she and Mike were smiling at each other and holding hands, they could have been the bride and groom at this party.

Lizbeth Parker had made it, too, and was present with her photographer, who snapped pictures while she interviewed the various guests. She stopped by Riley's table and interviewed Mom and Dad and Harold and Grammy.

Then Lizbeth approached Jo, who shook her head and refused to comment, saying only, "You'll hear what I have to say soon enough."

Soon enough came after dinner and before the cutting of the cake. Jo had already informed both the bride and the stand-in maid of honor that she was going to give the toast. "I claim the right as sister and almost matron of honor, which I would have been if I hadn't gotten pregnant."

She'd said it with a smile and Noel had been more than happy to hand over that duty, confessing that the thought of having to give a speech in front of all those guests just about had her in hives.

So, after the meal was finished and the champagne for toasting had been poured, Jo took the microphone and took center stage. "Of course, you all know why we're here. We're celebrating the fact that my sister is still single. So if any of you handsome men are in the market..." She paused long enough for everyone to chuckle. "Seriously, it's hard when you think you've got your life all figured out, when you've made plans and those plans don't happen. When you think you've found the love of your life and it turns out that maybe he wasn't, after all."

Here was a cheery little speech. Riley's eyes began to fill with tears.

"But that didn't keep my sister down," Jo continued. "She's Helium Woman and she was born to rise above her circumstances. And she's done that with grace and class. This may not have been the party she originally planned, but I'd say it's still a raving success."

"Hear, hear," called out Grammy, and everyone cheered and applauded.

"So here's to my sister, my hero. I can hardly wait to see who the real love of your life turns out to be. To Riley."

The tears were spilling over, but these were the happy kind. Riley blew her sister a kiss as Jo saluted her with her champagne glass.

"To Riley," everyone echoed.

The hero of the hour. Wow.

Not to be outdone, her brother took the microphone next. "As usual, my sister stole the words right out of my mouth," he teased, looking in Jo's direction. "But I want to add my two cents." He turned to Riley. "You look great, sis. Next time we're all doing this you'll be with the right man. Whoever that will be, he's gonna be one lucky son of a…gun," he finished, seeing Mom's warning frown. "You're really something."

"Amen to that," called Grammy.

Her father was the last to speak. "No man likes to see his daughter suffer, and I know this has been hard on you, Riley. But as your sister said, you've risen above your circumstances and I couldn't be more proud. We all are. We love you," he finished and raised his glass to her and once again everyone applauded.

Who knew being rejected would turn out to be such a good thing? Except all these wonderful speeches were going to end up ruining her makeup.

She stood and grabbed the microphone before anyone else could catch speech fever. "Thanks, family, for those kind words. That's enough already, though. You all are making my head swell. I threw this party because—what can I say?—I didn't want to waste such a nice dinner." Everyone chuckled and then she surprised herself by adding, "You know, I was so into planning the perfect wedding I almost forgot it's more important to have the perfect life. You can't do that if you're with the wrong person. In fact, I'm not sure you can do that with any person if you're not happy with yourself first. Well, tonight I'm pretty happy just being me, so I think I'm onto something."

The crowd burst into applause, confirming that, yes, indeed, she was. Everyone was happy and her heart was full. Did it get any better than that?

Maybe it did when you included a groom. The right groom. But for now this was enough.

"I'm so glad you could all join me and I hope you have a wonderful time. We've got plenty of cake and lots of champagne and I want to see it all gone by the end of the night, so enjoy. Now, let's dance."

"I claim the first dance," her father called out, walking out onto the floor to join her.

The DJ played "What a Wonderful World," and as she smiled up at him she was struck by how true the words were. It really was a wonderful world when you lost the self-pity shades and opened your eyes to everything around you that was good.

"Looks like you're doing okay," Dad said.

She smiled. "I am. I'm going to be all right, Daddy."

"I never doubted it," he said.

The music ended, Dad bowed over her hand to much clapping and hooting, and Harold took his place as the DJ started the only other song she'd requested, Bruno Mars singing "I Want to Marry You."

Most of the guests got it, but after the song was over Grammy approached her, very concerned. "What a thoughtless thing to play! You shouldn't pay that man and I'm going to give him an earful."

"It's fine, Grammy," Riley said. "I asked for it. It was a joke."

Grammy frowned. "Some joke."

"Okay, everyone," the DJ said, "we're going to do the Electric Slide."

The staple of all weddings. Riley knew it would put a crowd on the dance floor. It did indeed, and many of them were from the senior center.

"That's my song," Grammy said and hurried to join the others.

Riley saw that Jack's grandmother was out there, too, and once the music started she proved that she still had the moves even if they were slow, shimmying with her walker as the others moved around her. Grammy, queen of the senior center's line dancers, was right next to her, and the two women exchanged smiles. *Oh, yeah, we're good.*

When it was time to cut the cake she let her niece do the honors and feed her a bite.

After that, the DJ played "Better When I'm Dancin'" by Meghan Trainor and they all hit the dance floor again. Meanwhile, Lizbeth Parker made notes and her photographer happily recorded everything for posterity. Or at least for the Whispers section of the paper.

"Look at you," Jack said when the music slowed down and he pulled her away from the cake and onto the dance floor. "You're not exactly the picture of a jilted bride."

"I'm having fun."

"I can see that." He drew her closer and started them swaying. "Me, too. This is the coolest nonwedding reception I've ever been to."

She cocked an eyebrow. "How many have you been to?"

"None. But I can't imagine anything being as good as this. You'll have a hard time following it when it comes to the real thing."

Her smile faltered slightly. "If there ever is a real thing."

He lowered his face, kissing close and whispered, "There will be. Your brother was right. You really are something." Then, before she could form a reply, he kissed her. What a kiss it was, hot enough to melt the frosting off her lips. "You taste like cake," he said with a grin.

"That may be all the cake you get. It's going fast."

"Well, then, I'd better have a second helping."

The second helping was even tastier than the first.

The dance ended and old Andy from the golf

club was on hand to tap Jack on the shoulder. "Here, sonny, let someone with a little more experience show you how it's done." He spun Riley away and dipped her, and two of the older women standing nearby sighed.

"Don't hog him all night, young lady," said one.

They didn't need to worry. Andy never got another chance, not with Jack monopolizing her.

The gang from the nursing home left around nine, and Riley sent all the women home with carnations. By ten o'clock many of the seniors were starting to wear out.

"It's getting past my bedtime," Mrs. Wooster said to Riley. "When are you going to throw the bouquet?"

"Right now," Riley said and was glad she'd had the florist go ahead and make her a small bouquet of red roses.

The DJ made the announcement, and cousins and friends, including Noel, gathered for the time-honored custom. Grammy and Mrs. Wooster were both there, too, trying to nudge each other out of the way. With all their nudging, they missed the big moment and Noel caught it. Blushing furiously, she glanced at Ben Fordham.

So did Riley and she saw that he was smiling. It looked as if Noel was going to have a very merry Christmas.

Riley was beginning to suspect she was going to have a pretty good one, too. "Got your phone num-

ber from your grandma," Jack said to her when he
and his grandmother came to say goodbye. "Think
we can arrange to run into each other again? Only
without the cars."

"I think that could be arranged," she said, and he
smiled and kissed her on the cheek.

"Thank you for a lovely time, my dear," Margaret said, taking both of Riley's hands. "You're a
wonderful young woman and I hope we'll be seeing more of you."

"You will, Gram," Jack said, winking at Riley.

Jo left, too, anxious to get home to the baby. "It
was fun, sis. Don't know how you'll ever top this."

"How about by having a groom next time?" Riley
cracked.

"Good idea," Jo said.

The party went on for another couple of hours,
but after Jack left it all felt a bit anticlimactic. Once
everyone had gone, the presents were loaded into her
trunk and her backseat, as well as her parents' trunk.
Then she was driving home alone in her wedding
gown and the sad realization hit that she was not
going to get her wedding night or her honeymoon.

So she decided that on the first long weekend of
the New Year, she'd book herself a short trip somewhere for a non-honeymoon, even if it meant digging out the old credit card. She'd find someplace
affordable, some quaint B & B in Victoria, perhaps.
She'd take the Victoria Clipper and go have high tea
at the Empress Hotel. If Noel went with her they

could split the cost. Or she could go to the ocean and storm-watch. Something. She'd do something.

Back at her apartment she took one last look at herself in the bedroom mirror and admired her finery. She'd had fun and she'd given a lot of pleasure to a lot of older people. All in all, a memorable evening.

What were Sean and Emily doing now?

She frowned at her reflection. "Who cares, right?"

Right.

Her phone rang at eight the next morning. "You're in the Sunday edition!" Jo announced. "That reporter made you sound like a cross between Wonder Woman and Joan of Arc. And the pictures are great. You need to call her and ask for copies. Meanwhile, Mike's out buying another paper for you. You're probably in the online edition, too."

Riley hurried to the little desk in the spare room where she kept her laptop and brought up the page. Sure enough, there she was in the Whispers section. The article was captioned Who Needs a Groom?

Riley grinned. Who, indeed?

Although she still wanted one, down the road. But next time she was going to be really sure. Any future groom would have to sign a contract. In blood.

Everyone at church was talking about the big bash, and when Riley stopped at Pineland afterward to pick up some rolls for dinner at her folks', the checker could hardly stop gushing about how clever and brave she was.

"I just found out that my boyfriend cheated on me. I'm gonna kick his ass to the curb," the woman said.

"Do it," Riley told her. "You deserve better." So did she and she was willing to wait for it.

The family was about to have dessert when Jack called.

"I bet I know who that is," Jo said as Riley hurried away from the table.

"So, you had your non-wedding reception. I was thinking you might want to do something for your non-honeymoon."

Sex.

They'd just met. Where had that come from? Oh, yeah, the whole honeymoon thing. *You're not in a hurry*, she reminded herself and tried not to picture Jack and her checking into a honeymoon suite in some fancy hotel in Hawaii.

"What did you have in mind?" she asked.

"I was thinking maybe dinner at La Rive Gauche Paris. You can pretend you're in France."

Ooh, la, la. "That sounds great."

"They're closed tomorrow night, so how about Tuesday?" Jack Logan didn't waste any time.

She liked a man who was efficient. "I just happen to have Tuesday night free."

They made their arrangements and she returned to the dining room.

"I know that smile," Jo said, pointing at her. "Somebody's got a date."

Harold frowned. "Don't you be rushing into anything, sis."

"Don't worry, I won't." *Define rushing.*

Tuesday night, dressed in a black dress she'd borrowed from Jo and wearing Noel's heels of death, she tottered into the fanciest and most expensive restaurant in town on the arm of Jack Logan. Fancy chandeliers and drapes, elegantly carved chairs gathered around linen-topped, candlelit tables. The whole place screamed, *If you want to eat here, you'll have to sell a child.* The restaurant had been in business for two years but she'd never been inside it. Sean had certainly never taken her here.

"This is beautiful, but it looks expensive," she said, feeling guilty about Jack spending so much money on a first date.

"It's your honeymoon. You do stuff like this on your honeymoon," he said.

The maître d' seated them at a table for two in a quiet corner. Actually, the whole place was quiet. There were very few people here on a Tuesday evening.

The sommelier appeared and he and Jack consulted on wines and pairings. "What do you think?" Jack asked Riley.

She thought she was a long way from The Rusty Saw. "I think you know your way around a wine list. Carry on. That was impressive," she told him after the sommelier had left.

"Was it?"

"You must come here a lot."

"Never been here in my life. If you want to know the truth, The Rusty Saw and The Tree House are more my style."

"Mine, too," she said. "Still, this was really kind of you."

"Not so much kind as trying to make a good impression. Improve my game from the first time we met," he added with a grin. "Seriously, I wish I hadn't been such a shit on our first encounter."

"Our first two encounters," she couldn't resist saying.

"Not my shining hour. But you gotta admit, they were memorable."

Memorable. Yes, they were.

"Like your party Saturday night. Too bad your ex didn't get a chance to see you in your dress and get a look at what he missed."

"Actually, he did," Riley said and told him about her flat tire.

"Oh, man, that's classic," he said when she'd finished. "Guess I'm gonna have to go online and read all about it."

Their wine arrived, along with the appetizers. She took one bite of artichoke tartlet and was in heaven. "I could get used to this."

"What, being out with me?" he teased.

That, too.

As dinner progressed, so did their conversation. They covered everything from why he became a golf pro ("Love the sport but knew I'd never be bringing it at Pebble Beach. This is the next best thing.") to what she wanted to do now that her life was wide-open again. ("Travel and see the world. Sean was so busy with the gym we had a hard time setting a date for our honeymoon.")

"I hate to question your taste, since you're out with me, but what did you ever see in that guy? He sounds like a real asshole," Jack said around a mouth full of Duck à l'Orange.

Riley pushed away her plate. "You know, he's really not. It's been so easy to put all the blame on Sean, but if we were perfect together, we'd probably still be together."

"Or not. Let's stick with him being an asshole."

She couldn't help smiling. "I'll drink to that," she said and raised her wineglass in salute.

Dinner finished and the bill paid, Jack said, "Okay, ready for the next part of your honeymoon?"

Sex? She nodded.

"Let's go, then," he said and escorted her out of the restaurant.

"Where are we going?" she asked as he tooled his Hummer down Pine Street.

"To a sandy beach, of course."

The sandy beach turned out to be the boat launch at the park. The wind was cold and mean, batting her hair in all directions and sneaking up her coat with icy fingers.

"Just like Hawaii," she quipped as he pulled her close for warmth.

"Okay, some ideas are better in your head than in real life," he admitted.

"How about you come back to my apartment and warm up with some hot buttered rum? And cookies. Did I mention that I like to bake?"

"No kidding. Did I mention that I like to eat?"

Back at the apartment she made them both drinks and put some cookies on a plate. Then she turned on her electric fireplace and they relaxed on the couch. "Did anyone tell you this is fake?" he joked, pointing at it.

She shrugged. "It's better than nothing." She stared at the faux flame and wondered if that was how she'd wound up with Sean. He'd looked like the right man for her, but really, they hadn't had all that much in common. Had she settled? Had he? She looked at Jack. "I seem to settle for less quite a lot. I don't want to do that anymore."

"I don't think you should. At least find someone who wants to get away for a weekend," he added with a smile.

"Or for a non-honeymoon. Thank you for a wonderful one tonight."

He set down his mug and began playing with a lock of her hair, which started a fluttering in her chest. "Honeymoons usually last more than one day. What are you doing tomorrow?"

"Making you dinner."

"I could go for that," he said. "I could go for you. But then, you've already figured that out, haven't you?"

Suddenly shy, she focused on the plate of cookies sitting on the coffee table. *How many cookies will Riley and Jack eat before Jack kisses her?*

None! Merrrry Christmas.

Chapter Twenty-One

The Tuesday before Christmas was the annual children's holiday party at Whispering Pines Public Library. That meant treats and a guest appearance by a special author. This year's special author was going to be Noel, who'd be reading from *Marvella and the Lonely Little Tree*, which had been published the previous year.

She loved doing events like this. Back in the spring she'd gone to Liberty Bay Books in Poulsbo when her spring release, *Marvella to the Rescue*, had come out, to read and sign copies. She'd also done several school visits and enjoyed them immensely. While she wasn't keen on performing for big crowds of adults, children were another matter entirely. Like her, they loved Marvella. And since Noel was Marvella's creator, they loved and respected Noel, always sitting with rapt attention as she read from her books.

This afternoon she came bearing party favors— small coloring books that Noel had designed herself. They featured Marvella, of course, and some of the

characters she'd helped, with inspiring sayings be-
neath, such as "When you're afraid, it's okay to call
for help," and "You can do so many things!" This
last one was under a drawing of Marvella in the
center ring at a circus, wearing a tutu and standing
one-legged on a cantering horse, a big smile on her
face and her dragon arms thrown wide.

She arrived to find a crowd of young children
waiting for her, trying to curb their impatience for
the fun to begin while their parents chatted. Yes, this
was her world. She smiled as she walked in the door.

"Noel, I'm so glad you could do this," said Tina,
the librarian. "We've got a great turnout. But then
I'm not surprised. Everyone loves Marvella. I can't
keep the books on the shelf. We're going to order
more."

This was good news. She wasn't Dr. Seuss yet,
but like her friend Suzanne Selfors always told her,
it took time to make a name for yourself. And meanwhile, she was a bit of a celebrity right here with the
children in Whispering Pines.

A little girl came bouncing up to her, a book
clutched to her chest. "Hi! I'm Lola. My mama
bought me your book."

"Well, that was very nice of your mama," Noel
said.

The mother was right behind her daughter. "She
loves your books."

"I'm so glad."

"I'm not afraid of the monster in my closet anymore," said Lola. "Mama and Marvella chased him away."

"I'm glad to hear it," Noel said with a smile.

She happened to look up and, oh, yuck, speaking of monsters, in walked Mrs. Fordham. Noel's smile caved in on itself. Just the person she didn't want to see. Honestly, the only thing that kept Ben from being perfect was his mother.

She had her grandson in tow, and Timmy was jumping up and down, either high on sugar or very excited to be at the kids' party. Ben had said he was coming tonight to hear her and bringing Timmy. Where was he? Had his mother drugged him so he'd miss the event? Noel wouldn't put it past the woman.

"We're ready to start," Tina said. "Shall I introduce you?"

Noel dragged her gaze away from the lizard and nodded. "Sure," she said, trying to inject fresh enthusiasm into her voice. Suddenly she wasn't so thrilled about this evening.

Oh, for heaven's sake, get a grip, snapped Marvella. *Show her what you're made of.*

Noel squared her shoulders. She knew she was worthy of Ben, even if his mother didn't think so, and she wasn't going to let the woman intimidate her.

Tina gave her a glowing introduction and everyone clapped eagerly as Noel moved close to the children, who were sitting cross-legged on the floor. "Are you all excited for Christmas?" she asked.

Some nodded, some yelled out, "Yes!"

"You know, Marvella and I like to celebrate the holidays, too."

"Santa's coming to my house," announced a little girl.

"He's coming to my house, too," said a little boy, not to be outdone.

"And I hope he'll come to my house, too," said Noel.

"You're a grown-up!" Timmy laughed at the silly notion that Santa would bother with someone so old.

"Yes, but even grown-ups like seeing Santa," Noel said. "And they like to have fun, just like you do. And you know what else? They like to be loved just like you do." She shot Mrs. Fordham a quick glance and saw the woman frowning in disapproval.

She hurried on. "So I'm going to leave out cookies for Santa."

"*I'm* going to leave cookies for Santa!" a girl shouted.

"Me, too!" cried another. This was followed by a chorus of children all sharing their intention to contribute to Santa's weight problem.

"You know what Marvella's going to do?" Noel asked her audience.

Several children shook their heads. "She'll be checking to make sure everyone goes to sleep right away on Christmas Eve so Santa can come. Just like Santa, she wants you to be good and do what your parents ask."

As she surveyed the room she caught sight of Ben slipping in. He gave her a nod and a smile and she smiled back. Out of the corner of her eye she could see his mother frown. Again.

"Would you like to hear the story about Marvella and the lonely little tree?" Noel asked.

The children responded with an enthusiastic *yes*, and she opened her book and began to read. "Marvella didn't like to see anyone lonely, especially the sad little tree that sat out in Bella Brown's backyard."

"'I'm so lonely,' said the tree. 'I know I'm little and I don't have many branches, but I could be so pretty if someone dressed me up with Christmas lights. If I was wearing Christmas lights, then maybe someone would pay attention to me.'"

Noel read on, chronicling the adventures of the lonely little tree, using a different voice for each character, and the children sat in rapt silence. As she read, the words of encouragement she'd written for children encouraged her, too.

"Wasn't it good that Marvella could see how special that tree was?" she finished as she closed the book.

Her audience nodded solemnly.

"We're all special," she added and wondered if Ben's mom would get that message. She'd probably never think of Noel as special but if she could just move from antagonism to some level of acceptance, that would be enough.

"So if you ever feel lonely, just remember, there's always someone in this world who cares about you. Okay?"

Again, everyone nodded.

"Okay. Now, guess what? I brought a gift for each of you."

That produced much excitement and squirming as Noel reached into her tote bag and produced the coloring books. "I like books," said the same little girl who'd greeted her when she first came in.

"Me, too," Noel said, and handed her a coloring book.

"Thank you!" Timmy crowed when she gave him his.

"You're welcome," she said.

"I'm sure we all appreciate Ms. Bijou coming to join our party," said Tina and started the children clapping. "Now we have a Christmas guessing game," she continued and a moment later the children were all deep in the game.

Noel moved to the back of the group where Ben was standing. "Thanks for coming," she said.

"I wouldn't have missed it. You were great."

"I like doing things with kids."

"It shows. They obviously like you. And you're popular. I had trouble finding a place to park."

Which would explain why he was late getting in.

"Kids always like a party."

The game was over now, and cookies and punch were being served. Several moms came over to tell Noel how much their children enjoyed her books, and Ben stood next to her, smiling. Mrs. Fordham kept to the other side of the room.

But soon the party was ending, and she came up

to Ben and Noel towing Timmy along behind her. "I'm going to take Timmy back to the house now before he eats any more cookies."

"Okay. Oh, by the way, Noel, has Mom told you she's been working on a book for Timmy?"

One about witches? "Really?" Noel said politely.

Mrs. Fordham now looked distinctly uncomfortable. "Just a little something to entertain him," she said stiffly then added, "You read very well." No comment on Noel's writing abilities.

"Thank you."

"And that was a rather clever story," Mrs. Fordham said reluctantly.

"I try to write stories with a moral in them," Noel said. "I think everyone needs encouragement."

"Well, yes," Mrs. Fordham said, apparently at a bit of a loss.

"Can you say goodbye to my friend?" Ben prompted his son.

"Bye," Timmy said. "I like Marvella."

Ben smiled at Noel. "And I like Marvella's mommy."

Timmy was astonished by this statement. "Does Marvella have a mommy?"

"We need to go," Mrs. Fordham said and started hustling him toward the door. "I'll see you soon," she said over her shoulder and Noel knew the woman wasn't talking to her.

"I don't think your mother is ever going to like me," she said with a sigh.

"Oh, yeah. She will," Ben said. "Meanwhile,

Timmy likes you. And so do I," he whispered and kissed her on the cheek.

We can always poison the old bat, Marvella whispered.

Tempting thought, but no. *The party's over for you*, Noel told her. *Go away.*

I will as soon as you promise not to let that woman get the better of you. Remember what you just read to the kids.

Good point. An Eleanor Roosevelt quote came to mind. "No one can make you feel inferior without your permission." Darn it all, she wasn't going to give Mrs. Fordham permission to make her feel inferior. Ben might have chosen some unworthy women in the past but she wasn't about to become a member of that club. In her own small way she *was* special. And someday Mrs. Fordham would come to realize that.

She hoped.

Chapter Twenty-Two

It was the twenty-first of December, first day of winter, and Riley, Jo and Noel had met for lunch at the Olympic View Café, which offered a view of Case Inlet and the mountains beyond. "My treat," Noel had said.

"Are you sure you can afford to?" Riley had asked her. Noel had been on a tight budget for the last year. It was strange to think of her actually having extra money to spend.

"Now that things are squared away with the house, yes. Anyway, I want to celebrate."

So did Riley, and Jo was up for a break. "Mike's been gone so much the last few days, he owes me," she said, slipping into her seat at their window table.

"What's with that?" Riley asked.

"I don't know. Navy business of some sort."

"You're being a good sport about him reenlisting," Noel said.

"It's only for a few more years. We can handle it. And the signing bonus will be nice."

"There is that," Riley said.

"So," Jo said after the waitress had taken their orders. "I'm getting a bonus, Noel's getting a house and it looks like my little sister's getting a new man for Christmas."

It did look that way. Riley and Jack had been spending a lot of time together since her party, and each evening they seemed to discover something new they had in common, the latest being that they were both fond of games. That alone, she knew, would endear him to her family. They'd already played Gin Rummy and were now playing Word Scramble back and forth on their phones, and she was beating him soundly. He'd helped her decorate her tree, a chore she'd been putting off, sure it would depress her. There'd been nothing depressing about doing that with Jack. There was nothing depressing about doing anything with Jack.

"I keep thinking about when we went to see that Santa at the mall," Noel said.

"Pretty woo-woo," Riley said.

"Just lucky guesses," Jo said, choosing a tea from the selection of tea bags on the table.

"For you, maybe," Noel said. "But how did he know about my house? And..." Her cheeks turned pink. "Ben."

Jo looked at her speculatively. "So, that's heating up, is it? That would explain the earrings and the new top," she said, and the pink on Noel's cheeks deepened to red.

"How are things coming with his mother?" Riley asked.

"Well, she came to my reading at the library and frowned the whole time. But I have discovered some common ground. Ben told me she wants to write a children's book. I'm going to offer to help her."

"Brilliant," Jo said.

Noel shrugged. "Hopefully, I won't live to regret it."

"Maybe now she'll appreciate you," Riley said.

"I don't know about that, but I'm hoping she won't be quite so, well, so…"

"Bitchy?" Jo supplied.

Noel nodded. "After the party at the library, Ben had a talk with her and told her she'd better start being nice to me. I think he really cares about me."

Both sisters burst out laughing. "Ya think?" Jo said. "He practically gave you that house on a platter."

"I'm paying for it," Noel said, insulted.

"At the rate you guys are going it'll be community property within the next two years," Jo predicted. "Seriously, Noel, he seems like a great guy."

Noel's expression turned dreamy. "He is."

The waitress appeared with their orders—clam chowder all around and salads. After she'd left, Noel brought them back to the subject of Santa. "He couldn't have guessed *everything*. That Santa, I mean."

"Sure he could. We all know there's no such thing," said Jo.

"I suppose that's the curse of growing up," Riley added.

"Or of having a clumsy dad who trips hanging your Christmas stocking and falls on your Barbie Dreamhouse and breaks it," Jo said, digging into her chowder.

"He tripped over the clothes you left on the floor," Riley reminded her. "It is weird, though," she said. "Santa did know an awful lot about us."

"He sees you when you're sleeping," put in Noel.

Jo made a face. "Eeew. That is a serious ick factor."

"I'm just glad things have worked out for all of us," Riley said.

"You especially," Noel told her. "You're inspiring."

Not really, but… "Aww, thanks."

Jo batted her eyes at Riley. "You…complete me."

"Ha, ha."

Noel frowned at Jo. "I loved that movie."

"I loved Tom Cruise." Jo sobered. "Seriously, sis. We're all proud of you. And it looks like you might have found someone who deserves you. Make sure, though," she said. "Don't be rushing into anything."

"No rushing," Riley assured her. Just because she and Jack had hung out every night since the party, that didn't count as rushing. Right?

And it wasn't rushing to bring him to Mom and Dad's for Christmas Eve dinner three days later. Or to plan to spend Christmas Day with his grandma and parents, who had flown up for the holidays. She'd already met his sister via Skype and received her stamp of approval.

He seemed to be fitting in well with her family. The poor guy endured a grilling from Dad and Harold over seven-layer dip and chips and survived it. He took a turn holding little Mikey, although Jo didn't let him keep the baby for long (germs were everywhere), and listened respectfully while Dad read the Christmas story from the family Bible before dinner. Once everyone sat down to eat he complimented Mom on the prime rib and her garlic mashed potatoes. Of course she insisted he have seconds of both.

After dinner he was a good sport when the family played their favorite game of stealing presents back and forth, and Harold stole the slingshot he'd lifted from Mike. He wound up with an egg separator shaped like a face that oozed egg white from the oversize nose and claimed it was the coolest present he ever got.

"You are full of it," Grammy told him and he grinned.

After the gag gifts, it was time for the real thing. He'd come prepared, bringing Sweet Dreams Chocolates for all the women and six-packs of IPA beer for the men. Caitlyn got bubble bath. As for Riley, "You'll get yours later," he promised.

Jo received a sapphire necklace from Mike. "Groupon," he joked as everyone oohed and aahed over it. "Open the card, babe."

She did and read it, and her hand flew to her mouth. She stared at him, shocked. "What's this?"

"I'm not re-upping."

Silence fell over the living room and now they were all staring at Mike.

"Why?" Jo asked. "We talked about this."

"I know, and then I thought about it some more. I think you're right. I've served. I'm ready to let someone else step in."

"But you love the navy."

"I do. I love you more."

"Oh," sighed Mom and Grammy in unison.

"Whipped," Harold teased.

Jo shook her head. "I can't let you do this."

"It's a done deal, babe."

"That's what you've been so busy with."

He nodded.

"Oh, Mike. Are you sure?"

He looked down at their son, whom he was holding, and smiled. "Oh, yeah. Anyway, the navy isn't totally rid of me. They need volunteers to work with the Sea Cadets."

"What's that?" asked Grammy.

"It's a program for kids, teaches them about seamanship and exposes them to public service," Mike explained. "It's a good program."

"It's a good compromise," Mom said.

"But you said yourself that you'd never be able to find a job here," Jo pointed out.

"Got that solved. Dad wants to retire early. I'm taking over the hardware store."

Harold grinned. "All right. Do we finally get a family discount?"

Mike ignored him. He was too busy with his wife, who was hugging him ecstatically.

"Who needs to go to a Christmas movie?" Jack whispered to Riley. "This is the real deal."

Yes, it was. Her whole family was the real deal.

So was Jack Logan, she thought as they sat side by side during the Christmas Eve candlelight service at church and he took her hand and held it.

Later, when it was just the two of them back at Riley's apartment with the little fireplace cheerily pretending to give them a fire, he said, "I sure like your family."

Hearing him say that warmed her even more than the hot chocolate she'd been drinking.

"And I sure like you," he added. He picked up his sports jacket, which he'd discarded on the back of the couch, pulled out a small box tied with a red ribbon and handed it to her.

"And all I gave you was cookies," she said, looking at the plate on the coffee table.

"I happen to like cookies," he said, taking a second one. "Open your present."

She did and found a red crystal heart pendant with a sterling silver chain. "Jack, it's lovely."

"So are you," he said and kissed her. He tasted of chocolate and mint, and the way he was running his fingers through her hair felt like heaven. Jack Logan was the perfect Christmas present.

Much later, after he'd finally left, she sat on the couch enjoying her cozy living room and the sight of her cute little tree all lit up and hung with ornaments her mother and grandmother had given her over the years. She certainly hadn't envisioned herself having such a happy moment only a few weeks ago. When Sean dumped her, it had felt like the end of the world. Instead he'd set her free to find a whole new world of joy and promise.

She and Jack had been so engrossed in each other he'd gone off without his cookies. She took one and vowed to replenish the supply in the morning. Then she snuggled under a blanket and relived the last few days and all the fun she'd been having with Jack. It was still early, of course, and anything could happen. Or not. Maybe what they had was a fast fire that would burn itself out.

No matter what, she now knew that even when bad things happened they could turn out to be a door to something better. "All things work together for good," as Mom liked to say. Warmth and happiness lulled her into a doze before she could get up and go to bed, but she woke with a start when she heard the sound of sleigh bells. She sat up, blinking, in time to see the Santa from the mall bending over the cookie plate and helping himself to one.

"You!" she stammered, pointing a finger at him.

He jumped and dropped the cookie, then shook his head. "You're supposed to be asleep, young lady."

"You're not supposed to be real," she retorted.

"Who says?"

"Everyone over the age of twelve."

"Cynics and doubters," he said in disgust. "What

do those people bring to the world? What do they contribute to others' happiness? One of the joys of Christmas is the wonder that drives children to the tree every year to see what I've brought. There's a reason parents tell their children about me."

"Nobody's going to believe me if I tell them about you."

"Do you believe, Riley? Did you find your perfect man?"

"I think so."

He nodded. "Good. I love seeing girls get what they truly desire—both little ones and big ones. You know, I hear people complain about how commercial this holiday has become, but presents aren't a bad thing. They remind us of God's greatest gift. Remember that when you have children of your own, and do your part to keep the happiness alive."

Riley was only half listening. She was up now, looking for her phone so she could take a picture of her late-night visitor.

"You never did get your photo at the mall, did you?" he said as she grabbed her purse and dug into it. "But there's always next year."

"Wait, let me take one now."

He laughed and when she whirled around, phone camera aimed, he wasn't there anymore. She put the phone back with a sigh and returned to the couch. Nope, no one was going to believe her. Noel maybe but not Jo, that was for sure. She pulled the blanket back over her and stared at the fire.

At four in the morning she woke again. The fake

flames still danced in the fireplace, the tree was still lit and the leftover cookies were still on the plate. Of course, there was no sign of Santa. Had she dreamed him?

She shrugged and turned off the fire. Shut down the tree for the night. One thing she knew for sure, she hadn't dreamed Jack. So maybe it didn't matter whether she'd actually seen Santa or only dreamed him. Either way, she was a believer.

"Thanks, Santa," she murmured as she headed off to bed.

She might have imagined it, but she thought she heard the distant echo of a "Ho, ho, ho."

Epilogue

A CHRISTMAS WEDDING... AGAIN

Riley did have the perfect wedding two years later. The reception wasn't at the golf club, although she probably could have gotten a deal, considering who she was marrying. She didn't have winter colors and she didn't wear a long white gown or a faux fur stole.

Instead she wore a short, strapless lace tulle number, and her groom wore white pants and a navy linen shirt. Her bridesmaids all dressed in pretty summer dresses and the entire wedding party went barefoot. Perfect for getting married on the beach in Hawaii.

It was a smaller wedding than she'd originally planned on—immediate families and a few close friends. Jo was pregnant again but only three months and this time she was Riley's matron of honor. Noel, who had just gotten married in August, stood up with her, too, and Jack's sister made up a third. Noel's new son, Timmy, acted as ring bearer. Margaret had died right after Riley and Jack became engaged, but

Riley was carrying her lace handkerchief, along with a bouquet of tropical flowers. No silver bells were heard. Instead a conch blower celebrated the union of Riley Erickson and Jack Logan. And two doves winged their way skyward once the couple had been pronounced husband and wife.

Everyone agreed that the reception afterward was great fun, especially when one of the uncles arrived on the scene dressed as Santa after the bride had tossed her bouquet. (Grammy caught it.)

"You're gonna miss Santa," Jo teased as Riley and Jack started for the door.

"He already brought me everything I wanted," Riley said, smiling at Jack.

Oh, yes. She was a believer.

* * * * *

Acknowledgments

I absolutely must thank some of the people who so generously helped me with this story. A huge thanks to Jacy Teele, Linda Morton, and Rose Patrick for answering my questions about the life of a Navy wife and giving me a glimpse into the workings of the Navy. A special thank-you to Randy Schroeder from the Silverdale Navy recruitment office for taking time to explain the ins and outs of reenlistment. All I can say after talking with him is "Go Navy!" And any facts I've gotten wrong are all on me. Also, thank you Elsa Watson for helping me with some of those details of birth that I have wiped from my memory. Things have sure changed since I had my babies (back when the pterodactyls flew). Love my critique group! Thanks Susan Wiggs, Kate Breslin, A.J. Banner and Elsa Watson for all your insights. I'm also grateful to my agent Paige Wheeler for her wise guidance, my editor Paula Eykelhof who works so hard on my behalf, the art department at

Harlequin/MIRA Books for this lovely book cover and all the people at that wonderful publishing house who do so much for me.

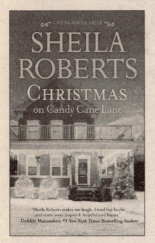

New York Times **Bestselling Author**

DEBBIE MACOMBER

National Bestselling Author

SHEILA ROBERTS

Can Christmas bring the gift of a second chance?

The Christmas Basket
by Debbie Macomber

Ten years ago, Noelle and Thomas secretly fell in love. Their mothers had been locked in a bitter feud for decades, but despite the animosity between them, Noelle planned to elope with Thom. Until he jilted her.

This Christmas, two things happen when Noelle comes home for the holidays. The feuding mothers find themselves working together to fill Christmas baskets for charity. And Noelle and Thom discover they're still in love.

Merry Ex-mas **by Sheila Roberts**

Cass has been looking forward to her daughter Danielle's Christmas wedding—until Dani announces that she wants her father, Cass's ex, to walk her down the aisle.

Then her friend Charlene arrives at her house in shock. She's just seen her ex-husband, Richard, who left a year ago. Now he wants to kiss and make up. Hide the mistletoe!

Available now, wherever books are sold!

Be sure to connect with us at:

Harlequin.com/Newsletters

Facebook.com/HarlequinBooks

Twitter.com/HarlequinBooks

MIRA®

www.MIRABooks.com

MDM1917R